Seven Blackbirds

Seven Blackbirds

A NOVEL

To Michael, my first purchaser! Thank you! Helen

Helen Winslow Black

Seven Blackbirds

Published by
Four Elk Press
Portland, Oregon 97298

Cover design: Angie Martorana
Page Design: Anita Jones, Another Jones Graphics

Library of Congress Number: 20079004250

ISBN: 978-097966230-0

To my father, my husband, my sons

Contents

The Phone Call

I WAS IN THE BEDROOM WHEN HE DID IT. He swung his arm from the shoulder like a baseball bat, palm open, and hit me in the face. When my head came back down from wherever it got sent I found myself quiet and still on the edge of the bed, watching while he began again with the other arm. He backed up, almost as though he were about to walk out, then circled, pulled in, let go, and slammed me again. The room was painted green, I'd done it myself, and the woodwork white; thank God the shades were down. I was watching his arms the whole time but the arms I felt were my own, cradling the baby nursing at my breast. Those were the only arms I knew because they held my child.

I couldn't breathe. Utter silence reigned, for two slow beats. Then Nathan pierced it with his screams. So it wasn't me. It wasn't my own voice, summoning me back to myself, but his voice, the voice of my child.

Later on I edged into the back room. The plantation blinds were closed against the southern exposure; it was early May in Tulsa and our bungalow had no air-conditioning. Larry sat at his desk, ramrod straight, elbows akimbo, with a textbook, ruler, and half a dozen sharpened pencils. My psychological universe had just been shattered, and he was studying juvenile justice in his running shorts.

"I'm hungry," I said.

"Make something then." He didn't even turn around.

Every morning on our honeymoon Larry had made me breakfast. We'd lived in Vermont together for two years before the wedding, but the honeymoon was different, the marriage had made a difference. He seemed light-hearted. We rented a cottage on Lake Champlain. Every morning that week, Larry rose before me for his hour-long run, as usual, but afterwards, he'd come down to the shore and just sit there, watching me swim. He never got in; the water was icy even in July, and he wouldn't put up with cold water unless there was a medal to be gained. Halfway through, he'd smile and wave and disappear, and when I got back up to the porch, there it would be, a big, hot breakfast, and Larry, grinning.

"I'm hungry," I repeated, still addressing his back. It was pale, but his neck showed the beginnings of a summer tan; his shoulders and arms were beautifully sculpted. I leaned against the door frame. "I'm too tired to cook," I whispered.

He heaved a sigh. "I'll go get some burgers." He pulled on a tee shirt and gave me a withering glance as he passed. "You look awful. Why don't you lie down?"

As I put the baby in the bassinet and collapsed on the bed, all I could think was *I used to have abs, too.*

The doorbell woke me up. The sun was filtering low through the trees, gleaming on the brass handles of my grandmother's dresser. Beside it, Nathan lay quietly in the bassinet, eyes open. What time was it? I hadn't replaced the clock radio yet, the one Larry had thrown out the front door when I came home from school "late" one day last week. It must be close to six. Maybe he'd had gone to the gym. As soon as I became pregnant, Larry had begun training seriously for a triathlon. Any triathlon.

"Is Larry home?" The weatherbeaten reel mower Andre had pushed eight blocks to our house stood behind him, at the bottom of the porch steps.

"No, but...what time is it?"

"I dunno."

"Go ahead if you want." I shifted the baby to my other shoulder. "He should be back soon."

2

Andre shook his head. "I want to do it when he's here. He said he'd take me for ice cream after."

He pushed the mower back down between the twin silver maples to the street.

Little Andre had resumed mowing our tiny lawn when Larry came back to town. Last week they'd gone out in Larry's new car and returned with a remote-control dune buggy. The toy wasn't actually given to Andre but stayed in our garage for safekeeping; nevertheless, this went straight into LARRY'S ECCENTRICITIES, a mental file folder I'd opened halfway through the pregnancy. Larry had taken a leave of absence from his LLM program in Seattle to help me with the baby until my semester was done. How did buying expensive gifts for young boys fit into this?

I saw myself in the mirror next to the door—limp hair, dark circles—and closed my eyes reflexively. When my sister and I were little, our neighborhood nickname was the Breck Girls. *Blondes have more fun*, I thought grimly.

Outside, dusk gathered. I sat on the porch swing, rocking it gently with one foot, and nursed the baby. At six weeks of age, his activities were limited to two: eating and sleeping. I was hungry as well, but too sapped to do anything about it.

It was almost dark when Larry returned. "I did some other shopping while I was out," he said, handing me the fast food bag as he went through the door. Silently I detached Nathan, ripped the bag open one-handed and shook the wrapper off the burger.

The first bite knifed through my jaw. I jumped up, stifling a cry, baby clutched in one arm. Fries spilled everywhere. Our next-door neighbor was relaxing on his porch with a beer after a long day of yard work. He stood up. "You okay?" He stepped down and walked over to the yucca between our unpaved driveways. "Everything all right?"

"Yes, thanks." I scuttled inside, head down, and plopped Nathan in the bouncer. Then, gingerly, I took a tiny bite on the left side, then another, and another, small careful bites until the food was gone.

Larry walked into the kitchen with his hamburger as I stood at the sink, canting my head to swallow some water.

3

"What are you doing? Why are there fries all over the porch floor?"

"Nothing." I put down the glass. "Sorry, I spilled them."

"Well, now I can't eat them. They're dirty." He shot his wrapper into the wastebasket and left.

That night I took the phone into the bathroom and locked the door while Larry played Chopin preludes on the piano. I called Dana and told her I'd just chipped a tooth. I had to lie. Wouldn't my best friend think it was odd for me to call on Easter evening asking for a dentist referral without giving a reason? The next morning I lied in answer to all the dentist's questions. He said I had nerve damage, and handed me a tiny x-ray sheathed in a manila cover on which he wrote *Kim Baltakis, 19 April 9-*. He told me to take it to an endodontist. I never did. I went home and shoved it into my dresser, underneath the flowered wrapping paper my grandmother had used to line the drawers. The pain faded after a week, but my ear was never quite the same.

When I moved out a month later, I took only the things that even Larry had to admit were mine: my clothing, the old maple twin bed in the back room, my grandmother's dresser, the kitchen table. Not even the car seat or the baby swing—I'd only paid for half of them, and dignity prevented me from giving him money. As time passed and reality grew, I shed everything in my possession that he'd even touched. But the x-ray—I couldn't bring myself to get rid of that little envelope. I had to protect it, this tiny, vulnerable thing, the only concrete artifact from a time of invisible pain.

I MADE THE PHONE CALL from the pay phone at 21st and Riverside. Not a booth; just a pole with two hoods on it back to back, exposed, in the open air. I faced away from the Arkansas River, so I could watch the street while I dialed the number inked on my palm. I'd written it down, so I must have planned it. Yes, I had to have planned it because the baby wasn't with me. I'd left him with a sitter because I didn't want him to hear. He was only six weeks old.

"My husband hit me a couple of days ago and I want to talk to someone."

4

"Are you in a safe place?"

I looked around for Larry in his new car.

"Honey, are you still there?"

"Yes," I said. "Yes, I'm in a safe place."

"Hold on, I'm going to transfer you to a counselor."

I scanned Riverside Drive.

Someone named Drew came on the line. I waited while two joggers ran by. "I'm sorry to bother you because I know there's not a real problem here and everything's fine but my husband hit me the other day and I want to know what I should do if it happens again."

"If it happens again you have to call 911."

"Why?" I was riveted to the ground. Saying the words aloud to this person named Drew made it something that had really happened. I looked at the phone in my hand. Too late, I realized *I can't go back from here.* "Why is it?" I babbled. "Why?"

"Because it's against the law."

"But he's my husband."

"It doesn't matter who it is. It's against the law."

"I'm sure he'll never do it again."

"If he does, you have to call 911."

"He won't do it again. He was just angry. I'm sorry, this is…I shouldn't have called."

"Listen, people do all kinds of things they may not mean later when they lose their temper. The point is, it's dangerous. You could get really hurt, even unintentionally. He could hit you again and you could lose your balance and fall and crack your head on a piece of furniture."

The baby could crack his head on a piece of furniture.

"Hello?" said Drew. "Are you still there?"

A man jumped out of a truck and picked up the other phone. I turned to face the river. "I'm worried about the baby," I whispered, cupping the receiver in my hand. "I don't care about me, but if he loses his temper again, he could hurt the baby. By mistake."

"Are there any other children?"

"No, just the baby. He's six weeks old. I was holding him."

"You were holding the baby?"

I said something wrong. Now he's mad at me.

A bum lurched out of the bushes, rail-thin, blood running down his face into his beard. He staggered toward me.

I moved around the open kiosk as far as the cord allowed, and said "Could you help me, please?" The other caller didn't hear. He had his elbow up on the metal hood, the other hand stuck in a pocket. I could see the back of his crew cut. He smelled like cotton, detergent, and sun. "Help me?"

Drew's tiny voice called: "What's going on? Are you okay?"

I lifted the receiver. "Just a minute, there's this drunk guy, I'm at a pay phone."

The drunk advanced, mumbling, bottle in hand, and when he reached out the air went dim and eerie like tornado season and while I thought *what the* hell *is going on here, here I am in Tulsa where even men who don't wear cowboy boots open doors for you and this punk on the other phone won't even help me* I banged my hand on the metal hood and cried, "Hey! Help me out here!"

The man looked up, dropped his phone and headed off the vagrant, who pivoted back toward the trash bushes on the riverbank. "Geez," he said, rolling his eyes. "Where's the park patrol when you need 'em?"

"Thanks." *Broad daylight,* I thought. *Broad daylight and in the park. Anybody could see me. Larry could see me.* I'd broken a sweat. Probably another post-partum hot flash. I wiped my forehead with my sleeve and picked up the phone again. "But he's working on an advanced law degree!"

Drew said: "Even doctors and lawyers hit their wives."

"I need to go now. You've really helped me. Really. Just talking to you has been a help—"

"Listen," he was talking fast, "I know it's hard, but unless you pick up the phone, there's nothing anyone can do to help you. And you're a smart girl. If you feel a bad situation developing you take that baby and get out of that house. Take the baby and get out of the house. Remember, that baby is the priority."

I got back in the car and threw up in an empty shopping bag that was on the floor. I wiped my mouth on the cuff of my sweatshirt and rolled it over before sitting up. No one was around. I got out, threw away the bag, and rinsed out my mouth in the public restroom.

When I returned I saw my wallet out on the seat in plain view. I jammed it into the glove compartment, unrolled all the windows, and rested my head against the steering wheel. Then I sat up and gripped it with both hands to stop the shaking, staring across the Arkansas at the thicket of refinery stacks behind the electric plant. It was mounted with huge block letters, neon-white at night: PUBLIC SERVICE COMPANY OF OKLAHOMA. I was shaking not just from the phone call, but from the encounter with the drunk: my own vehemence startled me. How had I been so bold with a total stranger? With strangers, I could be strong. With Larry, I was a cripple.

A breeze sifted over the riverbank. I thought of another cottonwood I'd seen recently; when was that? Then I remembered: on the Arkansas as well, further south, below 41st Street, where the river is a shallow mud flat on the days the Army Corps of Engineers doesn't open Keystone Dam. Riverparks is not as pretty there as a mile further north, where people fish and picnic, and nineteen-twenties apartment buildings on the bluff overlook sculptures nestled between the sycamores. But it was less crowded on a weekend, and Larry preferred that.

The cottonwood I remembered crowned the edge of the bank with some of its roots exposed. Cottonwoods aren't the strongest of trees, but this one was big, big enough to withstand the partial erosion. We'd climbed down around the roots, off the path, to a spit of sand. We stood there, and Larry sneered at me.

"You look woebegone," he said. Then he laughed.

We'd lived together for five years. His infant son was strapped to my chest.

I sat in the car with the sour taste of vomit in my mouth, staring at the electric plant, and the memory slid into place. I remembered when that happened. It was that same day, the day he punched me. That same afternoon, an hour later, and my legs had suddenly become weak and started to shake so I said we had to stop and rest, and then we'd climbed down to the river bank. We were on a walk together. He'd gotten what he wanted: he'd hit me because I'd insisted on taking a walk alone.

〰〰
〰〰

2

Living in the World of the Hypothetical

IT WAS MID-AUGUST, SCORCHING, northern Oklahoma's ugliest season. I was sixteen weeks pregnant. Larry came out the front door and looked down at me. "Off the couch, I see."

I gave the swing a push, and watched the shriveled yucca blooms bob back and forth. This was when things had been going to change, I'd told myself. When things were going to change. When I could hold down food, when I was back on my feet.

Larry took his car keys from his pocket and jiggled them in a cupped palm. His khakis were perfectly creased; the drycleaners did a much better job than I ever had.

"I need more boxes," he said finally, and left.

Maybe that was just my imagination, I thought. Maybe the sarcasm had just been in my imagination. He knew I had a meeting with Courtney to set the law journal agenda for next week.

When Courtney drove in she whipped off her sunglasses and gasped. "Oh my gosh! You look fantastic!"

"First trimester diet. I wouldn't recommend it."

"You are *so* funny." She peeked through the screen door. "Where's that handsome redhead?"

"Courtney, he's hardly a redhead."

"Oh, yes he is. He is in the sunshine!"

"He's out getting more boxes."

She sat down on the swing. "Are you going to be okay? I mean, all alone like this for that long?"

"I'll be fine."

She fingered her pearls and looked doubtful.

"He's going to visit every month," I said.

"It's just…if you weren't…I thought maybe he'd postpone starting his program. Or you'd change your mind and transfer."

"Not when I have an internship with a federal judge lined up this semester. And I'm on the journal. I couldn't get on the journal anywhere else at this point."

She still looked troubled.

"It'll be easier," I reassured her. "I'll only have myself to take care of."

She swatted me lightly on the arm. "You are such a joker. How's your tummy?"

"Better, thank goodness. I have to start next week and I didn't want to be spending the whole time throwing up in the ladies' room on the third floor of the Federal Building."

"Good. How does hot food sound? I don't know why, but I feel like hot food." We got in the car. "You seem back to your old cheerful self, too," she added, flipping open the sunroof. "You sounded kind of depressed on the phone over the summer."

"*Hyperemesis gravidarum* will do it to you."

"What in the world is that?"

"Severe dehydration."

"Well, those feel-good hormones ought to start kicking in now." She sped through a yellow light at 21st and Harvard. "I can't believe I'm back here in little old Tulsa. I can't believe we made it through another year."

"Says little miss 4.0."

"Oh, that's not what I'm talking about and you know very well. It's just so…what? So *male*."

"Relentlessly male."

"Yeah! Relentlessly! A Kim word." She lifted a hand from the steering wheel and jiggled her wristwatch. "Look what Daddy gave me."

"How'd that happen?"

10

"He asked me what I wanted for my birthday and it just popped out. I didn't think he'd really do it. I don't know why he spoils me like that."

"Because he loves you?"

"He feels bad because I won't let him pay any of my tuition, but why should he? Honestly. I earned my own living before law school. And, well, I got some money from the suit in New York." She pulled into a parking space, giving the miniscule boxwood hedge a bumper kiss.

"Why won't you ever tell me what actually happened?" I asked, when we sat down inside.

She emptied two sweetener packets into her iced tea. "Men are pigs," she said, wiping her fingers on a paper napkin. "Arrogant pigs. Some men," she amended. "I was just this yahoo from Tennessee, y'know? But not any more."

"Courtney, you were *never* just a yahoo from Tennessee. You went to Harpeth Hall. Your father's a trustee at Vanderbilt."

"But my granddaddy was a coal miner." She looked up. "Y'know all my life I've been taught to shut up and smile. It was embarrassing enough in the first place. Thank God we settled. I just have this policy. To put it behind me. If I talk about it, it's still there."

I nodded and unwrapped another packet of saltines. Two painters in overalls slid into the booth across from us, one with an eagle's head tattoo big as a fist on one skinny bicep.

Courtney whispered, "I just can't stand big tattoos. They're so redneck." Then she slid out of the booth. "I think I'll just have one more slice. I can afford it. We broke up twice this summer and you know I always lose weight when we break up."

"I thought you looked different!"

She beamed. "You did notice! One size smaller. I'm not going to say which size." She waltzed off to the pizza bar, the painters staring after her.

"So which is it now, with Howard?" I asked, when she returned. "On or off? I can't keep track."

"On. It's never off for long. The longest was three months."

11

"I guess you could interpret that as continuity."

"I know it would be different if we got married. Like you. You know, commitment and everything."

I tried a carrot penny. "No. I think when you get married, it's just like it was before, only more. Whatever it is, there's more. Larry and I have the same relationship as we did before. Nothing's changed."

"Except the ring." She tapped it with her finger. "Listen, I have three requirements for the perfect marriage: good-looking, *and* good in bed, *and* has money. Now, I've never found a guy that's all three. Howard's not that great-looking, but the other two are there, and the bottom line is it's *okay* for a guy not to be great-looking. It's *not* okay for a girl not to be good-looking, but if a guy has a good career it kind of makes up for that. People overlook it."

"You make it sound so calculated." I ate another carrot. "I never met a yahoo who was so cynical."

She smiled. "Remember, I lived in New York for two years."

I turned my ring around on my finger. It hung loose after the weight loss. "Maybe that was a mistake. Maybe I should have been more analytical. I am usually. But when it came to guys, I could never be calculating. Larry asked me to move in with him, and I did. I quit school and moved to Vermont. Maybe I should have thought about it more. It caused a lot of problems with my family."

"Oh, that's another thing. Your family has to love him. I guess that's number four. Otherwise there's just too much goin' against you."

She dropped me back at the house. I walked straight to the bathroom and threw up four saltines and a tablespoon of raw carrot into the toilet. Then I ran cool water in the tub and sat on the floor as I waited for it to fill, thinking about all the things Courtney didn't know. She didn't know what it was like to pray for each day to end so you could cross it off on the calendar and escape into sleep, what it was like to regurgitate ten times daily while your husband stood on the other side of the bathroom door and complained about having to do the grocery shopping himself. She didn't know about Larry's refusal to discuss baby names or buy a crib. She didn't know that although I could barely stand I'd driven myself to the emergency room on the instruction of the midwife when I couldn't hold down even the liquid sucked from ice chips, and that when Larry showed up two hours later he'd looked at me flat on my back with the IV drip in my arm and said: "You'll be okay to drive home, won't you?"

She didn't know that after I'd crawled back into the house that night, Larry said that if I was *that* sick it had to mean something was wrong with the baby; she didn't know because I hadn't told her, and I hadn't told her because I was ashamed. Just as she wouldn't talk about the details of what had turned out to be a ground-breaking sexual harassment settlement with the law firm where she was working as a secretary. Because she felt ashamed, thought she ought to have picked up on the signs, reacted or not reacted and thereby prevented it; and thus, because it had, indeed, happened, she herself had, of necessity, done something wrong.

Just as she didn't tell me, I didn't tell her. I was afraid she'd ask, "Why did you get pregnant in the first place?"

I heard the mailman walk in and pushed the bathroom door shut. Larry must have been in the front room. We had a small house and a friendly mail carrier; if our door was open and he saw us, he'd step in and hand us our letters.

When I came out Larry was in the kitchen with the mail. He thrust something into my hand. "Look at this."

His tone alarmed me. Blood test results. I scanned the print-out. "What? What?"

Impatiently he put his finger on a line of type. Next to the number 1 in 250 was printed *Heightened risk for Down's Syndrome.*

He said: "I think you should get an abortion."

I sat down at the kitchen table, an old library desk from my grandmother's house. I smoothed the tightly-grained oak with my hand. "It's a screening test, not a diagnostic one," I explained. "It means you should go for further testing. It has a very high rate of false positives for Down's, but it's the only screen for spina bifida, that's why they still give it. That's why I took it. The test."

"I think you should get an abortion."

13

The leaves on the little apple tree outside the window were browning. The sawgrass in the backyard was high. Suddenly I realized that Andre had not been mowing the back yard, only the pocket-handkerchief-sized square of lawn in the front.

Larry said, "I already called the midwife. I already called her and asked for an abortion."

"You what?"

"Don't yell at me. I called the midwife and asked for an abortion."

I sat down again. "Just now? What did she say?"

He stuck his hands in his pockets and slouched. "She acted a little weird. She said she doesn't do abortions. That's okay, you can get one somewhere else. But I think you should get one."

Our back-fence neighbor came out to take down her laundry. She folded and sorted as it came off the line: towels and sheets on the bottom, clothes on top, socks tucked into the edges. I always dumped everything inside to fold. *Maybe I should do it her way,* I thought, *maybe it would be neater.*

I closed my eyes.

"Go away," I said to Larry, and for some reason he did what I asked. When I opened my eyes, I was alone in the kitchen, holding the piece of paper.

I took it to the bedroom and put it in the top drawer of my dresser, under the flowered paper. I looked in the mirror and thought *If my father were alive this wouldn't have happened.* Not true, perhaps; adult children are on their own trajectory. But before he'd died, my father and I had actually been talking. Extrapolating from that, I imagined conversations in which, sensing something wrong, he would have gently questioned in a way that might have hastened analysis and insight. And then, maybe then, I wouldn't be pregnant right now. I wouldn't have asked for a baby, wouldn't have allowed it to happen.

I shut the drawer. Maybe I was right, but what good did that do me now? I was beginning to see, dimly, that it was living for too long in the world of the hypothetical that had trapped me in the first place.

~~~

Six days later, Larry stood on the porch again, jingling the keys. Before, he'd spoken of coming back for a visit in October, but he didn't mention it now. "All right, don't get an abortion," he said. "But it's your choice. If there's anything wrong with the baby, you're on your own."

He got in his rental truck and drove off for Seattle. It was Labor Day weekend. Classes had been in session for a week. I lay down on the bed and cried myself to sleep.

≈
≈

3

The Road to Tahlequah

I LAY ON THE TABLE LOOKING AT THE CEILING. Luke was beside me at the counter, doing something I couldn't see. "I feel funny," I said. "I think I'm going to throw up." A massive wave hit, and I broke out in a sweat, speechless with pain. He grabbed a small enameled basin and knelt by my head. I blinked my eyes no. It wasn't nausea anymore.

Try to hold on for just another minute: his voice floated by, up past the light that dangled from the ceiling. I rolled my eyes toward him. I saw his burly shoulders and the long, graying ponytail trailing smoothly down his back. Then he swiveled around with a piece of paper and started fanning me.

I anchored myself on his calm face. I was going beyond pain into a kind of state where I coexisted with excruciation. "I can take it," I croaked.

"No, that's enough." Luke dropped the needles one by one into a small bowl. He nodded. "You just made a major shift. Like your spirit got pulled back down to another part of yourself, where it needs to be now."

"Strong medicine," I joked weakly.

"In twenty years I've only seen that once before."

"It wouldn't hurt the baby?"

"No, no," he said softly. "It didn't hurt the baby." He chose a few plastic bags of herbs from the wall, where they were clipped in rows

16

all the way to the ceiling. "Make sure you get up slowly," he reminded me as he left the room, then turned back and put his hand on my arm. "You're a pretty strong girl, you know that?"

I didn't feel strong as I walked out. My knees were weak and the light coming through the storefront window knifed through my head. There was a gurgle from the floor. I looked down, and just avoided tripping over a baby lying on a blanket at Jeff's wife's feet. "This is our grandbaby," she said, shaking a cloth bunny at him. He was a startling baby: cocooned in fat, with intense blue eyes in a huge head topped by a wispy thatch of black hair. She looked up at me proudly. "He's a fullblood."

"A fullblood?"

"Oh, yes. Didn't you know? Cherokees can have blue eyes."

"Ho, Alvin." Luke greeted his next patient, an elderly *abuelo* in suspendered jeans. He put the herbs on the counter. To me he said, "Don't do anything energetic the rest of the day, Kim."

"No risk of that," I smiled, using the counter to remain upright.

His wife got out her receipt book. "Luke wants you to make tea out of this and drink it twice a day for the next week. That'll be five dollars extra. That okay?"

"Sure." When I got in the car I stuffed the carbon copy into the glove compartment. My health insurance was not going to reimburse for a Native American acupuncturist anyway.

I drove slowly down Muskogee Avenue under a sun still unnaturally bright, pausing at the corners to admire the Cherokee script on the street signs. I stopped at the Holy Smoke Barbecue for a diet soda before getting on the highway. It was a hundred-and-fifty mile round trip to Tahlequah but I enjoyed the excuse for a long drive into the country once a week. It was worth every minute; Luke was the only one who could provide me with relief from the back pain that had begun in the fifth month.

After the Broken Arrow Expressway, the highway was a narrow two-lane road that wound through fields, woods, and pastures dotted with black cows and cattle egrets. When I drove through Wagoner, Victorians set back on big lawns reminded me of the

Midwest and I always started to feel better, even though, each time, I hadn't realized I didn't feel good to begin with.

But then there was another place. After the rusty suspension bridge over the reservoir, past the boat ramps and the Indian Lodge Motel with its sign *Refrigerated Air*—after that, there was a place where the road ran high on an embankment through a swamp. It was like being on the edge of a very long dam. That was the spot, on the way out, where I'd get the sudden, repeated urge to jerk the wheel off the road. It came and went with such ferocity I tried not to think about it; I knew my body was awash with hormones that affected my mood. The urge never reappeared on the way back; I always felt better after seeing Luke.

This time it was different. I didn't feel better, or worse. I didn't feel like myself. I felt disembodied. I drove all the way home as though I were hovering over my car, looking down on it, until I rolled into the driveway and turned off the engine, the driveway of the house I now occupied alone. "My husband has left," I said. I said it aloud, staring at the sliding doors of the old garage we never used because it was too hard to get them open. Then I went inside and fell asleep in my clothes.

In my dreams I was a young man, out at sea with another young man in a storm of waves. Rescuers came. *Take him first because he is weaker,* I said, and they did. I sank into the depths below a thirty-foot wave, but some time later the very same wave washed me back up on shore. I was a different person, though. No one believed it was me.

Then I dreamt of playing the cello again for the first time in years. The music was like a human voice speaking to me, rich, deep, and true. The sound resonated in my bones, as though my whole body had been hollowed out and filled with an ancient and powerful force. I realized simultaneously that I had been away for a long time and that I had come home. Joy and relief flowed through me with overwhelming intensity, mingling with, inextricable from, the flow of music, and the words came to me, *This is your true voice, the voice of your soul. Never let it go.*

Eleven hours later I awoke to intense quiet. It was still dark; the birds had not yet begun to sing. I showered, put on old baggy sweats that still accommodated my shape, and started a saucepan of water to boil, with a handful of Luke's herbs thrown in. Then I sat down at the kitchen table and drew pen and paper out of the little brass-handled drawer to prioritize my work.

In the lightening of the dawn the apple tree surfaced, then the fence, then the neighbor's empty clothesline, pin bag flapping. I'd joked to Courtney about it being easier to be alone, but it was true: it was a relief that Larry was gone.

I got up with my mug of Luke's tea. I tried striking a chord on the Steinway upright in the dining room. It made me wince; it was Larry's piano, it sounded too much of Larry. I walked into our bedroom, then through a glassed-in door to the living room, connected to the dining room by an arch, then back to the bedroom. I was pacing, pacing in a circle round and round our pattern-book bungalow, understanding now, finally, that the emptiness I felt was freedom from Larry, from the tension that always accompanied him.

I was flooded with relief, then guilt. Larry was tense. He was tense about everything. The edge had always been there. I'd attributed it first to one thing, then another, assuming that at some future point these issues would resolve. But this generous, hopeful logic, this living in the world of the hypothetical, had failed spectacularly when it came to pregnancy. How could I not have known? Why did I believe him when he said we could have a baby?

I came to rest on the sofa where I'd lain all summer, too nauseous even to read, watching cartoon reruns on cable television and listening to his accusations that I'd promised the pregnancy wouldn't change anything, but look! His stock of organic carrot juice was depleted! The laundry wasn't done!

I'd promised him the morning sickness wouldn't last long. Unfortunately, it did: I was one of the ten percent. After awhile, he began to ignore me completely. He worked out, he wound up with his few remaining portfolio companies, took his laundry to the cleaners, went shopping for his advance move to the West Coast. I convinced myself that when I felt better, he would too. And I thought I'd seen it begin to happen.

I remembered the exact moment. It was the day in week fifteen, when I started holding down flatbread crackers, one at a time. Larry walked in the door with a bag of peaches from the farmer's market. He handed me one, and smiled when I bit into it.

That was the Larry I wanted to believe in: the Larry who handed me a peach and smiled. That's the one I had to believe in. I could not allow myself to think the pregnancy had been a mistake. That was one mental file I wouldn't open. There was still time for Larry to grow into fatherhood, there was still time. I could still taste that peach. I held onto that peach. It was a miracle.

〰〰

4

Things to Think About Later

I TOOK ONE HAND FROM THE steering wheel, grabbed my purse, and thrust it at Larry. "I need a carrot. Can you get me a carrot?"

"What?" He caught it like a football.

"I need to eat something quick."

He found one and I bit into it. "Sorry," I sighed. "You wouldn't believe how much it hurts if I get hungry. It's like morning sickness in reverse."

"We'd better keep the car well-stocked then," he said. I caught the hint of a smile. It was a relief, since he'd had no visible reaction, when I picked him up at the airport, to seeing me in maternity clothes for the first time. He just got in the car and starting talking about Seattle.

As he prattled on, I started noticing things: how empty the interstate was at midday, how the grass grew right up to the cracked cement of the Harvard off-ramp, how only three miles from downtown we were passing block after block of withered storefronts and dinky shopping centers, divided and re-divided into pawn shops and check-cashing outlets. On our reconnaissance mission three years before, we'd called Tulsa the Emerald City because it had risen, whole and beautiful, from the hazy distant plains as we'd made this same approach. Once upon a time, it had satisfied Larry's requirements: far from his family and mild in climate. He'd wanted to go all the way out to the West Coast but I had resisted; I didn't want to be that

21

far from my own family, in Chicago. Tulsa was our compromise. I should have known, when Larry agreed, that it was only an intermediate stop on the way to his ultimate destination, and I was trying not to notice how unperturbed he had been to decamp for Shangri-La without me.

At home I tied an apron snugly beneath my breasts and began energetically cranking opening cans of organic tomatoes.

I heard thumps and bumps in the back bedroom. I went to investigate. Larry had pushed everything into a corner: bouncer chair, car seat, rocking horse, baby carrier. He was packing away all the layette items from Courtney's baby shower. They were mostly green and yellow, since I'd opted to forgo sex determination. That first ultrasound had been enough. But even without that initial, early scan, advised by the blood test—even without that, I wouldn't have done it. As I told my friends: *I like surprises.*

I stood in the doorway and threw the dishtowel over my shoulder. "All you need now is a dropcloth."

Larry knelt over the cardboard box, stuffing in the tiny clothes, studiously ignoring me. I remembered that he did that a lot, the studious ignoring. I'd forgotten.

"I thought this was going to be the baby's room," I persisted.

"The baby's not here and I am."

"But when the baby comes, can it be the baby's room?"

He arranged his books on the cleared desk, then started sharpening pencils. He liked to have a handful at the ready; he'd only use ones that were really sharp. I'd first noticed this at Columbia, where I was working on a master's in art history and he was in law school. No matter where we studied—Butler, Burke, Low, or Starr—he had a case full of needle-sharp pencils.

"While you're here..." I stroked my apron-covered stomach, making gentle circles with my hand. "Honey, when you're here, can we go buy the crib?"

"Why are you obsessing about the crib?"

"It's just what you *do* when a baby's on the way. You buy the crib. It's like the main important thing you do. To get ready."

"Well, I don't want to buy the crib yet."

"I just want to know where the baby's going to sleep."

"We have plenty of time." He turned around. "Why are you doing that?"

I looked down. "I don't know. I just do it. I'm patting the baby." I hurried out, suppressing tears. It was my fault. I'd broken a cardinal rule: don't bring up iffy subjects when he's hungry. I was out of practice.

After his first helping of pasta, Larry pulled a CD out of his brief-case. *Baby Brain* danced around a smiling tot's face in comical mixed type. "This is going to make him good at math," he said, handing it to me. "It's got a lot of Mozart on it."

"I wonder, if we played it now, if he could hear it. Or she. Do you think?"

"No." He took it back. "This is something for *me* to do with him. For bonding."

I filled his plate again. "Did you tell your parents yet?"

"No."

"But...you said you were going to."

"I said I was going to *think* about it. About when to tell them. I haven't decided. It's my decision." He twirled a clump of linguine against a spoon and shoved it into his mouth.

"When I talk to your mother on the phone," I said carefully, "and don't say anything, I feel like I'm lying."

"That's your issue."

After dinner, while I washed the dishes, I opened a new file and labeled it Good Signs. I always imagined the labels in large and small caps, the protocol for footnotes in the law journal.

Bought Baby CD.
Has decided to tell parents about Baby (just figuring out when).

THE NEXT MORNING I entered the kitchen in my single piece of career-looking maternity wear, a blue jumper over a wide-collared white blouse. It was internship day.

"Larry, I wanted to ask—"

"Can't you leave it alone?" he said. "Why do you always keep going? Why can't you stop?"

"No, no, it's not about your parents. It's not about that." I stroked his shoulder. "I made one of my checkups with the midwife for tomorrow, so you could come with me if you like. Maybe it would be interesting. You could hear the baby's heartbeat. Would you come with me?"

His eyes traveled over me, taking in the lipstick, the low-heeled pumps, the briefcase.

"What's wrong?" I asked.

He took a sip of coffee. "I am woman. Hear me roar."

The toast popped up.

I blushed and left without a word.

When I got home that evening he was going through my desk. I decided to ignore this; maybe he was bored. "Where should we go eat with Courtney and Howard on Friday?" I asked cheerfully. "The Lamplighter?"

"I don't want to go."

I stowed my briefcase in the closet. "But Howard's only up for this weekend." When I turned around he was brandishing some snapshots at me.

"You're supposed to be going to *school*," he snarled.

"That's the Halloween party. We've always gone to the Halloween party, remember?"

"*I* didn't go to any Halloween party."

You could have if you hadn't cancelled your visit in October. I didn't say it aloud. I shuffled through the pictures of the journal crew in various costumes and levels of inebriation. I stopped at one: Courtney as a cat-woman, in a skintight black body suit and whiskers; John in a wig, apron, and lipstick, with a two-day growth of beard and a cigar clenched between his teeth; Chris as a pirate, with an eye patch, and me in men's clothes: white shirt straining over my belly, suit vest, tie, and fedora. We all had our arms around each other's shoulders. It struck me: I looked happy. Why did I have fun with my friends, but not with my husband? I filed this away in Things to Think About Later.

"Sweetie, what's Courtney going to think if I cancel? You haven't seen her yet. Remember how much fun we had in Grand Cayman last year? We did, didn't we?"

"And I don't like what you wrote about my parents in your diary." He thrust a piece of paper at me. My handwriting, and it had a jagged edge.

"How could you do that?" I cried. "That's mine!"

"No, it's mine. It's about my parents."

"But it's *my* writing. Maybe you can read it, but you can't rip it out. That's stealing."

"Stop with the pregnant woman crying thing."

"That's not true!" I blew my nose, folded the handkerchief over and wiped my eyes.

"Baloney. This is like the fourth time you've cried since I got here. And I've been here four days."

"Is it?" The handkerchief was smeared with black; I wore mascara on internship days. "I'm sorry. Sometimes at night I feel so tired I just start crying."

He held the paper up in front of my face and ripped it in half. Again, and again, and again, and again. "Just know," he said, "my relationship. With my parents. Is my own business." Paper flakes snowed onto the floor.

I sat down on the bed, knees wide to accommodate my belly. "But it is my business. Something between you and your dad is causing problems in your life right now. In our life."

"What about *your* dad? He didn't approve of our getting married either."

"My dad not approving of us," I yelled, "obviously has no effect whatsoever on my desire and enthusiasm to have a family of my own!" I beat my fists on the bedspread. "It is not *keeping* me from being *happy* about this *baby!*"

I grabbed my keys. I did a three-point on the street before I realized: I had nowhere to go. I couldn't go to Courtney's. I'd hinted at problems a couple times before but she'd always glossed over it. I could understand that someone on the fence about getting married

25

herself didn't want to confront the spectre of a pregnant friend with marriage trouble. Dana was my best married friend, but I couldn't go to her house either; she had already told me, kindly, and only once—the day she accompanied me to the hospital for that nerve-wracking ultrasound—that Larry should have changed his plans once I got pregnant. I knew no friend on earth would say "I told you so" under such circumstances, but I still couldn't face it. So I took Riverside Drive twenty miles to Jenks and back. I had a sandwich and a root beer float at Weber's, then fell asleep in the car. With the second trimester had come the ability—almost the compulsion—to nap on the turn of a dime.

When I woke up, I thought: the law library! At eight o'clock on the night before Thanksgiving it would surely be deserted. I drove back to school.

The front desk was empty, but when I knocked on the counter the clerk appeared, one I didn't know. I never studied there at night. Actually I rarely went to the library at all; I went to campus only for classes and always studied at home. Now I wondered *why did I do that? Why have I always done that?*

"I should have something on hold that just came in from Cincinnatti," I said. "Under Baltakis."

He went away and came back smiling, hefting the tiny book in one hand like a piece of fruit. He laid it down and gently paged through to the frontispiece. "*The Law of Nations.* Seventeen hundred fifty eight." He looked up. He had grey eyes, striking and unusual in someone with such dark skin; a long, slender face, and the highest cheekbones I'd ever seen.

"I'm doing—I'm doing an article on the historical development of transboundary water law."

"I see," he glanced at my card while handing it back, "Kim."

"I…uh…need to go through the whole backdrop of how international law emerged from post-Enlightenment ethics, that kind of thing."

"It's just a little different from the usual stuff," he said, scanning the bar code on the book. He took in my physical state over the counter. "Oh, my. Got any sisters?"

I grinned back.

"Nice to meet you, Kim and company. I'm Morgan."

"Are you from Tulsa?"

"No, no, no," he chuckled, as though the idea amused him. "Atlanta, most recently."

"I just haven't seen you before."

He leaned on the counter, put his chin on his hand and smiled at me. "I followed my girlfriend here. Five months ago. We broke up. Four months ago."

"I'm sorry."

"I'm not." He raised an eyebrow. "Anymore."

I put the book in my bag. "So—what else do you do? I mean what's your day job?"

"Oh, this *is* my job." He adjusted his cuffs with a grin. "I'm assistant director. On the strength of one audited course in library science at Emory. Pickings must have been slim. If I like it I might go for my master's."

"That's serendipitous of you."

"Serendipity is my middle name. You'll have to get out at night more often," he added. "I fill in at the desk a lot then. It's nice and quiet here in the evening." He raised an eyebrow again.

"I bet that made you real popular in third grade."

"That and wiggling my ears."

That evening, Larry told me he'd changed his return flight. The next day, at the airport, he bent down and looked at me through the open car window. "We do better," he said, "when we're apart."

ON SUNDAY I LAY on my bed and stared at the books stacked against the wall, each with its neat pile of notecards on top. I hadn't spoken to another soul, even my neighbor, in three days. Dana had gone to New Orleans for Thanksgiving. Courtney thought that Larry was here, but had the flu and I was nursing him. Lisa, our friend from Larry's office, was a possibility, but she enjoyed griping about him and I didn't want to deal with that at the moment. I had no one to talk to.

27

Even Chris was gone, up to Pawhuska to spend the long weekend with his Osage grandmother. I got out the law school directory and looked up John, the new journal board member who'd put my screen door back on a couple weeks ago after a meeting.

There was no answer. He was probably taking last night's date out to breakfast.

I turned over and stared at the woodwork. It was a good job on the casement windows. My father had taught me to be thorough. There had been five layers of wallpaper and three colors of paint in the breakfast room at our house, and the stripping had taken him forever. "If you do the preparation right," he'd told me, "the actual job is easy."

I rolled to the edge of the bed and pushed off. In the back room, a drinking glass of sharpened pencils still sat on the desk. The box of baby clothes was in the corner, the maple twin bed still unmade. I went in the kitchen, took the uncooked turkey out of the refrigerator, and dumped it in the garbage.

〰〰
〰〰

5

I'll Be Home for Christmas

CHRISTMAS AT MY MOTHER'S WAS a string of leaden days, of course without Larry, who was doing an Ironman training session in Hawaii. He'd promised to do a layover in Chicago if he finished in time, but how did one define "in time?" It had never been our habit to travel together—he said this represented healthy independence—but I'd been hoping things might change, now that we were a family, or almost a family. But Chicago wasn't exactly on the way from Oahu to Seattle, so I wasn't holding out much hope.

The day before New Year's, I awoke to a promising aura seeping around the edges of the curtains. I swung my feet down, levered myself off the bed, and opened the drapes. The sun was shining, and the stale, waist-high mounds lining every driveway, every sidewalk, had been transformed by a few fresh inches into pillowy, inviting snowbanks, dazzling beneath a cloudless blue sky.

I pulled a sweatshirt over my nightgown. The pine swags roped to the mahogany banister were crisp to the touch. Downstairs, my mother, Bobbie, was alone in the breakfast room, wearing corduroys, and a Fair Isle sweater whose predominant color matched her wheat-colored hair.

"I'm definitely taking a walk today," I said, lowering myself into a chair.

Bobbie swallowed her spoonful of shredded wheat. She shook out the *Tribune*, folded it back to the front page, and put her finger on the weather report: *Fourteen degrees without wind chill.* She looked up at me dubiously.

"I'll wrap up."

I took a sip from my mug of Apricot Ambrosia Delight and sighed. It tasted like steeped oak leaves. I was tired of herbal teas in calico print boxes made from ninety percent post-consumer recycled material with Buddhist aphorisms on the package flaps. I longed for a good strong cup of hot coffee like my mother was drinking. At five weeks from my due date, the aversion to coffee, which I'd been convinced I would never, ever, want to drink again, was steadily fading. The chair was a tight fit too.

"What's this?" I said, looking out the side window, narrow as a battlement crenellation. Someone was cutting through the bushes from the neighbors. He high-stepped onto one shoveled track of the driveway and trudged up, holding a thick wad of plastic-encased shirts on hangers.

Bobbie rose halfway and looked out. "The new people." They'd moved in eight years ago, but they were still the new people. She'd never forgiven them for thinning their bushes so drastically. To tease her my father had once gotten out his binoculars and claimed he could read the channel settings on their large-screen TV through the glass wall of their kitchen remodel. Now she got all the way up and leaned on the table to push in her chair. "The man always brings their dry cleaning over here when they're not home. It's such a nuisance. I don't know why they have it delivered. They're never home. He's going to ruin my euonymus."

"But Mom, it's wintertime."

"It's the principle of the thing. He'll make a habit of it." She adjusted the fold on her turtleneck, then limped through the kitchen to open the door. "Just put it right there on a coat hook," she directed.

"Sure thing, Mrs. MacLean."

"And do me a favor, will you call and leave a message on their machine, because I may not remember about it."

"Sure thing. Thanks, Mrs. MacLean."

She sat back down. "Your father would never have allowed me to have the cleaning delivered. Such a needless expense."

My sister Karen bounded down the stairs and put a bagel in the toaster. "Did he cut through the bushes again? Why didn't you tell him not to?"

"Oh, what difference would it make?"

Karen and I rolled our eyes at each other.

"I *have* mentioned it before," Bobbie said defensively. "He does it anyway."

My sister flipped her hair over her shoulder and started to braid it. She looked like a Swedish skiwear model. I suddenly realized I was the only one not wearing a Fair Isle sweater. "I can't wait to get out on the golf course with the skis," she said. She patted my belly, and joked, "Want to come?"

"I was thinking more along the lines of a walk to the lake."

"Okay. It'll be a warm-up." She stuck her left hand under my nose. "Does this prong look bent? This one."

I took her hand and steadied it. "No."

"I'm just not used to it yet. I get nervous. About outdoor sports. Even with a six-prong setting."

"Karen, it's not going to fall out."

"I guess I could turn it around inside my glove."

Four months ago, my own ring had flapped between my knuckles; now it wouldn't budge. Courtney had told me to take it off and wear it on a chain around my neck, but I had hesitated, because Bobbie told me once she'd never taken her ring off since the day Dad gave it to her. Now it was too late. Every cell in my body was swollen. I would never complain about PMS again.

"So you're still having the baby at home?" Bobbie asked. She was now stamping book club postcards.

"Yes."

"Is this what everyone does in Oklahoma?"

"Mother, I'm ten blocks from the hospital. We'll just get in the car if we need to."

Karen chewed her bagel, looking from one of us to the other as though she were watching a tennis game. She played it straight-faced most of the time, but I knew she had dimples. They brought her porce-lain complexion, her perfect bone structure, down to earth.

"Well." Bobbie tapped the cards into a pile, smoothing the edge with her thumb. "I always thought anesthesia was over-rated. I didn't have it for your brother because he came so fast and I felt much better afterwards."

Karen jumped up and rummaged in the fridge. "What else can I eat? Oh, goody." Raffia crinkles from a gift box sifted onto the floor. She came back with a plate of salami slices and cubes from a nut-studded port wine cheese ball.

"How can you *do* that first thing in the morning?" I asked.

"Mmmm." She smacked her lips.

"Give me that," I snapped.

She grinned and pushed it over. "You're up early," she said to our brother, who'd just walked in.

Doug ignored her and took a handful of cheese cubes. "Hey, a Wisconsin breakfast. Where's the six-pack?"

He leaned against the doorjamb, where two decades of height measurements were notched and initialed in my father's hand, and flipped his car keys back and forth. "When are you going to take those garlandy things down? They're dead as doornails. Done with this?" He picked up the plate, tilted the remaining tidbits into one hand, and with the other shook a fresh cellophane-wrapped cylinder of crackers out of the box.

"Where are you going?" Bobbie asked.

"Out." He tucked the crackers under his arm, went to the door, and unhooked his ski jacket. "What the heck is this?" he said, poking the neighbor's dress shirts with his finger.

"Don't go out with wet hair, Douglas," Bobbie implored as the door slammed. We listened silently as his car labored down the drive-way to the street.

Bobbie picked up the stack of postcards, put them down. "I guess...I guess we should." She looked out the window, and then down to her lap, as though the sight of the neighbor's clumsily overthinned and now denuded forsythia had filled her with pain.

"Would you...would you girls take down the decorations today?"

"Sure," we said quietly.

She closed her eyes and pinched the bridge of her nose. "I don't know which is harder," she said, "putting them up or taking them down."

Our father had been born on Christmas.

The streets of Hubbard Woods were hard as iron and bleached with salt. Karen and I crunched silently toward Lake Michigan, breathing painfully even through scarves. I could just see the tips of my boots bobbing alternately from beneath my red wool-clad belly. *He hasn't told his parents yet, he hasn't told his parents yet.*

Karen took my arm. "I can't believe that coat still fits you."

"I was just thinking that."

Uptown there were few cars on the street and the stores were closed except for both delis and the coffee shop, windows completely fogged up. We crossed Green Bay and stopped on the train tracks, arm in arm, looking first all the way south toward Chicago, then all the way north to Milwaukee, drinking in the long stretch into bleak distances. We'd always done this. As girls, out of curiosity and longing; but since we'd grown up and moved away, had occasion to live in places that were not flat, we'd discovered that what we actually craved was, simply, that ability to see for a distance. It was something we'd had and taken for granted, but now desperately needed in order to feel we had a clear grip. The world was no longer so mysterious, but a good deal more complicated.

At the end of the street we stood beneath naked trees on the bluff overlooking the beach. A wedge of frozen whitecaps rimmed the sand, buffering it from waves angry with wind as far as the eye could see.

"So," Karen said finally. "Remind me. If you're not moving to Seattle now, how are you going to make sure Larry is there when the baby is born?"

"He's going to book a ticket for my due date and stay a week. He says, statistically, more first babies come after the due date than before."

She gave me a look. The Karen look. The look of someone who'd

33

managed my dad's office for two years while taking auditions and had done it so well he'd told her she could have had a great career in the military. The look of someone who'd had virtually all her wedding preparations in the bag within a month of her engagement. But the look, nevertheless, of someone who knew the limits. I avoided it and adjusted the scarf over my nose. "I can always call him if I go into labor and he can jump on a plane. First labors are usually long. Statistically."

"Statistically." She tucked her arm through mine and put her hand in my pocket. Far away, beyond the horizon, invisible, lay the state of Michigan. When I was little, I thought Lake Michigan was the ocean. Later on, our grandparents bought Elmwood, a big, rambling turn-of-the-century house on a tiny lake in Wisconsin, so that the entire extended family could vacation together. I was ten when I saw Elmwood and then for the first time I understood: a lake was a small body of water you could look across to see the opposite side. But this was part of what it meant to grow up on the North Shore. Horizons were boundless. Everything was bigger and better than anywhere else but you didn't know that until too late, until you'd left it behind and couldn't go back. Until you'd gone out into the world with an unrealistic sense of proportion, and unrealistic expectations as well.

"Well," Karen said finally, tucking me closer. "He certainly sounds organized."

I squeezed her hand in my pocket. When Karen left home for college, I missed her desperately. I still missed her. I missed living with my sister. I missed playing cello with her.

The last time I'd played was together with her, in Chicago's Civic Orchestra. Every afternoon, the summer I graduated from high school, we drove the station wagon to Wilmette, then rattled south on the El, bracing our instruments, watching the asphalt roofs of brick three-flats shimmer with radiation as we jolted past. Orchestra Hall was air-conditioned, and this was a new and wonderful experience, to come in off the hot downtown pavements, through the lobby down to the basement, to unpack, tighten and rosin the bow, tune, then ascend to the stage, all the while adjusting from heat-dullness and sweat to the sharp, swift clarity of other seasons, to spend the next few hours rehearsing in the miraculous suspended atmosphere of coolness. Three years earlier Karen had departed for college, leaving me to navigate alone. But now we were playing together again, and all was right with the world.

My first two years at New Trier High School I'd clung to her side. Then she graduated and went to Julliard and I was alone. When I was a senior I was first chair, too, but I knew I didn't deserve it; I was just all that was left. Sometimes I panicked, the way I had at fifteen when my teacher said, "You're better than your sister was at your age"—and Karen had agreed. For years I'd followed in her footsteps, from *Tune-a-Day* to Sevcik to Kreutzer, each exercise with bowings and fingerings already penciled in. Not just in music but in everything else: I wore her clothes, had her teachers, got her grades. Now both of them had thrust me beyond this safe terrain. I forgot about it as quickly as I could.

Two years later, though, Mr. Baumgart said it again. He was accompanying me to Ravel's *Pavane for a Dead Princess,* not a difficult piece, but one in which tone and phrasing were therefore all the more important. When we finished, he closed the music and sat on the piano bench, frowning out the window, framed in antique lace by his violist wife Lucinda, with whom I sometimes played duets.

"You have the potential to become an even better player than Karen," he said. He spoke to me as one adult to another, a gift that, under his tutelage, I'd awaited for years. Now, as he looked wistfully out the window, chin in hand, I almost regretted it. But you can't give back an inheritance.

I wasn't going to continue in music. I wanted to explain my decision, but I couldn't, because I couldn't articulate it to myself. So I remained mute, miserably aware that I was now fully and completely responsible, all on my own, for those moments when I disappointed others who cared. I walked out of that familiar house, full of upholstered furniture draped with antimacassars and smelling of rosin and old sheet music, and turned away into a future I'd chosen which excluded all I'd ever known.

But that summer, the summer of Civic, I hadn't yet begun to live out the consequences of that decision. We played Mahler's Ninth that summer. I'd never played Mahler before; it was a revelation. It altered my molecular structure. As we rode home in the gathering dusk, Mahler rolled around the car, swam around the seats, the poles, the CTA maps, wrapped itself around me when I closed my eyes, slipped through the cracks in the door, changed colors. I was cocooned in music.

Finally, though, at the end of that summer, as I stood on the stage of Orchestra Hall and looked up in surprise as it filled with applause, because the space was so immense, and we had filled it—finally I realized, standing there, looking up, that the whole world was not going to be like this. The whole world was not steeped in music, and, because of my decision, this was as good as it was ever going to get for me. And I had just realized I had talent.

My very first night at Wellesley College I dreamt I threw my cello over a cliff. I cried out and sat up to find myself in a fourth-floor double with a tiny dark-haired girl from New Jersey who had played The Talking Heads nonstop since her parents left that afternoon and whose mother had folded me in her arms and kissed me goodbye even though I was a virtual stranger. I was not at Julliard, or Oberlin, or Indiana. I was at a liberal arts college in Massachusetts without an orchestra to its name, and it was there the second-guessing started, later, and later, and later, as I felt the loss, the lack, over and over again. Why did I give it up? Time passed, but I was still haunted by the question.

I didn't have my music anymore. I didn't play with my sister anymore; I didn't live with her anymore. I was out there alone, in the wilderness of this world. No one but me, however, knew that. The wooded bluff, a tangle of blackened twigs and branches, was not a sheer drop but sloped down to the beach, otherwise I could have taken one step and gone down a hundred feet. Instead, I turned around, still holding Karen's hand in my pocket, and we headed for home.

Bobbie was sitting on a high stool at her Bartleby the Scrivener desk when we got there, paying bills and listening to Heinrich Schütz's *The*

Seven Last Words of Christ, which my brother, out of her hearing, always asserted were *Oh my God, this really fucking hurts.*

"Someone called for you," she said. "You Kim. About ten minutes ago."

"Larry?"

"No, not Larry. He didn't say. Someone from school, I think."

It wasn't Larry. It was Morgan, from the law library. "How did you get my number?" I blurted when he called again.

"You gave it to me, remember?"

"Of course." I didn't remember. "I'm sorry. I meant, how are you?"

"I'm flying back to Tulsa this afternoon and I have a two-hour layover at O'Hare."

"From Atlanta?"

"No, no, I'm in Indianapolis. Visiting my sister. Want to get a cup of coffee?"

"I can't drink coffee."

"Want to get a cup of water?"

It's not like I had anything else planned. Except having a baby in a month or so. I met his Great Lakes prop plane at three o'clock and we went to the café in the United concourse. I couldn't remember the last time I'd sat in public at a table for two with a man other than my husband, but Morgan acted as though it were the most normal thing in the world. He sat there drinking coffee and grinning like a fool.

"I completely forgot I gave you my phone number in Chicago," I said. "Isn't that weird?"

"No, you're pregnant. Pregnant women are forgetful."

"And what's your experience with pregnant women?"

"My mother. She had six."

"Well, I don't think I'm very good at it." I picked at a shard of cinnamon stick glued to the tabletop, probably a stir-stick from a holiday latte.

"Oh, you'll be great. You're an Amazon."

"I'll try to remember that."

"Of course it also depends on who you're having them with. You appear to be having this one entirely on your own."

37

"Not far off. We're pretty close to a virgin birth here."

He scrutinized his paper cup. "If you were my wife, I wouldn't leave you alone for a minute."

"I think…Larry's having a little trouble dealing with fatherhood."

He raised an eyebrow. "Children do."

I leaned forward. "Don't say anything to anyone. Nobody knows at school. I haven't really talked about it. Well, to Courtney a little."

"The journal editor? The sorority sister?"

"I don't know why I'm saying anything now." I raised a hand to ward off a garment bag as someone squeezed past. "It makes it sound worse than it is."

Morgan wouldn't stop smiling.

"You seem happy," I said.

After a while I said, "Ever dated any single mothers?"

"There's always a first time."

"I'd better go. You probably need to go."

"Let's take a walk." He picked up his backpack. We walked straight out to the garage and didn't speak until we were in the back seat of my mother's Buick on the fifth parking level. It was thirty degrees outside.

"I just wanted to get away from all the people," I said.

"Me, too."

I looked straight out the windshield.

"How are we doing on time?" I said finally.

He pulled a wristwatch out of his pocket. "Fine." He put his arm around my shoulder. "You're a great woman and you're going to be a wonderful mother."

I nodded.

"Also, I am very attracted to you. Just wanted to get that out," he said, and kissed me.

It was the first time in almost six years I'd kissed anyone but Larry, who didn't like to kiss anyway, so practically speaking it was the first time in six years I'd been kissed at all. When he got his hand inside my shirt I shot bolt upright. The car windows were fogged up. It reminded me of high school.

38

"We have to stop." I readjusted my size 40D maternity bra.

"I didn't ruin anything, did I?" Morgan asked. "We're still friends?"

"No…ah…yes. I mean, I never did this before."

He put his hand on my stomach. "Well, at least once."

"You know what I mean," I said, tapping my wedding ring.

"Listen, I'm on your side one hundred percent. I'm there if you need me. For anything. Even if we never have sex again."

"We didn't *have* sex," I replied in alarm.

"*You* almost did," he retorted. "Okay," he said, when I laughed. "Even if we never make out in the *back seat of your car* again."

I kissed him once more, so I could remember the smell of his skin.

〰〰

6

The Bargain

I WAS BRIEFING *New Mexico v. Mescalero Apache Tribe* under the blossoming apple tree when Larry came out with papers in his hand. "You have to sign this," he said. "I'm putting the listing in tomorrow."

It was four in the afternoon and I was still in my bathrobe. Beside me, eight-week-old Nathan slept in a wicker basket. My sister and brother and I had each, in our turn, been toted around in this basket like an oversized picnic by our mother, who'd been more agile then, her polio limp barely noticeable.

"Please can't I stay in the house?" I asked. "Until December? When I finish my last credits. I'm paying the mortgage anyway."

"No. We had a plan. We agreed to put the house on the market at the end of the school year."

I shuffled through the papers. "But I didn't know I'd need to stay an extra semester. I really want to stay in one place until I finish school."

"I'm selling this house. Now. I don't want to own property in Oklahoma."

"Larry, it's an assumed mortgage. The payments are really low. Rent on an apartment half the size would be twice as much."

"You're *not* renting an apartment here. You're moving to Seattle. You're just spending the summer with your mother until you can get over this postpartum thing."

I busied myself with the baby, tucking his teddy-print blanket more closely around him.

40

He raised his voice. "If you're not moving to Seattle now, you're not staying in this house. You're not getting any help from me."

Our neighbor stepped out her back door with a laundry basket.

Larry grabbed the papers. "Come inside."

"I think Karlene wants to see the baby."

"Come *inside*."

As soon as I crossed the threshold my legs felt weak. I subsided into a chair.

"Listen," Larry hissed, "these are the ground rules. Remember? You do all the shopping. All the cooking. And give me sex whenever I want. Or I'll kick you out of the house. *Before* the end of the semester. This is *my* house. Now sign the listing."

I signed. He smiled sarcastically. I'd never noticed before how thin his lips were. I looked out at the basket. "You remember I have my evening seminar today."

"Right. I'm watching the baby. That's fine."

"So I'm going to get ready now, okay? He shouldn't wake up for another hour, but you'll keep your eye on him while I'm in the shower, right?"

"Right, fine, fine."

"So...are you driving me, or can I drive myself?"

"You can drive yourself tonight." He ran two hands through his hair, an habitual gesture which had recently taken on the look of someone trying to anchor his head to his shoulders. "But you have to come home right afterwards. You have to be home by eight forty-five. Exactly."

THE STALE SMELL of marijuana hung in the air when I climbed up into the attic the next morning. Larry was lying half-in, half-out of a sleeping bag. Since he'd taken a leave from school a month after the birth, his square footage requirements had mysteriously increased. The back bedroom was still his office—the baby slept beside me in a bassinet—but the unfinished attic was now his music room. In all our time together I'd hardly ever seen Larry smoke a joint. Was this the West Coast influence?

"I have to run to school because I forgot the Morgenstern paper," I said. "The deadline's tomorrow. I'm sorry."

He rolled over. "You were just there last night."

"I know. I'm sorry. Courtney had it in the journal office for me. I just forgot."

He groped for his battery-operated shaver, flipped it on, and started on his jaw. "I thought you only had to go to school once today."

"I'm really sorry."

"Just make some coffee."

"Already done."

"Great." He pulled his lip down over his teeth and addressed the moustache area.

I perched on the edge of the doorwell, my feet on the ladder, and looked around. Four amps, a sitar, a djembe, a steel-string guitar; it was quite a magpie's nest. The disarray was unusual for him.

The instrument Larry really played well—brilliantly, in fact—was the piano. I found that out soon after we met at Columbia University. We'd been introduced, briefly, by a mutual friend at the Presbyterian church near campus, the one that ran a lunch café out of its guild room. The next day we ran into each other there again. This time, I was standing in the narthex, eating my sandwich, so I could listen to the organist practice a Bach Toccata and Fugue. He invited me back to his apartment, where he played it for me on his upright and had a hard time convincing me he'd never heard that particular piece before. He was a savant. Now I realized: this was lucky, because he didn't have the discipline necessary to become a practiced musician. He did it not because he loved music, but because it came to him easily, because it was a novelty, because it was one for the scoreboard in his perennial competition with his brilliant brother and sister.

I noticed an electronic keyboard. "Didn't you take your Kurzweil to Seattle?"

"Yes. That's another one."

"Another? How much was it?"

He stared at me. "Eight hundred dollars."

"Do you...do you really need two electronic keyboards?"

"This is a better one. What do you care? It's my own money."

"But you said you couldn't split any of the groceries with me any-more!"

He snapped off the shaver and felt his chin. "That's different. I decided that since you were living in this house, you should pay for the groceries." His eyes, which had once been warm, attractive, needy, were glaring at me like a gorgon's. I backed down the ladder.

I dressed in a maternity jeans skirt and tank top, then switched to a tee shirt in case Larry objected. All the self-possession I'd had as a preg-nant woman living alone had evaporated when he had returned. Since that Sunday, since the Phone Call, I could still do the difficult things: brief cases, proofread journal articles, navigate complicated board discus-sions. It was the simple things that were hard now. My brain had col-lapsed like a telescope, and I operated from moment to moment, all my attention concentrated on a new kind of radar that had sprung up in my head, which tracked Larry's position in the house at every moment.

I was sitting on the bed, nursing Nathan, when he emerged from the back room, fully dressed. He picked up the travel mug of coffee I had waiting for him and walked out the door. I tucked Nathan in the crook of my arm and scurried after him, refastening my nursing bra with the other hand.

We drove the five minutes to school in silence.

"This is a yellow line area, honey," I said when he pulled up to the curb.

"I'm staying with the car. Just hurry up." I leaned in the back to kiss the baby. Had Larry always been this impatient? I added that to THINGS TO THINK ABOUT LATER.

In the journal office Courtney was munching on a sausage-and-egg breakfast biscuit.

"How can you *eat* that?"

"I know, I know," she said, swiping the wrapper into the waste-basket. "We're up against it now. I don't have time to eat right."

A junior editor stuck his head in the door for a nanosecond to check his mailbox. Courtney caught him. "Did you finish the footnotes on the Rudnick?"

He stuck his head back in again. "Not yet. Don't worry."

I said, "I just came to get the Morgenstern. I forgot to pick it up last night."

"Can you get it done by tomorrow? —Hey, Professor!" She turned on a bright smile and waved through the door, then turned back. "We're still getting together tomorrow, aren't we? You and me and Maureen? For the final edit."

I took the paper out of my box and tossed a Spring Luau flyer into the circular file. "Do you think we could meet at my house instead?"

"But y'all don't have air-conditioning."

"I know." I put the file folder in my bag, took my time with the clasps. "I don't know if I can get away from the house for that long. With the baby."

"Well, okay. I'll write it down but don't forget to tell Maureen." She erased the last box in the "Morgenstern" category on the marker board and replaced it with "Baltakis 4 p.m." She fiddled with the marker. "You know, he called me yesterday. About you."

"About me?"

"Well, he knows Howard's a doctor and all…"

"He's a *foot* doctor, Courtney."

"He's concerned about you." She capped the marker and put it away. "He just wanted to know about pregnancy hormones, and when they go away, and stuff. Like he said you were tired and cranky all the time, and had temper tantrums, and you wrote some mean things about his parents in your journal."

"Don't you think that's weird, that he would read my journal?"

She threw her hands up. "I don't want to get in the middle of this. I just wanted you to know he called. And it was embarrassing. I didn't know what to say. I just said basically nothing. I wish he wouldn't call again."

"You mean—it's happened before?"

"Once."

"If you don't want to talk to him when he calls, just tell him."

"I know." She fiddled with her pearls. "It's just, he's, well, hard to say no to, you know?"

"I know."

We contemplated the situation silently.

"I have to go," I said finally. "They're waiting in the car."

"They're in the car? Why didn't you say so? I have to see that baby." She brushed crumbs off her suit and followed me out.

"Hey, Larry! Y'all are in a no parking zone, you know. I'll be your lawyer when you get that ticket." She leaned into the back seat and put one hand on either side of Nathan's blue-capped head. "Oh my gosh, I just can't believe how fast you're growing!"

"Look what he can do now." Larry guided the baby's palm toward Courtney's finger and he gripped it instinctively.

"Well look at that," she cooed. "You are just getting bigger and stronger every day." She looked at Larry coyly. "Little did I know when we all went to Grand Cayman after finals last year this would come of it."

He grinned at her.

I buckled my seat belt and stared out the windshield.

"Y'all have fun with that baby," she caroled, as Larry drove away.

"Please come to visit again," I begged Karen. "I really need to see you. Wait a minute." I took a bite of tomato sandwich.

"Are you eating?"

I wiped my mouth. "Sorry. Nursing mothers are always hungry."

"I remember Dad said he learned never to get between Mom and a plate of food when she was pregnant."

"Dad said that? To you? In what context?"

"I don't know. We were just joking around at the office. He said he made Mom cry once when he said her dress looked like a circus tent."

"Jeez. Even Larry never said anything like that to me." I took another bite. "Probably because he rarely saw me pregnant."

Karen was silent.

"You were supposed to laugh there."

"Are you sure you're okay?"

"I'm fine, I just…I want to see you. I'm tired."

45

"Oh, sweetie. Listen, I can't do it right now. *Carmen* starts tomorrow and that'll tie me up for two weeks. After that opera season is over. We'll get to spend more time together after the wedding. I promise. You know we're not doing the honeymoon until July." They were tacking it onto a ten-day symphony tour of Russia.

"Okay," I sniffled.

"I thought you were managing. Getting plenty of rest. Every time I call, Larry says you're sleeping."

"You've been calling?" I took the phone outside and stood with my back against one of the silver maples. "When did you call?"

"I don't know. Twice yesterday. Before that, I don't remember."

I said goodbye without hanging up, and heard two clicks on the line. I went back in and tapped on Larry's door. I put my phone down on the desk next to his. "If you wanted to talk to my sister, why didn't you say so?"

He kept his eyes on his book. "I just wanted to hear what she had to say."

"No, you just wanted to hear what *I* had to say."

"It's my phone."

"And it's my conversation."

He turned around. "I need to know what you're saying about me."

"I wasn't saying anything about you."

"You were about to. I haven't done anything wrong. I'm your husband. If you say anything bad about me to anyone, I'll have a few choice things to tell your friends myself."

"Such as?"

"Such as...who's Chris?"

"Chris?" I shook my head. "You mean Chris from the Journal board? Chris in my IP class? Black hair, glasses?"

"I don't know what he looks like. He just leaves messages on the machine."

"We were going to study for the exam but he never got back to me..." I trailed off as I realized why.

"Why are you always studying with guys?"

"Larry, it's statistical. Even at Columbia it was less than half."

Where he'd gotten his law degree. Not that he'd ever used it. "At this school only twenty percent of the students are women."

"I know. That's a problem. I already told Courtney to put you in an all-girl editing group for this issue."

The Morgenstern article: me, Courtney, Maureen. "You 'told' her?"

"I asked her. Yes. She agreed it was a good idea. She said she'd been concerned too. That you'd been acting strange. That people were noticing."

"I need some fresh air."

"You can't go out."

"That was part of the bargain. You *said* I could take my walks alone."

"All right, don't get hysterical. Go ahead. But you have to take care of me first."

Nathan fell asleep in the sling to the rhythm of my steps. He looked like a pea in a pod in his green plaid romper, his closed eyes tiny slits, his cheeks fat and rosy. "At least you're a well-dressed baby," I said softly, tucking his cap back down over his ears, then lifting my fingers to my nose. They still smelled faintly of the antiseptic I'd taken to pouring over my hands after obliging Larry.

On my third round someone got up from a bench as I walked by, a tall, angular man with a blond ponytail and a friendly smile. "My God, that's a baby!" he exclaimed. "I thought it was a purse."

I dipped the edge of the sling to show Nathan off.

"How old is he?"

"Nine weeks."

He put down his newspaper. "Can I hold him? I'm certified."

I handed him over.

"What's his name? Nathan? Look at him. He's so smart."

"How can you tell?"

"Oh, the look in his eyes. The shape of his head. You can tell he's a smart baby." He handed him back. "So, are you married?"

"Of course I'm married!"

"Just my luck. If you weren't married, I could ask you out."

"I'm glad you have scruples."

"I don't always. What do you do?"

"I'm a law student."

"With a newborn! A Power babe. I'm just an artist. A lazy good-for-nothing."

I sat down. "Is that the Sunday Times? You get it delivered?"

"They don't *deliver* it here. Not in this town. You have to go *get* it. There are two places, Bigelow's or the newsstand at 41st and Yale. So are you sure you're married?"

"Last time I checked." I hesitated. "I have to check frequently."

"That sounds familiar. I've been there too."

"Do you have kids?"

"Two, one in college, one out. I was a child groom," he added in response to my surprise, and made me laugh again. "I know it gets hard. Stuff happens. But just to show you my heart's in the right place, I won't ask for your phone number."

"That's big of you."

He pulled a flyer out of his pocket. "But I do have an exhibit opening on Friday. Maybe you and your husband can come."

"We'll see." I tucked it in the sling and stood up. "Thanks for making me laugh."

He gave a gentle salute. "Anytime."

I stopped at the Git'n'Go for a soda. When I got home Larry was in the dining room stacking books on the piano. The table was clear except for paper and pen.

"Oh! You're starting the make-up exam." I set down my soda and slipped Nathan out of the sling, feeling his bottom for dampness. "Say hi to Daddy," I whispered, waving his arm. "Larry, I just met this guy, he's an artist, he couldn't believe it was a baby when he saw Nathan in the sling. He said, 'I thought that was some kind of purse.' He said, 'You can tell he's a smart baby.'" I held Nathan up and away. "Sweet pumpkin." He blinked at me lazily. I turned him to face Larry again. "I think so too, but how can you tell?"

"I want to go with you next time," he said harshly.

I stopped breathing.

"It's *my* baby, you know." He got up, sat down, realigned his pens. "Could you make some more coffee, please."

Maybe it wasn't too late.

I put Nathan in the swing, cranked it up, started the coffee, got into the shower. Ten minutes later, I emerged in clean sweatclothes, my hair wrapped in a towel. Maybe the cup of coffee had calmed him down. Maybe it was going to fizzle out.

"Where—the hell—have you BEEN?" It started slowly, but ended in a shout.

In the swing, Nathan sat motionless, tiny legs jacked out, staring at us with a finger in his mouth. One of his booties had fallen off.

"I'm waiting for my coffee!"

"It wasn't ready yet." I kneeled down, swiped up the bootie and tied it back on. "It was just brewing. I'll get it now."

"It's been ready for ten fucking minutes!"

I cranked up the swing. "Okay, okay, I'm getting it now." I tried to walk by him but he grabbed my arm.

"You should have waited until it was done!"

"I'm sorry, I didn't realize, I'll get it now."

"You didn't *realize*?"

"I mean, sometimes you pour your own cup, don't you? You pour your own cup, don't you remember? You pour your own cup."

He twisted harder. I bent my knees, and the towel fell off.

"That's the deal. You're my wife. You're supposed to take *care* of me. Not go out with friends for a soda." He used his free hand to sweep the paper cup off the table. Soda splashed on my face. "I'm trying to get ready for an exam now. I have to take a fucking *exam*."

He had me down to the floor. "I'm sorry! I'm sorry!" I cried.

He let go.

I straightened up and picked up the towel. "Larry, you never, you never used to swear like that, please don't yell like that in front of the baby, it's not good for him, it upsets him."

"Don't tell me what to do!" he yelled, loudly enough that a string in the piano vibrated. He took Nathan roughly from the swing, pressed him to his chest. "It has absolutely no effect on him! He doesn't know what's going on!" He went into the back room and shut the door.

I opened it.

"Go away!" he screamed, standing in the middle of the room, still clutching the baby.

I shut it quickly and stood there. Only for a moment. My baby was behind that door. I had to disobey. This is what that man Drew had meant on the phone, when I made the Phone Call, this is what he meant.

I ran to the kitchen, hopping over the puddle of diet soda on the floor. I poured a mug of coffee with trembling hand, added cream liberally, stirred in four spoonfuls of sugar, picked it up, slopped it onto the back of my hand, carefully wiped off the rim with a clean dishtowel, carried it back with two hands.

"Go away!" he roared, when I knocked again.

I opened the door a crack.

"GET OUT!" He was still standing in the middle of the room.

"Now, Larry," I advanced, holding out the mug, "let me take the baby, you're upset, you've got a lot of work to do, let me take him off your hands and you can be alone." I set the coffee down on the desk, swiftly removed the baby from his arms, surprisingly, thankfully, encountering no resistance, all the while soothing, wheedling, backing out of the room, shutting the door.

I buckled onto the sofa, laying my cheek against Nathan's, stroking the faint down on his tiny head with one hand. My own head blossomed with a pounding so hard I thought at first the room was moving. I didn't notice I'd burned my hand. There was nowhere I could go. This was my home. There was nowhere I could go, without giving it all away.

〰〰
〰〰

7

Make No Snap Decisions

DANA WASN'T HOME FROM WORK. I parked at the curb and sat, while the baby snoozed behind me. A bower of maples arched above us, branches lacing gracefully over the wide, gently-curving cement street. The soft-looking yellow-green leaves were losing their new-born tinge. Bruised blossoms from a big-leaf magnolia littered the lawn. I hadn't noticed it until now, but the season had turned. The forsythia was long past flower, and the time of the lilacs was gone.

There was a car in Dana's driveway with Louisiana plates. A woman emerged from the house and took a suitcase from the trunk. I knew it was the sister I hadn't met yet. Seeing me, she set it down and came straight across the lawn.

"You must be Kim! I'm Trish." She enveloped me in a hug. "I hear you're one worn-out mama. Hey, little cricket!" She poked her head in Nathan's window. "Did you just wake up? You are coming with me." He gazed at her rapturously.

I followed, the portable playpen banging against my hip. As I unfolded it in the living room Dana came in, lugging the suitcase.

"You left your trunk open!" she scolded, dropping it and hugging her sister.

"Hello to you too."

"I had a close call. Sheri forgot she was covering for me tonight. I had to call her up and yell at her. 'My big sister that I haven't seen in two years is coming up from Loosiana with a cooler full of crawfish and shrimp and you're not going to let me get home when I covered for you last month so you could drive to Dallas for your brother's wedding because you're too cheap to fly?'"

"What did she say?" Trish asked.

"Said she'd be right there. What else could she say?" She pulled a rattle out of the pocket of her scrubs. "Look what Auntie Dana's got for you," she crooned at Nathan, closing his fingers around it and shaking it gently. His eyes widened. "That'll be good for about three minutes, won't it, Mommy? I'll be right back."

"We might get a few more out of it," Trish said. "It makes noise."

Dana returned in jeans and a black tank top appliquéd with red velvet lips. "Now we're ready. Time for Girl Talk." She danced through the kitchen, pedaling her arms. "The Cate Brothers are going to be at Cain's Ballroom tomorrow night."

"Do I know them?" Trish asked. She set a stockpot on the stove, pulled a plastic bag of crawfish out of the cooler and slung it into the sink.

"They're from Fayetteville," I said.

"Last time the older one was looking at you."

"He was looking at a lot of girls."

"He was looking at *you*. A lot."

"We were right in front of the stage," I protested.

"Mostly at you."

I handed her a glass of wine. "Well, if you'd worn *that* to the concert, it might have been different."

"I was."

Dana was the one who got me into R&B. I met her at the Indian Territory coffee house back in the days when I had freedom of movement, relatively speaking. It was close to the hospital where she worked, and I saw her there a few times before she plopped down next to me one day and tapped my stack of books with a polished fingertip.

"Medicine or law?" She pushed them around to read the spines. "Law. You look too mellow for a lawyer." She started telling me all about her attorney, Ludger Steinhauer, who was, she swore, the only lawyer in town who rode a Harley. As his primary vehicle, she meant. Then she invited me to go see Delbert McClinton with her the next weekend.

"And the best part," I told Trish, "is that Larry hates R&B. Really hates it."

"You gotta have something you do that's your own," Trish said. "Something separate."

"True. Preferably not child-rearing."

Dana's twelve-year-old came in with his gang of friends and his guitar and grabbed a bag of corn chips.

"Aren't you forgetting something?" Dana asked.

He waited until the rest of his band had filed past, then gave his aunt a quick hug. The garage door shut heavily behind him, cutting off the drummer's warm-up.

"Thank God we soundproofed that door," said Dana. She poured a glass of water and put it in front of me. "Drink this, and slow down."

I sipped it obediently. "It's hard to believe you're sisters. You look so different." Dana was skinny and pale, with straight black hair, but her sister was big and broad-shouldered. You could see Indian blood in her somewhere.

"We're steps," Trish said. "Same Mama, different daddies. I had the nice one, Dana got the mean one."

"The one that pulled the heads off all my Barbie dolls and put'em in the garbage."

"Why?"

Dana shrugged. "He said I was too big for them because I was twelve. But really he was pissed 'cause he thought I wasn't his. He just had this idea stuck in his head and he was taking it out on me." She leaned forward. "You know, what I want to do is, DNA. They can do it on dead people now. If they can do it on Billy the Kid who's been dead that long I want to do it on my dad. He got a lot of people in the family convinced. Just because it was a shotgun wedding."

And her first child had been stillborn, a blue baby. I chewed a breadstick silently. My own situation was paling rapidly in comparison.

"That Barbie collection would be worth a lot of money today," Dana sighed, lifting a restless Nathan from the playpen.

Her son returned and took a liter bottle of cola out of the fridge.

"Y'all use cups with that," Dana said, as she jiggled the baby on her hip.

I looked out the front window at my car. "You know what he did the other day? Larry. I was driving home, I was about ten minutes late, supposed to be home at two-thirty, just turned off 21st onto Des Moines, so I was, I don't know, how many blocks away…"

"Three, four." Dana sat down with the baby.

"And Larry drives past me, in the other direction, and waves. So I'm a little confused, because he's supposed to be watching Nathan, but he doesn't have a car seat in his car, we only have one in mine. I mean, he just bought a new car, but we only have one car seat."

"He took the baby in the car without a car seat?" Trish asked.

"Well, that's what I was wondering. Did he borrow one or something, so I get to the house, and there's Nathan, swinging away in the baby swing."

Trish looked from me to Dana and back again. "I don't get it. Is this guy retarded or something?"

Dana put her hands over Nathan's ears. "No, he's just making the slowest transition to fatherhood I've ever seen."

"Well—what did he have to say for himself?" asked Trish.

"He got all mad at me for asking about it. He said he had an appointment, he knew I'd be there in a while, so he left. He said, 'What could have happened? He was strapped in.'"

Dana leaned forward. "I'm getting worried about this man."

"I guess he was right," I said. "The baby didn't get hurt or anything."

Trish said, "Sounds like he needs a childrearing class."

"It's parenting now." Dana passed the baby to Trish. "That's what you call it. But this guy doesn't know what the word parent means. What he needs is an attitude adjustment. And I'm fixing to give it to him when he gets back to town." She spread her arms out flat on the table, palms down. "What. Is. His. Problem."

"I think…I don't think…I don't think he's ever going to make that transition to fatherhood."

Dana's husband arrived. He dropped his briefcase, and gave us each a kiss. "How was the drive?" he asked Trish.

"Fine." She stretched out her arms, then smoothed back her thick hair with both hands. "Long. Not fast enough. The crawfish kept me company."

"And we're glad for that." Dave took off his American Airlines ID and hooked it over the back of his chair. "I notice a folding crib in my living room, so I'm guessing it will be a long night."

"We're sleeping over," I said.

Dana patted my arm. "This girl ain't driving tonight."

"Where's your hubby?"

"He went to Boston for a few days to see his mom."

He nodded.

We sat in silence for a moment, listening to the faint thump of the band from the garage.

"Did I interrupt something?" Dave asked.

Dana picked up his guitar and held it out.

"Is that a hint?"

"Jam with them awhile, supper isn't ready."

"You think they want me?"

"According to Penelope Leach we've got about four point five months before he's not going to want to see either of our faces again for about a decade. So do it now."

"I thought Penelope Leach only went up to age five."

"She's expanded her territory. Now get your butt out of here and teach them those changes to "Stairway to Heaven" right before I go crazy."

"Okey dokey." He slid the strap over his head and picked up his glass, exiting with a practiced one-heel delay to keep the door from slamming. Dave was always calm and quiet, even on stage with his band on the weekends. He might bend his knees a little during a solo, but that was about it. I opened a new file folder: QUALITIES TO LOOK FOR IN A MAN. There might be something to Courtney's checklist concept.

"So," Dana said.

I looked out the window. "I missed the lilacs this year."

She leaned forward. "What's going on?"

I had a postpartum hot flash, and closed my eyes.

After my father died, my mother got out her knitting bag one night and along with the yarn pulled out a piece of paper. She looked at it, then handed it to me:

1. MAKE NO SNAP DECISIONS.

We were at the hospital, she said. *He wanted to make me a list.* She gave a faint smile. *He wanted to make me a list...but then he got too tired.*

I opened my eyes. Larry was far away, not just out of town but out of state. There was no way he could hear me. I took a long deep breath, but it came out empty.

"So," Dana said again. Dana was Nathan's godmother. She was by my side all twenty-five hours of labor. She was the one who told me I could do it; she was the one who cried, *It's a boy!* It was her voice. Hers: *It's a boy!*

"I'm getting a divorce," I said.

She raised balled fists slowly to her temples. "Thank God," she exhaled. Then she pushed back and was up, spinning around and pumping her fists. "Oh, my God, finally! I'm so happy! Now I can tell you how much I hate him. I kept my lip zipped for three whole years! What a snake! What an absolute snake! I'm so happy. You're not going to Seattle. You're *not going* to Seattle!"

Dave put his head through the door. "Everything okay?"

"Everything's great! Kim's getting a divorce!"

"Oh, gee, sorry to hear that, Kim."

"Congratulate her, you doofus."

"Okay, congratulations." He ducked back out.

"You know when you had the baby, it was about noon of the second day, and I couldn't take it anymore, I was freaking out, I was like, 'Okay, we've tried the home birth thing and it ain't working, told you that midwife should have been carrying oxygen, can we go to the hospital now?' You were running out of gas. I went into the kitchen and there he was sitting there reading a book. With his legs crossed. And I said, 'Where's the liquor?' And he said 'On top of the fridge.' And I grabbed a bottle, I don't even know what it was, and I took a shot, and he looks at me and says, 'Is something wrong?' And I was just snarlin'. I just couldn't believe it. I said, 'Why don't you get the fuck out there and hold your wife's hand for Christ's sake? She's been in hard labor for twenty hours. Why don't you give her some fucking support.' I must have scared him, 'cause he got up."

"That's why he came. I remember he came in and held my hand once but he was reading a book and that bothered me so much I told him to go away."

"I may have even used the word asshole. I can't remember. I think I did."

I smiled ruefully. "I always thought that was one of the things we had in common."

"What?" they said together.

"We both liked to read so much."

Trish got up to stir the gumbo.

After a moment she said, "Sounds like you need a lawyer."

"A good one," I agreed. "I can't just look in the yellow pages. It's got to be a really good lawyer, someone Larry can't push around."

"Good lawyer. Good lawyer. Best lawyer in town is what you need." Dana said. "I'll ask some of the doctors. You need a rich people's lawyer."

I KNEW I WAS in the right place because of the hunting prints. Larry thought I was taking a run at Riverparks, but I was actually on the sixteenth floor of Tulsa's tallest office building, in the waiting room of the best family law firm in town. I'd driven to the parking lot at 21st and Riverside—the same place I'd made the Phone Call—and scanned traffic for a full ten minutes before sprinting into the public restroom with the bag containing my navy suit and heels. For some reason I felt I needed to wear a suit. I was glad for it now; I'd already sweated through the blouse. I sat in a wingchair, smearing the ink on the same two pages of *Southern Living* and watching the door, frantic to get inside Hal Duncan's office before Larry walked through it and ruined my last chance.

Then, suddenly, I was sitting in another armchair in front of Mr. Duncan's desk, looking over a credenza-top studio portrait of his children at a panoramic view of downtown. At this hour the lowrise buildings were all in shadow; only the tops of the skyscrapers still caught the sun. *How nice,* I thought, *he gives his guests the view,* then corrected myself: *clients.*

"So." Mr. Duncan smoothed his hands over his desktop, a large expanse of burled walnut completely empty save for a blotter, and a tiny bronze statuette of a bronco buster just managing to stay in the saddle. Mr. Duncan was balding, with a long nose and full lips, a big man but he carried it well, and a fastidious dresser; his shirt had enough starch in it to withstand a gale force, and he wore a silver bar in his repp tie, an old-fashioned touch that reminded me of my dad.

After a moment he drew a yellow pad toward him and uncapped a fountain pen. "I take it you want to file for divorce."

I nodded.

His suit jacket hung on a coat tree in the corner, not draped, but on a proper hanger. This attention to detail was reassuring.

He started asking questions and I watched his hand move down the yellow pad. Name, address, where and when we'd married. No joint property except the bungalow which was already under contract. One child born, on such and such a date.

"He doesn't want custody," I assured him. "He's totally uninterested in the baby."

He looked up at me, then down, flipped to the next yellow page.

"How long will this take?" I hazarded.

"Without children, thirty days; with kids, you're looking at ninety, assuming settlement proceeds at a reasonable pace." He took off his glasses and sat back. "Have you talked to him about this at all?"

I tucked a loose strand behind my ear. I'd done my hair in a French twist, like Karen. I wanted to look as normal as possible; I needed this man to take my case. "Uh, he's kind of…he's got it in his head that we're going to separate for a while. The house closes next week so I'm going to spend the summer with my mother in Chicago and he typed up a separation agreement—"

He sat forward. "Himself?"

"Yes. It was just something he wrote. He typed it up and we signed it yesterday."

Another note on the pad.

"He put down that I had full custody of the baby for the summer and he'd visit us in Illinois a few times" —another note, underlined— "And that we're not getting divorced—"

Here he put the pen down.

"The thing is," I rushed on, "he *knows* it's going to happen and we almost talked about it a couple times but he just needs to get used to the idea and he doesn't want to do it yet, because he said *his* psychotherapist didn't get divorced until *his* son was eight, so I want to file the papers and have him served after I've left for Chicago, because I'm a little afraid of what his reaction might be." I concentrated on the carpet. "So I signed that paper just to keep him from getting mad. That's why I want the petition filed after I leave."

There was a long pause, during which I worried that he was going to kick me out of his office.

"We can do that. You *are* coming back to Oklahoma?"

"Yes. I signed a lease on an apartment at Riverview Gardens yesterday. For August fifteenth. He doesn't know about it."

He pulled over his calendar. "We'll get everything written up for you to sign, then we'll do service by mail. There's plenty of time for that if he's staying in town until the closing. We'll get a court date when we file, although that usually changes. After he's served he'll get a lawyer here and we'll work out the details." He passed a hand over his chin. "The only real problem I see is visitation, if he lives on the other side of the country. We'll just have to see who the judge is."

"You know, I'm not even sure he'll want any. He's not interested in the baby. The baby is why we're getting divorced."

"You'd be surprised at the number of dads who suddenly perk up when a divorce is in the works. You may be right, but I don't want to make any assumptions."

I put the check for the retainer on his desk. "Just, ah, I just want to make sure he's not served until I'm out of town."

"We can do that."

"And maybe don't call me in Chicago because my sister's getting married in a couple weeks and I don't want to tell anyone until after that."

"We can do that too." He wrote down my departure date.

That was it; I was done.

As I stood up to leave I noticed a set of butterfly prints on the wall.

"My wife got me those," Mr. Duncan said. "I was getting tired of Audubon birds. I used to collect butterflies when I was a boy." He got up and stood next to me. "We had a Monarch migration through Tulsa about nine years ago—that's this one—I'm trying to remember...the year my youngest was in kindergarten. Their path varies, you know. It was quite a sight." He shook my hand. "Give us a call from Chicago after you get there and we'll see where we stand with the service. Wait a few days, it'll probably take a few days."

I changed back into my running clothes at the public restroom and took a real run in order to work up a convincing sweat. I thought about Hal Duncan. I liked the way he kept saying, "We can do that." This man was an expert. He'd done this for years. All I had to do was give him the retainer, and I'd be divorced in no time. Two days later I packed up the baby, threw my wedding shoes into a Salvation Army bin, and got on a plane for Chicago.

8

Member of the Wedding

AT EIGHT O'CLOCK IN THE MORNING the day before her wedding, Karen was in the kitchen at Elmwood. Clad in leotard and headband, she'd already completed her video workout. I counted thirty-two slices of bread on the kitchen table.

"I want lunch to be ready," she said.

I unlatched a cupboard and selected a creamware mug from a middle, frequently-used shelf, ran my finger around the inside, then filled it with coffee. "You could have saved a lot of money and catered your own wedding."

"Don't hate me because I got the domestic engineering gene." She dealt out iceberg leaves. "Where's the baby?"

"He's upstairs. Sleeping. Now."

"Poor Kimmie. Don't worry, he'll be sleeping through soon. It's right about time." She started slicing on the diagonal. "Do you think I should quarter them?"

At the age of twelve, Karen had told our mother she was going to get married at the Wisconsin lake house, and ever since then they'd sparred about it, because Bobbie felt that a wedding wasn't official unless it took place in a house of worship. But by the time the event actually materialized, the issue no longer seemed so vital. I hadn't even had a ceremony; at least Karen's plans included a priest. Our mother decided to quit while she was ahead.

My sister and I had driven up earlier in the week with various pieces of equipment and luggage wedged around Nathan's car seat, and my dress spread out in the trunk. Karen's dress was coming up with our uncle, Will, and his wife Ginny; we wanted to keep baby and wedding gown as far apart as possible.

It was unseasonably warm for southern Wisconsin in May. All through the preparations the heat continued to rise, and all through the preparations Karen remained unflaggingly cheerful. She managed everything: the arrival of out-of-town friends, the lawnmowing, the grocery runs, the rehearsal, the rehearsal dinner at the Red Circle Inn in Nashotah. Impending bride-dom had done nothing to obscure her inner drill sergeant. She was confident the weather would be delivered as ordered on Saturday.

But late on Friday night, after everyone had gone, or gone to sleep, she came into my room and sat down on the bed. She rubbed her thumb across her top lip, a habit from earliest childhood.

"I'm getting nervous," she said.

I pulled the curtain across the closet and sat beside her, buttoning up my pajama top and thinking fast. At the moment I was at a low ebb of confidence about the institution of marriage in general, not to mention my qualifications as an expert in particular. "If you're not sure, you can put it off. You don't have to do this. Not until you're completely ready."

"No, no, no. I *am* ready. My birthday is in September."

"So?"

"So I'll be thirty. I have to get married before I'm thirty."

My heart sunk.

"I mean, I want to marry Frank, so why put it off? That's what I mean. It's just...how do I know I'm doing the right thing?"

I looked at my confident, talented big sister, who always knew what she was doing and did it better than me. For my own sake as well as hers, I desperately needed to feel that she knew what she was doing. That I was the only failure, that my impending divorce, the first ever on both sides of the family, was an anomaly.

"I don't know Frank all that well," I said finally, "but all the different times I've been around, I never got that false step feeling. He's never once done anything to give me pause."

"I know. It's not him, it's just…"

It occurred to me: maybe I just needed to be quiet. All she needed was to talk. "What?" I asked.

"Well…Dad never met him. I'll never know what Dad would think about Frank. I can't talk to Mom as well as you can. You're more like her. I always talked with Dad more. And now he's gone. You still have your parent that you can talk to. But me…I have to use my own judgment." She caught back a sob. "When big important things in your life happen, that's when you realize. He's never going to see you get married or have kids or anything."

With me it was a mixed bag; there were a few things I didn't want him to see.

I smoothed her hair off her forehead. "Here. Sit up." I turned her so we faced the beveled mirror over the dresser. I put my cheek to hers. "Look."

When we were little we used to stand at the bathroom sink at bedtime after washing our faces, looking in the mirror pressed tightly cheek to cheek, wondering if we could pass as twins. "You've still got me," I said. "You've still got me to talk to. And Mom, and Doug. And we'll just have to make do with that. You've still got us."

She pulled a tissue out of her pajama pocket. "The difference between you and me," she said, "is that I need answers to my questions. But you, it doesn't bother you. You're more patient. You can keep going without the answers. You can *not* know all the answers and still be comfortable."

"There's a philosophy major for you," I joked.

She wiped her eyes and smiled.

"But I do have a question for you," I said, "and you have to answer it now." I looked out the window, tapping my lip with my finger once, twice, three times. She waited. I turned to her. "How do you truly, honestly, in the bottom of your heart—"

"—feel about Frank." She fell silent, unusually so; unlike me, Karen was never at a loss for words.

"The way..." she said, "the way I feel with Frank...is like when we were little, and we were just playing, together, you know, us, and Mom and Dad were there, somewhere, and we were all together." She looked up. "It's a family feeling. When I'm with Frank, I get that same feeling. With him I feel...at home."

I knew exactly what she meant. I'd had that feeling before, but not with Larry. Never with Larry. I'd sensed it with Andy, the quiet, intense boy from Wilmette I'd dated during college summers, who was now on his way to becoming a well-known composer. And recently, I'd caught a glimpse of it with John, who'd put my screen door back on after a law journal meeting last Fall. But I'd never felt that way with Larry. Relief flooded over me. I had to swallow to control my voice. "Then you're right on track."

After she left, I lay in bed watching the moon over the lake and listening to the shudder of a nighthawk's dive, first close, then further and further away. I was jealous: she had love. She was making the right choices. She could cry. I'd never felt older than Karen, even though I'd married before she did, had a baby before she did—I figured those were just things that happened when you all tumbled into adulthood. But now I did. For the first time in our life together, I felt older than my sister.

THE NEXT MORNING I found Angela, the other bridesmaid, in the dining room, rosining her bow in her nightgown.

"The heat didn't break, did it," I said, putting down the empty wicker basket and switching the baby to my other shoulder.

"That's okay. We'll leave off the jackets and wear scarves instead. I brought them as a back-up." Angela had sewn our dresses herself.

"Don't make me look like Isadora Duncan."

She sat down and opened her music. "You'll see. Don't worry. I'm from Indiana, I know from scarves." She pointed with her bow. "Isn't that supposed to be a baby carrier?"

"Yes, but I'm getting tired of bruises on my thighs."

Scale progressions of two-octave arpeggios followed me through the butler's pantry into the kitchen, where Karen was standing at the breakfast table, leafing through the *Milwaukee Sentinel.*

"I feel like I'm at summer camp for Type A's." I set down the basket. "It's like Oberlin without knee socks. Back page of section D," I told her.

She flipped the paper over. "'Continued humid, high of eighty-five...'" She looked up at me. "This is *not* supposed to happen in May. That was the whole point! Of doing this in the Spring!"

"You should have ordered monogrammed paper fans."

"This is it!" Karen decided. "There's always one thing that goes wrong at a wedding and this is it! Everything else will be fine. No missing cummerbunds. No lost rings. No music blowing off the stands."

"No babies throwing up on wedding attire."

"Let's stop right there. Is one of those for me?" She examined the bagel halves. "You didn't use the bagel slicer."

"There isn't one up here."

"Oh, yes, there is." She opened a drawer.

"No home should be without one. How does this stuff get here?"

Angela came in. "I just broke a D string," she said. "Do you have an extra D?"

"That wasn't supposed to happen," I laughed.

"What's so funny?" Angela asked.

"It doesn't count," insisted Karen, putting her hand over my mouth. "She's not playing in the wedding. If she were *playing* in the wedding, then that would be something gone wrong."

"You do have one, don't you?"

"Someone who remembers to bring a bagel slicer to her own wedding," I said, "would never forget an extra Jarger D."

"It depends if it's on the *Modern Bride* checklist," Angela smiled. She took the baby spoon and cup of rice cereal from me. "Can I try?"

"Laugh all you want," said Karen. "Someone has to do the organizing. In every couple, one is the organizer."

"That makes Frank the organizee," I said. "Is he aware of this?"

65

"All couples work that way. Look at you and Larry. He's off in his own little intellectual world. You do the grocery shopping."

I looked out the window. The florist's van was approaching. Over the years Uncle Will had extended the garden to the size of a small European principality. The pole row stretched a good sixty feet along the drive. Dew still clung to the fence. I'd been up twenty minutes and was already bone tired.

"Just you guys wait until you have a baby," I said. "Try to stay organized then."

"I'm sure you'll be there to answer my every question," Karen sang, going out to meet the flowers.

"You'd be better off with a magazine checklist," I called after her.

Nathan regurgitated cereal everywhere the bib wasn't: collar, shoulder, all down one sleeve.

"That looks like much more than I fed him," said Angela, cleaning him up with the speed, efficiency and cheer of someone who had been sleeping more than four hours a night.

"Let's just hope she didn't order him a boutonniere," I replied.

THE CATERER WAS LATE. Her van emerged from the woods into the clearing as the brass quintet finished Widor's Toccata; she shifted into neutral and coasted down the drive in silence, coming to rest under the silver maple near the kitchen. The servers crept out and sat in a row on the cement gutter of the old grass court to watch the ceremony. As soon as the first notes of the recessional sounded, they sprang up, but by the time the reception line was finished, all they had managed to do was to set up two bars on the lawn.

I unwrapped the scarf from around my neck and made a beeline for my brother and his fiancée, Cassie. They were strategically parked with our cousins Jim and Chas, Uncle Will's boys, beside a cooler the size of a footlocker.

Cassie fanned herself with a deckle-edged program. "It's going to be a long wait for food," she remarked.

"Who needs food?" Jim combed back the long blond hair he culti- vated to counteract the pin-striped banker image. "We have the bulk of the Wisconsin food pyramid represented right here. All we need is a small plate of cheese and sausage."

Jim's date cackled. She was wearing a flowered strapless dress, an incredible tan, no makeup but mascara, and a sloppy French twist. I could tell she was one of those people who could run off the tennis court, hop in the shower, and be special-occasion stunning five minutes later. She was what fashion magazines referred to when they used the word "effortless." I patted my dyed-to-match hair ornament to make sure it was still in the right place.

Doug palmed the cap off a bottle of beer and handed it to me. I gave him my scarf in return and took a long draught. "I'd rather climb in there," I said, indicating the cooler, "but I guess this'll have to do."

He draped the length of peach chiffon around his shoulders. "Thought about it myself," he said, "but it's not big enough to sit down in. Don't pass out," he added, as I took another gulp. He scooped up a palmful of ice chips, laved the back of his neck, and shook the remains into the hosta border.

"Don't get my scarf wet," I admonished.

"Weren't we roasting marshmallows up here this time last year?" Chas said. "I swear we were roasting marshmallows up here."

We moved away from the cooler, out of the foot traffic. I grabbed Cassie's arm. "See that guy? He's a trombone player. I dated him senior year at New Trier. He went to Northwestern. When we broke up he started going out with her, and they got married before they even graduated. She was skinnier then."

Doug pulled a bandana from his back pocket and mopped his brow. His hair had condensed into thick curls. "You know, a full fifty percent of these people, you're never going to see again in your entire life. So what's the point?"

"Doug," I said, "your friends are going to get married, you're going to get married, you're gonna have to do this, so just get used to it." He'd been engaged to Cassie for eight years, since freshman art class at De Paul.

"I know. But we're not having any decorations, or anything monogrammed. I made her sign a paper to that effect."

Cassie pulled the scarf off Doug's shoulders and tied a chiffon bow around a creosoted porch pillar. "What do you think?" she asked.

"Perfect," Jim's date and I answered in unison.

The men rolled their eyes.

"It needed something."

"Mmm. If we found Angela we could do the other side too."

"I don't know. The symmetry might be too precious."

We studied it again. "You're right," I said finally. "Symmetry is sometimes *not* the right thing."

Doug broke in. "The only thing I liked about this wedding was that there were no decorations. Now you've ruined it." He stuffed the bandana back in his pocket and poked Jim. "Let's go down to the dock. I want to have a smoke without Karen seeing."

"Will you bring us some chairs, Doug?" Cassie asked.

"And another one of these," I called after him, holding up the bottle. I turned to Cassie. "He's having fun."

"Mmm-hmm." Cassie was amply qualified to join the family, since she adhered to one of our cardinal rules: never use actual words if you can communicate sufficiently with your lips shut.

"Taking notes?" I asked.

She smiled and ran her hands through her short curls, shaking them as though to air out her head.

"On the other hand," I said, "why ruin a good thing?" Since they'd been engaged, I'd moved in with Larry, lived with him for two years, been married for three, had a baby, and filed for divorce. Maybe there was something to be said for taking things slowly.

Jim turned to his brother. "You know, that's one good thing. Our family is pretty laid back. In this situation, other guys would be getting hounded by everyone. 'When are you getting married? When are you getting married?' We're lucky."

"Mom says men should never get married until they're thirty, anyway," Chas replied.

"Yeah, no pressure there."

Doug detoured back and planted two lawn chairs in front of us. He handed me the beer, made eye contact with Cassie, and pointed in the direction they were going. Jim's date gamely followed them down the hill in her stiletto heels.

"Who was that girl again?" I rolled the new, cold bottle across my forehead. "He didn't introduce us."

"You've met her before, I think. Not a date," Chas said, looking around for somewhere to put his jacket. "One of his friends from Northwestern come out for reunion. Even Jim wouldn't be stupid enough to bring a girl to a family wedding on a first date." He pointed. "Is that Hudson Flame?"

Hudson Flame had the notorious distinction of being the only person in living memory to have been banned from Elmwood for life, after one of the boys' college parties where, according to Doug, he "had his dick hanging out of his pants" the whole weekend. He hadn't even been invited; his older brother was their friend. Hudson was someone's roommate's friend who'd happened to be hanging around when they were loading the car. Since Mrs. Flame and our mother were bridge partners the lifetime ban was a tidbit of information that had been successfully kept from them for years.

"Let's hope he keeps his pants zipped," I said.

"What do you expect? Broken family," Chas remarked. The Flames had divorced when we were in high school; Hudson had only been in sixth grade.

I drained my beer.

Chas drifted off to find the California cousins. Cassie sat down in one of the chairs and flapped her neckline. Only Cassie could wear head-to-toe vintage baby blue peau-de-soie and look cutting-edge. I stared at her sandals. "Are those dyeables?" I exclaimed. "Where did you get those?"

"I had to look. Not everyone carries them. A place on the Near North Side."

"Fetching."

That's exactly what your dad used to say. Whenever I went over to your house, in a new outfit, he'd stand up when I came in, which by the way how come Doug never does that, and he'd say, 'Cassie. You look simply *fetching.*'"

My bottle was empty already. My mother sailed by with her sister Thea. "Why aren't you using a cup?" she scolded.

"Your son didn't bring me one. You know," I said to Cassie, "I'm just realizing, you're the only future spouse that Dad ever liked. Spouse...of us. Spouse of ours."

"He got a kick out of my hats. Remember the hats?"

I spun the bottle on the grass. "Larry had two finals to finish, that's why he couldn't make it." In all the time we'd been together, Larry had only visited my home twice. I used to tell myself he wasn't family-oriented. Now, I made a new entry in LARRY'S ECCENTRICITIES: *Slightly misanthropic.*

Cassie put a hand on my arm. "Let's check on the baby."

We went inside. Upstairs in the children's room, the high-schooler from next door was holding Nathan and playing blocks with the groom's toddler niece, who was dressed like a ruffled macaroon.

"My God, a child bride," I exclaimed. I sat down in a small rocker and lifted Nathan onto my lap. He seemed to have doubled in weight. My energy plummeted to my feet and I was suddenly exhausted, barely able to muster even the strength to keep the baby from falling out of my arms.

Cassie asked the sitter to get a big cup of icewater and shut the door. "Kim," she said, "it's eighty-six degrees and you just drank two beers on an empty stomach."

"Gee. That was stupid." I rested my head on the back of the rocker. "But I was so thirsty."

"Why don't you nurse lying down? You can put a pillow under your arm."

I struggled with the zipper in the back of my dress. The whole thing would have to come down to the waist; this was one matron-of-honor outfit that wasn't customized for breastfeeding. "How do you know so much about nursing?" I asked.

"I've got three sisters, remember? Two of whom are married. Both of whom have kids."

"Guess that takes the pressure off you," I joked. "Not that there was any pressure on me," I hastened to add. "Our family's not like that. You know that. Not about marriage, or having babies…Chas was right, wasn't he? Our family is pretty laid back. That's a good thing, isn't it?"

"Of course. When you're an adult you have to be allowed to lead your own life. You have to make your own decisions."

And your own mistakes, I thought, as the baby settled in.

The sitter returned with the icewater. Cassie handed her the ruffled macaroon and closed the door on her again, then sat down in the rocker and gave me the glass.

I wouldn't let her take her hand back. "Doug will be a great dad," I blurted. "You don't have to worry one bit." I took a gulp of the water.

"Oh, I'm not! He just needs to finish his degree. First things first."

"That's wise," I said. "Maybe that was our problem. We weren't grown up."

She gently let go my hand and dandled Nathan's little foot, waiting tactfully for me to amplify.

"Larry never really earned a steady income. As soon as he got his law degree, he decided he didn't want to practice and all of a sudden he hated the city so we moved up to Vermont. He got into real estate, he was a silent partner in that organic farm, then in Tulsa he was an analyst at that small venture capital outfit. But the thing is, I don't think he was really working. I don't know what he was doing. I mean, how was I supposed to know, I wasn't home all day. In Vermont I was working at the library, and in Tulsa I was at school. He used to get checks in the mail, I guess he was pulling money out of a trust fund or something, I don't know, I just signed for the envelopes, I thought it was none of my business. He said the income was low on our tax returns because he had a good accountant. He said everything was all right."

"Isn't he going back to school now? To be a law professor?"

I sat up, put a clean diaper on my shoulder and burped Nathan. "He'll be thirty-nine when he's done. Isn't that a little old to start a career?"

"Maybe, but not to change one."

"He's not really changing, is he? He's beginning. I mean, if you've never really worked before, why start now? He never uses his degrees anyway. Except the MBA, a little. Well, maybe he is suited to be an academic. Or it's just an excuse to move to the West Coast. I don't know." I sagged. "Could you please hold him?"

"I'll take him downstairs. Why don't you rest?"

I wiped my nose. "Don't say anything, okay? Oh, wait! The shoes. Don't forget the shoes." I scrambled off the bed and rooted around in the diaper bag. "I got him the cutest little shoes, special to go with this outfit. And the socks. Where are the socks?" I pushed the tiny shoes and socks into her hand. "Make sure you put them on before you take him down. You'll put them on, won't you?"

"Of course I will."

She went out. The eyelet curtains lifted and fell as the door closed. I turned my face to the wall, and wedged a pillow under my head. I couldn't bear the kindness in her voice.

Right before Larry and I moved to Oklahoma, his younger sister had gotten married, and we'd driven into Boston for the black-tie dinner after a private ceremony in judge's chambers. Courthouse weddings ran in the family, it seemed; Larry's older brother had eloped, and we ourselves had been married by a justice of the peace in—because we thought it was funny—North Pole, New York.

At the end of our six-hour drive, a window-washer at a stoplight had ignored my gestures and banged his fist against the window three inches from my ear so hard I was deaf on one side. This gave the evening a surreal quality. I tilted around, sipping champagne as slowly as possible, waiting desperately for dinner to be announced so I could sit down. Why hadn't the window broken, I wondered, and how had he known exactly how hard he could smash his hand against the glass without breaking it? Handicapped as I was, I was not going to even try negotiating the complex dynamics of the Baltakis family: Larry and his sister Suzanne had sided with mother during the divorce, but older brother Josh had sided with Dad, and acknowledged Dad's second wife, but was still friendly with mother; Larry and Josh wouldn't speak, but both were on sparring terms with Suzanne; none of them would speak to mother's moocher boyfriend, who'd lost his Board seat in New York in the crash of '87 and was quietly slurping gin in the corner. I purposely attempted to chat only with strangers.

There was one failed attempt to join a group, women about my age, but they'd just discovered they were all Georgetown Law grads, and were busy trading restaurant names. When they found out I hadn't even started law school and even worse, was enrolled someplace in Oklahoma, they cut me out, even though I was the bride's sister-in-law. When Suzanne, in an ivory silk shantung suit, joined us and began to reassure her friends that the two-carat solitaire on her finger was just a starter ring, I skulked off and hung out near the harpist. I wanted to tell those women, "I only came to this wedding because I had to and the only reason I'm going to school in Oklahoma is because Larry wouldn't let me apply *anywhere* east of the Mississippi because he couldn't *wait* to get away from the family that your girlfriend is so desperate to ditch as well that she's marrying a cripple who went to NYU at night and who you're only looking at twice because he's now assistant general counsel at a major New York publishing house and wears suspenders! And in the Midwest, women don't necessarily *wear* black to weddings, even if they're in the evening."

But of course I didn't. And he wasn't really a cripple. He'd only lost two fingers off one hand at a petting zoo as a child.

At ten o'clock, we were finally seated and served a total of five ounces of food in three courses. I was placed next to brother Josh, probably because I rated as a neutral buffer and, a Midwesterner to the core, could always be counted on to make an effort. Josh had Larry's same reddish-brown hair and rosy complexion, but he was bigger and heavier, and the beautiful brown eyes were hidden by glasses. He'd graduated from the University of Pennsylvania at eighteen and was now a partner at Goldman Sachs, having adroitly sidestepped joining his father's firm; he had a good sense of balance. He and Larry had absolutely nothing in common except that they'd both married blondes.

"So what's this guy like?" he asked after the seafood mousse. He was referring to his new brother-in-law. He pushed his glasses up on his nose. "Does he share any of Suzanne's interests? Which I guess in this case means skiing and shopping?" He left out Russian literature, in which she'd obtained a doctorate from Yale before starting her import business. It must have slipped his mind.

"They're different as night and day," I stammered, flagging the waiter for another roll, and thinking, *Have they really never met?* "But from what I've seen, they get along really well."

He sighed and shook his head.

I put his pessimism down to the fact that his fifteen-year marriage, despite its legendary romantic beginnings, had produced nothing but a brittle, well-dressed wife to whom I'd almost literally never seen him address a word. *We're leaving in two weeks,* I thought, touching the pendant of my necklace, making sure it was centered in the gap between my collarbones. *In Tulsa, everything will be different. Everything will be better.*

Little did I know.

I lay on my side in the nursery at Elmwood with my arm under my head, staring at the chain of circus animals on the hooked rug. I should have left then, I thought. I should never have made that move. I remembered the rug from the children's room in my grandparent's house in Winnetka. They always kept a crib, for family gatherings. I remembered being put down to nap, studying the animals marching in a circle, listening to the comforting murmur of distant voices. After my grandfather died, the center of our family life had slowly, over the years, shifted from that house up to Elmwood, so that when my grandmother sold the other we hardly noticed. She'd spent half the year in Wisconsin, half in Florida. She was on her own for many years, always cheerful, productive, gardening, sewing, making soap. The women in my family all seemed to have an instinctive grasp of the natural order of things, how to arrange fulfilling and generally happy lives by controlling the circumstances they could and flowing gracefully with those they couldn't. All the women except me. My decisions were always mistakes—or at least they seemed so right now—mistakes I didn't recognize until too late.

In Tulsa, everything will be different. Everything will be better.

"There you are!" Bobbie frowned, catching me in the buffet line. "Aunt Thea's been looking for you."

"I was just lying down for a minute."

I took my plate and found Thea on the front porch with my California cousin, Jenny.

"You don't object to smocking for a boy, do you?" Thea asked, making room for me on the glider. Thea looked exactly like my mother, but less grey. Like my mother fifteen years younger, which she was. Except she talked more. "You can do some very cute smocking for a boy, in the right colors. I could do an overall with smocking on the bib and then embroider over it, a railroad train, or a little row of cars. I did one for Nels like that."

I took a bite of potato salad and nodded. Outside the porch, Angela went by with her cello, followed by a flutist. "Looks like we might be having a chamber music slam," I commented to Jenny.

"Oh, my dear!" Thea reached out and put a hand on my cheek. "I'm so glad you followed your mother's example instead of mine in starting a family. I worried a bit about that when you went back to school. Having a first baby at thirty-eight wasn't that difficult, but then the twins at forty-two! It's no fun having to find your reading glasses to read the small print on the baby ibuprofen."

"Isn't that your old boyfriend?" Jenny pointed at the trombonist with her fork. "I recognize him by his hair. I remember he was the first Jewish person I ever saw with an Afro."

"My God, is this a conspiracy? Did everyone bring their instrument to this wedding? I didn't know he still played." I stood up. "I think I'll get some more chicken." I edged my way back inside, through the dining room, the butler's pantry, and out the kitchen door.

Frank was sitting in a plastic chair under the silver maple, stealing a smoke. He'd probably thought he couldn't be seen; the tree trunk was four feet wide.

"I'll join you in that," I said.

He looked around with a guilty start. "I didn't know you smoked."

"Once in a blue moon. If I'm drinking." I pointed at his jacket. "Is that rented?"

He took it off the back of the chair and spread it out on the grass.

"I have to preserve this dress. You never know when someone's going to ask you to be matron of honor." I carefully arranged legs, cup, and plate. "Does Karen know?"

"She gave me the cancer stick lecture."

"Only once? That's a good sign." We sat in comfortable silence while I finished my chicken. I wiped my fingers on the grass. "Okay."

He lit a cigarette and handed it over.

A cardinal sounded his dive-bomber's call and sailed off over the court, over the abandoned chairs and makeshift altar, to the oaks in what would have been the narthex in a church. We contemplated the garden stretched out before us. Along the old beds, a new two-foot strip was partially turned over. Uncle Will had left a spade standing in it. "Welcome to the family," I said.

I'd gotten to know Frank a little over the last year or so, even though Karen and I didn't live in the same place anymore. He seemed more inclined than Larry to attend family gatherings, which I now knew to interpret as a good sign. My gut feeling was that he'd never hit her, but how entitled was I to faith in present judgment when my past had been so egregiously mistaken?

"Welcome to the family," I repeated, tipping my head up and blowing a plume of smoke over the long triple clothesline. "I guess you're the head of it now."

"Oh, I doubt that." He crossed his legs and tapped ash into the grass.

A man of few words, but then so was Larry. Slowly but surely, however—probably since the sound of blood rushing through my ears had died down—I was learning to tell the difference between "quiet" and "calm."

"Nevertheless." I sat up and leveled my cigarette at him. "It's incumbent upon me to ask a few questions. *In loco paternis,* if I may be so bold. As a matter of fact, if my father were still alive, you probably wouldn't be marrying Karen at all. He had a knack for scaring away friends of the male persuasion he didn't approve of. Which was most of them."

"You got married."

"Yes, but he made his disapproval unmistakably clear."

"That's right. Karen told me. I forgot."

I took another sip from my plastic cup. "I don't usually drink this much, by the way. Extenuating circumstances."

"I'm cool with that." He offered another cigarette.

I rolled it in my fingers. "Why is it that the occasional alcoholic binge is less socially acceptable than ingesting serotonin reuptake inhibitors by prescription for years on end?"

He tugged at his beard to hide a laugh.

"It's a racket, that's why." I lit the second cigarette from the butt of the first. "To continue. In my father's view, there would have been three insurmountable barriers to marriage with his daughter, Karen, and they are as follows: one, you're divorced, two, you're a musician, and three, you have a beard."

"In that order?"

"Probably the beard would have been first. Just kidding. The divorced thing would have been first. He never would have allowed Karen to marry a divorced man."

"Would it have been up to him?"

"You'd be surprised! I was once engaged to a guy, we went to my dad's office to break the news to him, and he said, 'Aren't you forgetting something?' And he kicked us out. Said he was busy. It took me a couple days to realize that he meant this guy—I'll call him applicant number three—"

"There were others?"

"Not that he knew about. This was the first one that ever rose to the level of parental notification. Anyway, what he meant was that he'd forgotten to request my hand from him before proposing to me— I kid you not," I said in response to his laugh, then added hastily, "It was other reasons that I broke up with him, other reasons."

He exhaled smoke toward the silver maple branches. "Just to

reassure you, it was my wife who left me. For a percussionist. She decided she didn't like family life."

"My God. A percussionist? She left a French horn player for a percussionist?" I digested this for a moment in silence.

"She's on her third marriage now. No other kids. Which is a good thing."

"And you raised your son on your own all that time. I salute you."

"I salute your sister. For taking on a nine-year-old boy in addition to me."

"A nine-year-old boy is nothing to Karen. She could chew one up and spit him out for breakfast. She could organize a whole dorm full of nine-year-old boys single-handedly. Of course," I added craftily, "she probably would have liked to get him younger, so she could knit him adorable little baby-blue garments and start him on Suzuki at age three."

"She'll have that chance with her own."

Satisfied, I crushed out my cigarette, unwrapped it, and began shredding the filter. "Actually, I don't think you can start Suzuki until age four."

"What are you doing?"

"Composting my butt. Removing the evidence."

He followed my lead and started shredding.

Shouts floated over the house. "Sounds like someone just went off the dock," I said.

"I hope it's not my son."

"If it was anyone, it was probably Hudson Flame."

Frank stood and helped me up. "Who's Hudson Flame?"

"It's a long story. I'm sure you'll be hearing it," I said. "One of these days." I took his arm, and together we strolled around the house to rejoin the party.

9

Caution! The Beverage you are About to Enjoy is Extremely Hot

"It's Svenga, the Swedish housewife!" Doug said. He sat down at the Mexican leather table on my mother's porch in Hubbard Woods and took a swig from the orange juice carton. It was three weeks after the wedding. I looked up from the couch where I'd been staring at my coffee.

"How can you eat pizza for breakfast?" I snuffled.

"Have you been crying again?"

I tapped the printed warning on my cardboard cup. "They have good corporate counsel. They've been doing this all along. Everyone else jumped on the bandwagon *after* that woman in Arizona burned her lap and sued."

"You've been crying again. Why are you always crying?" He took another gulp of juice and hooked the newspaper toward him with one finger. "Ever since we came back down from Elmwood you've been crying. Last summer when you were here it was business as usual—Larry was being obnoxious on the phone and you were taking it, like always. Which, by the way, is really weird because you never take it from anybody. So I don't get it. You should be happy now. And you're crying all the time."

I blew my nose and squinted into the distance with puffy eyes, considering this assessment of my personality. Through the fine mesh of the porch screens everything was fuzzy: the salmon-pink geraniums in the urns on the steps, the nodding branches of the locust tree, the massed bushes concealing the lawn from the sidewalk. I turned my gaze to Doug: untied sneakers, head bent over the paper, scalp bristling with his annual summer buzz cut. How could I explain Larry to someone like that?

The breeze wafted in, bringing the scent of fading lilies-of-the-valley.

Doug sighed gustily and turned a page. I was used to this impatience with my slow responses. Upstairs, the baby began to chirp. "I guess he just didn't like fatherhood," I offered.

Doug snorted. "He should've thought of that beforehand." He finished the pizza and looked around for a napkin. I fished one out from beneath the sports page and tossed it over, then I went up to get the baby. When I came back down Doug was still sitting there, elbows on the table, chin propped on clasped hands: our late father's meditative dinner table position.

"Paddleston!" he broke off and greeted his nephew. "Gonna wind him up?"

I put Nathan in his swing and turned the crank. Doug leaned over and pushed the plastic play-tray to set it in motion. He stood up. "I mean," he said, "he's a jerk. You should be happy."

"Don't leave your dishes out," I reminded him. "The house needs to be clean for showings."

He ignored me, went into the den and turned the computer on, then stuck his head back around the French doors. "You should be glad."

I prised up the plastic lid to see how much coffee was left in the cup and nursed it slowly. If only I could find the right words to make Larry understand the marriage was over. It never occurred to me not to take the calls; he was my husband. But he never listened. Why didn't he remember that he didn't love me?

I'll get a bigger apartment, he said. *The problem is we need more space.*

I'll get you an apartment of your own. I'll help you pay for the move. Can't you just come out for a visit? Why don't you bring the baby out for a visit?

Listen, drop the suit. We don't need lawyers. We can work this out between ourselves. We can save a lot of money. My therapist can mediate. This was his sometime psychotherapist in Newton, who'd responded with dead silence when I'd told him on the phone, in private, that Larry had hit me.

Finally: *You're making a big mistake! You're a sick person! You're clinically depressed and completely twisted.* And then, in a hiss: *I'm going to take your car.*

I gnawed on the rolled edge of my cup and thought about what Doug had said. Why was I always crying? Maybe when the divorce was officially underway, maybe then, these conversations with Larry would be stripped of their ability to upset me. That had to be it. That's why I was on edge: he hadn't been served yet.

I'd discovered that almost a month ago when I called Hal Duncan after the wedding.

"We did certified mail on him in Tulsa," he said on the phone. "After you left, just like you asked. Three times. He didn't accept it."

"Doesn't he have to?"

"No, not certified mail. With personal service, he'd have to."

"You mean a process server? Why didn't you use a process server?"

He paused. "It costs a bit. You told me he wasn't going to fight the divorce. I didn't want to do that without talking to you. And you told me not to call."

With my free hand I gave Nathan his plastic keys, and he shook them vigorously, first surprised, then gleeful. "He isn't going to fight it. Not really. He's just mad at me right now for filing without his permission. I mean...when he wrote up that separation agreement, he kept saying, 'This isn't a divorce. We're not getting a divorce, yet.'"

"'Yet?'"

"That's the word he used."

"Well, we've just sent the papers certified to the Washington address. He probably won't accept them there either but we have to try. It's an extra hundred dollars for a process server."

"That's okay. I don't care."

"They'll attempt three times and then send it back. We'll wait and see. Usually, this is the easiest way to do it. With certified mail it doesn't

81

have to be the actual party, it can be any adult at that address. If it comes back we'll have to find an outfit to do service in person. Just send me that income worksheet and I'll get started calculating child support from your end."

I'd done it right away, printed everything in neat block letters on the form, to make amends for my impatience on the phone. All the time, in my head, Larry's arm was coming at me over and over again, and I knew it wasn't going to stop until he was served with the papers, but I couldn't say that to Mr. Duncan, because Mr. Duncan didn't know. I hadn't told him. I hadn't told anyone. Karen was the one I really needed, but she was in Russia. I had to talk to Karen first. I couldn't say anything before she went on her honeymoon. Now I had to wait until she came back.

I heaved myself off the couch. I needed some fresh air; it was time for another pilgrimage to the lake. I stuck my feet in my sandals and headed uptown with Nathan. I was going to make a stop at the stationery store on the way, to fax the worksheet to Mr. Duncan.

I saw my retired nursery school teacher, Mrs. Engelbrecht, behind the counter, but I already had my hand on the door, so I had to walk in.

"Kim!" she beamed. "And the baby! How old is he now?"

"Sixteen weeks, almost seventeen."

I took off his cap so she could see him better, and tucked it into the sling behind his head, pushing the income worksheet further down. I'd have to fax that another day.

"Oh, isn't he beautiful. I know you're a boy, but we can still say you're beautiful, can't we?" She put on her reading glasses to look at the two ballpoint pens I'd pretended to need, and scanned the price card taped to the counter. "Your mother's so proud. She showed us pictures at bridge club. Now let's see, you're moving out to the West Coast, aren't you?"

"Seattle. My husband's doing an LLM at the University of Washington so I'm going to do my last semester there."

"That's right. My goodness, law school and a baby. You girls today are so amazing. I don't know how you do it." She slid the pens into a tiny green bag embossed in gold script. They came in ten sizes; at Olsen's Stationery you always walked out with a bag exactly suited to the size of your purchase. She folded over the pinked edges, creased them, and handed it to me. "A law professor and a lawyer! Good luck in Seattle."

The door jingled behind me. Mrs. Engelbrecht was one of my favorite people. Twenty-three years ago she'd shown me where to hang my jacket in the bright, tiled basement of St. Luke's, introduced me to finger painting, and fed me graham crackers and apple juice. At the age of four, hers was the first warm lap I'd known that did not belong to a blood relative. I wiped my eyes and gave my finger to Nathan, who gummed it as I continued down the sidewalk.

Someone whistled. It evoked memories: people used to whistle… it seemed a long time ago…I'd forgotten about it. "It's just what happens when you wear a short skirt," I explained to Nathan.

I crossed the tracks without stopping and walked past four more blocks of well-tended shrubbery and ornamental gateposts, offering glimpses of springy green lawns.

At the top of the bluff, I took the baby out of the sling. Lake Michigan's water was calm, an intense blue spread to the vanishing point all along that endless horizon. With my cheek pressed against Nathan's, I gazed out at it, searching for the exact point where water ended and sky began. I needed to know it. Lately, it seemed that Karen was wrong: I'd lost my ability to abide unanswered questions.

Why did Larry buy another car in Tulsa?

Why did he say he couldn't afford to give me money for the baby when he left?

And then, when I stood at the door looking shocked and indignant, and he pulled a twenty-dollar bill from his wallet—why did I say, "Thank you?"

I'd always given the lake my questions. Sometimes I didn't get answers, but even then, just giving it the questions had always been salutary. Today, I got no relief.

I tucked Nathan back in and walked away. Uptown at the coffee shop another young mother was trying to maneuver her navy and white double stroller out of the door. I held the door, and her latte, so she could negotiate. "You look unburdened," she cooed from behind her designer sunglasses, and I forced a smile.

At home I flipped through the mail while spooning rice cereal into Nathan's rosebud mouth. *Newsweek* had a cover article on domestic abuse. *He was like Jekyll and Hyde,* reported a woman. I rinsed off Nathan's bib, took him upstairs, and lay on the bed for a moment while he squooshed and squished and sighed in the old crib.

Two hours later I struggled upright. Nathan was inspecting me through the bars. I stared back, slack-jawed. It was my first deep, sound sleep since leaving Tulsa. I felt like I'd been hit by a truck.

In the breakfast room my mother was reading the *Newsweek* and drinking two inches of my reheated coffee. "I took a little," she said, lifting the cup.

"That's why I got a large." I put Nathan into her waiting arms and sat down. "All is well in the baby kingdom."

"Good." She pulled out a blue and white striped overall and matching cap with a locomotive on the brim. "Look what I found walking home from the club after the board meeting. It was in the window of the Hadassah shop." She handed it to me. "It was on sale. I couldn't resist it. Try on the cap and see if it fits."

I put it on while he sat in her lap.

"Don't put the elastic under his chin, it might hurt him."

I took it off, tucked the elastic under, and put it back on again.

"Grp," Nathan said.

"Aren't you a bonny boy," said my mother, in a sweet, musical voice that transported me instantly: I smelled her hair, felt her camel wool car coat with the old nappy collar, saw her getting out of the paneled station wagon looking like Ingrid Bergman in flat shoes with the groceries. She looked up. "Any news?"

"No. Forty-two days and counting. Mr. Duncan's going to get a process server."

"It's about time. It seems to me," she said carefully, "if Larry's reaction to the situation is mostly 'Kim's being a naughty girl and not doing what I want and I'm miserable,' then one has to question the depth of feeling there." She shifted the baby on her lap and took a sip of coffee. "It's not 'What can we do about this, what can I do about this,' it's 'She's making my life unpleasant.' "

I nodded. "It's a bit chilling."

"Chilling..." She took off the cap, stroked Nathan's hair, looked over his downy head at the mass of forsythia along the driveway. In thirty years her profile hadn't changed for me, but now I saw her blue eyes narrow, and in that moment, in the set of her face as she gazed along the inner distance, I realized she was no longer a young woman.

Ten years before, I'd sat with her in a diner in southern Minnesota, listening to her reminisce after a visit to her grandparent's home which was now the Cottonwood County museum, where other people, other families, walked through the rooms, touched the furniture, listened to the gramophone. Suddenly she'd stopped, gazing out the window; then swiveled, looked directly into my eyes and—in what? Defense of wistfulness? Rebuke for perceived inattention? Apology for the inescapable exclusivity of memory?—said to me, in the gentlest of voices: *The past is just the present of another day.*

I was seventeen years old.

This time, she only sighed and pressed her lips together.

After a while she said, "My friends and I, we've talked a lot about this over the years. Some of the girls, when they got married, you just knew the man was not very mature...sometimes it worked out fine. We all came to the conclusion that so much of marriage was just dumb luck."

"What do you mean?"

She shrugged. "Luck. What kind of person he turns out to be. Whether the marriage is happy or not. That's probably not the best thing to be saying to you right now. People are so completely different today. Marriage is different, expectations are different. I was just thinking," gently again, "about Larry, you know. I was thinking at the very least, if you understood what his attitude was, it could help. Help you to deal with him."

She pressed her lips together again in that way, bitter, and I felt a pang of guilt. Three years before when I'd come home for a visit and told her that Larry and I were getting married, she'd clasped my hands in both of hers and said earnestly, *I hope everything turns out well,* and I thought at the time, Why won't it? We've been living together for two years, we own a home together. What could change?

It was a moment for recreational shopping. I left the baby with my mother, and drove to Old Orchard. I walked around looking at merchandise inside under-lit counters. Everything was clean, everything was perfect, everything sparkled. I tried on a pair of sunglasses. With my eyes hidden, I looked great. Normal. Exactly how, I suspected, I had looked during March, April, May, bathing, dressing, brushing my hair, applying lipstick, climbing the steps of the law school with Nathan in the sling, casebooks under the other arm. I looked normal. Larry looked normal. Nobody would have guessed. Nobody guessed now. In a way, even I hadn't guessed. I'd lived with this man for five years. It couldn't be him! It was just a stressful phase.

Behind me in the mirror a man walked by. He looked like Larry. *Jekyll and Hyde. The past is just the present of another day.* I broke into a sweat. My mother was right. There wasn't any such thing as the past, there was only the eternal present. Everything that happens to you in your life matters. None of it gets left behind. You take it all with you.

I gripped the counter. When the tide of nausea subsided, I paid, walked out to the car, and locked myself in. "That wasn't so bad, was it?" I said to the rear-view mirror. "A bit of an over-reaction there." Dana would love these glasses. I started the engine.

A minute later, I turned onto Tower Road, and more words came: *Don't hit me while I'm wearing my glasses!* I had reading glasses, I'd worn glasses for reading since high school. He picked them up, I remembered, and bent the earpiece back into place, popped the lens back in—and I was grateful. We'd been living together, what? a couple months. I searched; one other time, near the fireplace: I remembered looking at the cracked floor tiles near the hearth. And there was another time, I realized. Recently, in January. In January, a week before my due date, he'd hit me on the head. That's why I'd had that sense of *deja vu.* He hadn't hit me again, until then, because he'd never had to; I'd learned my lesson. But then something new changed the equation. Threatened the status quo.

It's against the law, Drew said on the phone. *If it happens again you have to call 911.* I flipped on WFMT and Schubert lieder filled the car.

At home, when Bobbie saw the sunglasses, she said, "My goodness."

"Oh, Mom, they're not racy, they're just *cute.*"

She handed me the baby. "I think he's hungry."

I sat down, unbuttoning my blouse with one hand, while Nathan made little eager fish-blowing-bubble noises with his mouth.

"Take off those glasses," she said. "You'll scare him."

The doorbell rang at six o'clock. A man stood there, short and clean-cut, a stranger, but what gave me an odd feeling was his car. It was parked on the street. In this neighborhood, nobody parked on the street.

"Kimberly MacLean Baltakis?"

"Yes?" It was a cheap car too.

"I have some legal documents for you."

I opened the screen door obligingly, and into my hand he put a divorce petition filed in King County, Washington.

"There must be some mistake," I said politely, trying to hand it back. "This case is already pending in Oklahoma."

"I don't know anything about that."

"But it's a mistake!"

He was halfway down the flagstone walk.

"Well, uh, thank you."

I sat down on the doorstep and looked at the papers in my hand, trying to examine them in a professional manner. "Petitioner knows of no other pending litigation in any other state." Further down: "The child has lived in no other state than Washington." Printed on the back was a standard restraining order preventing either parent from removing the child from the state. I doubled over.

Dear Kim, please consider moving out here for a while, before we decide whether we want to divorce.

Dear Kim, please come out to visit. I'll pay for your ticket.

Dear Kim, divorce is out of the question. We need to talk about this in person. I will pay for your ticket.

In my imagination, I sat on a plane at Seatac waiting to go home; the flight attendant announced that take-off would be momentarily delayed, and two policemen boarded the plane, called my name, wrested my infant from my arms.

The house was too big. It had too many windows, too many doors, and I was alone. I locked them all and went down into the basement. In the corner of the laundry room was my father's workshop, no bigger than a large closet. I went inside. The heavy, pitted workbench was still there, and the pegboard with hooks and black felt-tip outlines of now-absent tools packed away by my brother, who was in the process of moving into a garage apartment in Evanston.

I sat down on a demoted side chair. Murky light filtered through the smudged casement window onto wooden shelves labeled in paint in my father's neat draughtsman's hand, black on white: NAILS. SCREWS. TAPE. DRILLS. I rocked back and forth, arms wrapped around my stomach, staring at my dead father's handwriting, shattered by evidence of deceit so final and overwhelming it could not be ignored.

Afterward, floating dully on the backwash of tears, I picked at a loose piece of braid trim. Dust rose. Would this chair, the pocked Hepplewhite varnish-tester with the frayed satin upholstery, be the odd stick left behind? There was always something left behind, something small and dusty in a corner, abandoned or forgotten; it was impossible to make a clean sweep. My father's writing was all I had left, and now someone would paint it over.

Bobbie had obeyed his instruction; she'd waited two years before deciding to sell. I'd been brave in front of Karen, but this was different. As long as we'd had the house, we still, somehow, had him, and as long as we had him, we still had that time when we were innocent, when we pressed our milky cheeks together in front of the mirror and tried to see the future, secure in the knowledge of guidance. How could I survive in a world where there were no longer any traces of my father?

After Bobbie returned with the baby, after we'd eaten the Chinese food she'd picked up because it was too hot to cook, I took Nathan to my room. I flopped on the bed while he practiced rolling over on the rug.

After high school graduation, I often lay here in the evening after supper, tracing the pattern on the chenille, waiting and listening for the moment when that promised future would begin, as it already had for Karen, who was off at Julliard.

My mother always went outside after dinner to pull a few weeds before dark, and Dad would take his coffee out to keep her company. Once, I heard him put on an Audubon Society recording in the den; we'd been discussing birds at dinner. Their voices floated through the house in the twilight calm, through open windows and doors, up to my room:

Barbara?

Yes?

Where are you?

In front.

Where?

In front.

Then the dry rattle of the screen door, and he'd found her, following the sound of her voice as though reeling himself in to a ship. I could hear their deep satisfaction in the telegraphic exchange of long familiarity. This was their private music, but we knew it too. We were born into its key, and it formed the diapason of our childhood.

I found it! he exclaimed joyfully.

Oh, good! She had no idea what he was talking about. *What is it?*

They were right beneath my window. My father was, I knew, standing on the front doorstep, beside the garlanded stone urn of geraniums, my mother looking up from the dandelions she'd caught infiltrating the euonymus. I could see the gloved hand resting on her knee, her face lifted, smiling: *What is it?*

At that moment, up in my room, staring at the ceiling, I suddenly saw them as they stood to each other, and with the force of a blow, I felt the physical weight of my body at the same time I realized I was about to leave the only place I'd ever belonged. What was I supposed to do now? Why couldn't I figure that out? Why was I going to college at Wellesley? Just because my mother had? I loved that bed: the old, extra-long mattress, the metal coils that sighed, the soft bedspread. Now gravity pinned my arms and legs to it while inside I teetered on the edge of a cliff. Listening to my parents' voices down below on that long-ago night, on the threshold of adulthood, I wondered: would I, too, succeed? Would I find the answers they obviously had—how to live, how to be happy? Would I find my place?

Ten years later I was still trying to answer those questions. I'd been out in the world for years, lived on my own for years, but I still hadn't figured it out, I was still learning lessons, ones that they'd begun—but they weren't here anymore. When I gave birth to Nathan, my mother was hundreds of miles away, my father dead.

What was the key to a happy marriage? It had never occurred to me that I wouldn't eventually have one like theirs, so in a way I'd never paid much attention to it. Now I wondered, should I have? Was that where I went wrong? Did I miss my lesson? Or was it unnecessary in childhood to be so deliberate, and had I indeed absorbed it unconsciously, like air, the knowledge that would surface instinctively when it was needed? If so, why hadn't it?

Why had I turned down others, and married the cold, unloving solipsist I did?

Nathan chortled joyfully. His head was off the floor: he was pushing up with two hands—he'd just discovered elevation. I rolled off the bed and joined him. He reached out for me, lost his balance, and went down on his tummy.

For years I'd lived with Larry in the world of the hypothetical, until motherhood jerked me back to reality, a reality I proved profoundly unequipped to manage. But now, as Nathan wrapped his tiny fingers around my outstretched hand, I felt his energy flow into me, and I began to see that fresh connections would augment those that had faded; that Nathan, by virtue of his arrival, had transposed me into a new key, and that possibly, just possibly, the strength to move beyond the evergreens was in my possession already.

10

Escape to Wisconsin

"IT DOESN'T MATTER THAT Larry has a lawyer in Washington state," Hal Duncan said on the phone, for the third time. "We cannot simply serve the Oklahoma papers on her. She's not required to accept service."

"So what do we do?" I asked, cranking the baby swing back up.

"You have to get a lawyer in Seattle. He'll file a motion to quash. Once it's granted, Larry will have no alternative but to accept the Oklahoma papers. There's no other jurisdiction where this could be heard."

"I'm sure he'll think of one," I said glumly.

"He is turning out to be a bit of a case."

"What about Illinois? In his Washington suit he's claiming Washington is the only appropriate jurisdiction because I've moved to Illinois."

"There'd be no advantage to him in that," replied Mr. Duncan. "Illinois isn't his home court. If it's anyone's home court, it'd be yours."

"I don't think he cares about that. He just wants to be the plaintiff and not the defendant."

Bobbie hovered in the doorway. I pointed, and she gave the baby swing a few more cranks.

"That kind of stuff doesn't matter anymore," Mr. Duncan said. "It's no-fault divorce today. You have two parties and you settle. We'll keep trying to serve him, Kim. We'll get him soon. Then when the motion to quash is granted we'll be ready to roll."

I scrabbled through the papers. "But the court date in Washington is in *December!*"

"Don't worry about that. That's the date they set for the divorce hearing. He's not going to get that far. A motion to quash is an in-and-out thing, the clerk will be looking for a hour-long slot, a forty-five minute or an hour slot on the docket. You won't have to wait that long. Remember what Mark Twain said."

"What?" I tried to smile at Bobbie.

"'I've seen a lot of trouble in my life, and most of it never happened.'"

It was the first time I'd heard him crack a joke.

"WHAT A *SCHLEMIEL*," my new lawyer said over the phone. Her name was Jessica. "I can't believe he did this to you. Where did you say he grew up? Weston? Spoiled brat."

"Are you chewing gum?"

"Sorry, it's a lollipop," she said. "I need to turn the volume down on this phone. It's too sensitive. I don't know about you, but I'm always hungry. Breastfeeding is the only time in my life when I've been able to eat all the time and not gain any weight."

"Same here." In my case, of course, there had been other factors contributing to drastic weight loss, such as panic, desperation, and insomnia.

"Okay, so what I'm going to do is make a special appearance," Jessica said. "Not a regular appearance, a special appearance, it's just nomenclature. It means we're not accepting the court's jurisdiction, because if we make a regular appearance, then we're accepting the jurisdiction of the court over you, which is exactly the thing we're contesting."

I was at Command Central—the porch sofa—scribbling notes on the basketweave coffee table, with my mother beside me. My pen kept going through the holes. Bobbie snatched a *Smithsonian* magazine and silently inserted it beneath my paper.

Jessica continued, "So I make a special appearance, and move that the court quash service because it has no personal jurisdiction over you because you've never lived in the state of Washington, you own no property in the state of Washington, the child has never lived in Washington, etc. etc."

"I forgot," I said. "How come my state has jurisdiction over Larry?" Bobbie was chewing on the rolled edge of my coffee cup. I tapped on her hand and she put it down.

"Because he lived there," Jessica said. "And owned property there at the time the divorce was filed. Because the child was born there and the child lived there." There was the crinkle of another wrapper, and an audible crunch. "Under the UCCJA, a court cannot take jurisdiction over a child until the child has lived there six months, that's to avoid forum-shopping, or in your case since birth, because he's younger than six months."

I imagined Jessica in her office, not a corner office but one rung down: spacious, with a good view, and the piece or two of statement art a rising star can afford. She had a solid-panel desk so she could sit comfortably cross-legged with her expensive heels kicked off on the floor. She had a ten-month-old baby. She had a husband.

"So what I'm going to need from you is a personal narrative of your relationship with this guy, where you guys lived, and when, and why you weren't together when the baby was born, and so on. Because I have to file a memorandum in support and I need to throw a lot of facts at them to make it absolutely clear that there's no connection to Washington, 'cause it's a little murky, you know, 'cause he's had a residence there for, you say, almost a year, and we have to prove that it wasn't *your* residence—"

"He attached a copy of the lease, but I didn't sign it. I didn't know even know my name was on it. The signature is not in my handwriting."

"That's okay then. And you didn't live there anyway. But now you're up in Illinois—"

"Because he sold the house out from under me."

"*I* know that, but he's going to say, 'See, we sold the house in Oklahoma, we don't live there anymore. So, Oklahoma, you can't make any rulings over this child.'"

The prospect of actually writing down the entire history of my relationship with Larry was revolting.

93

Jessica went on: "I'll express you the client agreement, you sign it and turn it around and put the Washington papers in there too. Copy them first. But I need them. Oh, and we need to discuss the retainer."

My stomach clenched. "How much?"

"Well, it's usually five thousand dollars."

"Five thousand?" I looked at Bobbie in dismay. "Uh, I'm not sure—"

"But this is just a motion to quash, it's not a whole divorce, so it'd probably fly with two thousand. Let me put you on hold for a sec." She came back quickly. "Yeah, that'll work, we can start with two thousand. So are we set?"

"Two thousand," I mouthed at my mother.

She flapped her hand and whispered, "We'll worry about it later. Just say yes."

"Yes," I said.

Jessica chuckled. "I'm kind of looking forward to this, actually."

Two months down, and so far the only thing I'd done was start a collection of humorous lawyers across the continental United States.

THE DAY AFTER Jessica's express packet arrived, I decided to take Nathan up to Wisconsin. I needed to concentrate, and Elmwood was nothing if not quiet. When my grandparents had started searching for a summer home, after Thea's twins were born, they'd been looking for square footage, but ultimately what they'd secured for us, decades later, was peace and quiet. The traffic, the planes overhead, the lawnmowers and leaf blowers—had they guessed the Chicago suburbs would become so noisy? Elmwood meant different things to each of us, but one of the things it meant most to me was silence. I needed that now.

Larry called.

"You've got nerve!" I exclaimed.

"You made me do it. I had to protect my interests."

"The only interest you have is in driving me crazy!" I yelled, and hung up.

"Good for you," Doug called from the den, where he was tinkering with the front elevation of an office complex. He didn't know Larry had hit me. Nobody did. But Doug had never liked him anyway.

The phone rang again. "Don't answer," I cried, but he picked it up. "It's what's-his-name," he called into the receiver.

When I came on the line, Larry drawled: "He's so immature."

"I don't want to talk to you," I snapped.

"Well *I* do. And I came all the way out here to do it."

"Here?" I looked out the window. The back yard was empty. I ran to the front door. Bobbie had taken Nathan for a walk in the stroller. I couldn't see anything. The sidewalk was completely hidden by the bushes.

"I'm at O'Hare. We need to talk this through. Face to face."

O'Hare to the house: thirty-five minutes without traffic. What time was it? Midday. Thirty-five minutes. "I don't believe it," I said slyly.

"I tell you, I'm at the *airport*."

"Where?"

"Right outside... gate 35C."

Still in the terminal. Forty-five minutes.

"Well, okay," I lied. "If you're already here. But you're not setting foot in the house. I'll meet you on the sidewalk."

I hung up the phone. My legs got wobbly, just like in Tulsa. Larry may have been mentally torturing me at my mother's, but at least until now I'd felt physically safe. "Larry's here, Larry's here," I cried, bolting from the kitchen to the living room and back again.

Doug came out of the den. "What the hey is going on?"

"Larry's here, Larry's here." I flung out an arm. "Here!"

"What do you mean?"

"He flew to Chicago, he's at the airport, he's coming to the house!"

"Kim! Shut up! What's wrong?"

"I'm *scared* of him!"

"Fuck. In. A." He grabbed me by the shoulders. "Calm down. You don't have to see him." He stilled my arms. "Leave the house."

"I told him I'd see him."

"Just get in the car and go somewhere."

"But I told him—"

"You don't have to do what he says anymore."

95

"Right, right." I looked around. "Just get in the car and go."

"Right. Jesus, Kim, don't go mental on me."

"I'm not mental. I'm fine."

"Weren't you going up to Elmwood?"

"Yes. Up to Elmwood. I've got to pack now. I have to get the baby in. Where's the baby? Come look with me." Holding his arm with both hands I stepped out the front door far enough to see up the street.

"Look, " Doug said. "There. It's all right, there they are." He peeled my hands off his bicep.

"Good." I started up the stairs, then turned around. "What will you do when he comes?"

"Tell him to shove it up his ass."

I started up again, then ran back down. "I have to call my lawyer. What's the number? I forgot the number. Maybe we can get him served. Maybe you can give him the papers. I mean, the real ones. The Oklahoma papers."

But it wasn't going to work like that. Larry was not going to be served in Illinois because a) neither the litigant, nor the litigant's little brother, nor an obliging police officer in the litigant's home town could serve the divorce papers on Larry, because none of these individuals was properly authorized by the court in Tulsa County, Oklahoma to serve notice and summons to said court and b) even if they were, giving him my copy of the divorce petition or giving him a copy faxed from my lawyer's office would not have constituted proper service because it had to be an original, that is, an original copy, and c) forty-five minutes was not enough time to engage a process server in Cook County and provide him with an "original copy" of a divorce petition.

"So I'd say, Kim, under the circumstances, it'd be a good idea to get out of town for a few days," Mr. Duncan said. "There's no reason for you to see him if he's not accepting service of the papers." He hesitated. "He might—well, has it occurred to you—he might be planning to kidnap the baby."

It had not, actually, occurred to me.

For the first time in my married life I was glad Larry's visits had been so rare. He'd never even been up to Elmwood. He didn't know where it was. He didn't even know the name of the town.

ELMWOOD HAD GATES. I'd never seen them shut, and they were probably rusted open, but their mere presence was a comfort. I felt safe the moment I'd driven through. As I pulled up to the house, Uncle Will came around the corner with a wheelbarrow.

"I had to get out of Dodge for awhile," I told him.

"Well, for once it's probably just as hot up here as it is down there." He set the barrow down in front of his van, which was loaded with zinnia flats. "Look at these. Got a hundred of them on sale this morning. Have to get them in now. Maybe you can help me." He took the baby swing out of my trunk. "We have to go back down day after tomorrow, I have a board meeting."

"Which?" I followed him.

"Field Museum." He rounded the corner. "Kim's here," he announced, setting down the swing.

Aunt Ginny looked over her reading glasses. "You mean the baby's here. You don't count anymore, you know." She held out her arms, and I deposited Nathan in them.

"I've picked up on that."

"Isn't this weather horrible? My brain is swollen." She fluffed her bangs. "I told Jim and Chas, don't even bother coming up this weekend. There's sun tea in the kitchen." She frowned. "Kimmie, is something wrong? Take a sip." She lifted her glass out of the wire holder staked into the ground and held it out to me.

"No, nothing's wrong." I dropped into a lawn chair. "My air conditioning doesn't work so well. Um...also...Larry filed for divorce in Seattle."

"What's the point of that?" She rolled her eyes. "Isn't a divorce a divorce? I'm so sorry you have to go through this, Kimmie. I've known a few cases where the guy kind of went off the deep end."

"How long did it take for them to come around?"

"Oh, it varied," she said vaguely. "Men are just more immature than women, I don't care if that's not politically correct. They shouldn't get married until they're thirty. Although—yes—he was, wasn't he. Well over thirty. Not an operative factor in your case," she said wryly. She checked Nathan's diaper. "Why don't you take your things in? I can watch the baby."

I went inside. Upstairs, I closed the shutters over the clawfoot tub and submerged myself in icy water. Bars of sunlight dappled the rag rug and slanted into the hall. I turned my head to follow them and looked straight into the branches of the silver maple through another window's wavy leaded glass. A month ago Frank and I had smoked a cigarette beneath that tree. *Welcome to the family.*

I smiled at my imaginary list of paternal objections to Frank; they were nothing in comparison to what Dad would say to Larry. *One, you twisted my daughter's arm so hard she buckled to the floor; two, you left your infant son alone and unattended in the house, and probably more often than my daughter realizes; three, you left your palm print on her face not just once, but twice. After you'd had time to think.*

When I was numb enough I got out. I opened the shutters to dress in the breeze. Aunt Ginny was below. I could see the afternoon sunburn on her shoulders and knees. She'd fished a book out of my duffel and was reading to Nathan in the crook of her arm. It was the book of English nursery rhymes she'd given him as a baby gift. She pointed at the illustrations as she read:

> Seven blackbirds in a tree,
> Count them and see what they be:
> One for sorrow, two for joy
> Three for a girl, four for a boy
> Five for silver, six for gold
> Seven for a secret never to be told.

I clutched the towel to my chest and leaned out the window. "Do you think he really understands?"

She tipped her head back and found me. "It's never too young to start. They can tell a lot just from your voice."

At five o'clock I joined my aunt under the hickory tree at the top of the hill. "How's the legal assignment going?" she asked.

"Okay. It's taking me longer than I thought." I put Nathan in his swing and spooned peaches down him as a martini boat trolled by. I leafed through Ginny's pile of reading matter: Calvin Trillin, Thomas Sowell, an Antonia Fraser, Heidegger. "Haven't you got anything light?"

She handed me a copy of *Woman's Day*.

"May, 1982?"

"This place is a firetrap," Ginny grinned. "You know Thea won't throw anything away. She brings it all up here and loads it into the butler's pantry when Uncle Hubby threatens to clean out the garage." Uncle Hubby was our nickname for Thea's husband Henry. It had been coined years ago, for reasons allegedly lost to memory. From time to time the younger generation offered conjectures—a small child's mispronunciation overheard, the fact they'd dated twelve years before tying the knot—but the older generation remained evasive. Perhaps it really was the case that they didn't remember. Regardless, the name had become affectionate, and stuck.

I found a megaphone under the pile. "What's this for?" I asked.

"Chas gave it to me for my birthday as a joke. He got tired of hearing me complain about the motorboats violating the No Wake rule."

"Is it real?"

"You bet. But it doesn't carry too far. It's kind of a junior version. Wait." She smiled wickedly and pointed at the boat pedaling back across our slice of waterfront.

"MOVE AWAY FROM THE DOCK!"

All heads swiveled, and we ducked down in our lawn chairs.

"Whoops! Wind must have been with us," Ginny said. "They should have known better anyway. The rule is twenty feet from a dock. Even non-motorized."

Uncle Will came out the kitchen door in his Madras plaid swim trunks with a towel around his neck. He held an empty tool caddy with a bar of soap and a can of beer in two of the slots. "Virginia, did you just use that megaphone?"

"Scared'em off."

"I'm going to have to take that away from you." He continued down the hill to the dock.

Ginny pawed through the newspapers. "I wanted to show you this book review. Here it is." She tapped it with her reading glasses. "It's about the link between television and ADD. Of course you know as a librarian that's my soapbox. Television caused the fall of communism but it hasn't done much else good."

I said flatly: "I know someone who has ADD with regard to child-care."

Ginny unclipped the pen from her bikini top and wrote the book title down in the margin of the newspaper. She ripped it off and handed it to me. "Add it to your list. In your free time. Ha!"

After dinner I went onto the porch to continue working on the affi-davit. I untied my chiffon scarf from the pillar. It smelled of creosote. I pressed my nose against the porch screen. The lawn rolled down the hill and the sunset glittered off the lake, through old growth artfully thinned by my father and uncles under my grandfather's direction many years ago. I sat down in a wicker chair, put my feet up, and uncapped the pen. I knew exactly how long this porch was: seventy-two feet, eight inches. My friend Andy and I had measured it one rainy weekend during a college summer. We'd spent most of the day on the porch reading old issues of *Life* from the thirties, left by the pre-vious family; they must have had an Aunt Thea too, someone who couldn't throw anything away. Toward suppertime the sun came out and we went canoeing; in the evening we went back and sat, as it grew dark. My grandmother had already gone to bed; we were the only others there. I lay in the hammock, rocking it gently with one foot while Andy told me the story of *Lulu*, Berg's opera about the rise and fall of a brilliant femme fatale. He must have studied it the previous semester. He sat resting his elbows on the wicker table between us, shuffling a deck of cards as he outlined the libretto. The birds fell silent, the crickets started, and it got darker and darker until Andy's white shirtsleeves and metal watchband seemed to glow. I closed my eyes and listened to the creak of the hammock, the cards, his voice. *"Du bist wie eine Blume,"* he sang. *You are like a flower.*

Andy was the only truly appropriate person I ever dated, in my old life. There was an ease between us I didn't know to value because it was so natural. He was the only male friend I had to whom my father was civil. He was the first man to send me flowers: a dozen long-stemmed roses on my nineteenth birthday. He was the first man who truly treated me with respect.

After that, I realized, I always went out with inappropriate people.

I put down the pen and pad. I couldn't write about Larry, on this porch where I'd sat with Andy; off the gravel circle where my father had taught me to drive; looking down at the dock where my grandfather had taught me to swim. It was too hard. I gave up and went to bed.

I was in the room over the kitchen this time, with a low ceiling and two sets of square windows that swung open like double doors on opposite walls, east and west, to afford the perfect cross-breeze. I leaned on the sill looking at the dark comforting shapes I knew were there, though I couldn't see them clearly: the fence, the clothesline, the zinnia border, the stately bank of oaks and maples wrapped around the property.

The Seattle hearing was a month away. After that I'd be divorced. It would all be over. I wouldn't have to think about it anymore. I'd just build a new life. I climbed into bed and listened to soft waves of wind in the crowns of massive, well-rooted trees, and I heard nighthawks, and fell asleep.

In my dreams I was waiting in a restaurant with a man. It was small and narrow, with only a few tables. We had a reservation but another couple pushed ahead of us and we had to wait for them to finish. When they left, we sat down at their table and I noticed the woman had left her watch behind, one of those expensive wristwatches with a jeweled dial, like Courtney's. *Oh,* I said, *she left her watch behind, I'd better run give it back to her.*

No, said my companion. *Look.* He turned it over and showed me there was poison on the dial. The watch was poisoned, so that when

101

she wore it, the poison would touch her skin and slowly kill her. *She was being poisoned by time.*

But I wouldn't believe it. *He's her husband and I'm sure she'd want to wear the watch.*

I awoke. My skin felt thin as parchment, hot to the touch. I took another cold bath, then stood in the open window to let the night air cool my skin.

When I slept again, I dreamt I gave birth to a round object. We looked at it, the midwives and Dana and I, trying to figure out what it was, because it wasn't a baby. Dana turned it around. It was an eye.

THE NEXT MORNING I waited for the coffee to brew with one side of my face pressed against the plastic tablecloth, a gaudy riot of fruit and vegetables. I closed my eyes.

I heard steps, and a soft laugh from Aunt Ginny. "Remember the cardinal rule of motherhood, Kim: sleep when the baby sleeps."

I opened my eyes. "I know, but I woke up in the middle of the night and I just had to get that writing down. I'm almost finished." The coffeemaker gave its death rattle and I roused myself to pour two cups.

"Did you think," I asked, turning the mug round and round on the laminated cornucopia, "was there anything…was there anything that made you think you saw this coming?"

"It's hard to say." She picked at a fraying patch in the buckled window screen. "Not really. I don't think so. He was a bit eccentric. I remember when he finished the law degree and then didn't use it— I mean in any way—I remember thinking that was odd. Usually people go into practice first, and then they might end up doing something else. But he hasn't used it at all. And then after that—to go for an LLM? Well, like I said, he's a bit eccentric." She glanced at me and took a sip. "But academics can be a safe haven for eccentrics."

Outside Uncle Will went by with a watering can, liberally dousing the potted fuschias. I poured another cup of coffee. Who was the man in the dream, I wondered. Was it Andy? Morgan? John from the law journal board, who'd leaned out his car window and given me a kiss before he'd left for Oregon after graduation? I constructed a hypothetical alternative reality in which I was ten years younger, got married young and foolishly to a wealthy octogenarian who impregnated me and then died in his sleep, upon which I enrolled in law school, met a handsome, kind, psychologically healthy man, and married him while Nathan was still in utero so I could put his name on the birth certificate.

We moved outside under the hickory tree.

"When I was still at the library," Ginny said, meaning Northwestern, "there was a gal whose husband was a tenured professor…in history, I think. When they got divorced, he quit his job and worked at an athletic club handing out towels to avoid child support. They had three boys between ten and fourteen. She saved every single sales slip in a shoebox. Every single bag of groceries, receipts for every single pair of shoes—three boys, imagine the shoes!—everything. 'One day he's going to get the bill,' she said."

Nathan pushed himself around in a circle. With his padded bottom and flailing legs, he looked like a beached turtle in a red romper.

"His arms are getting stronger," Ginny said. "He'll be an early crawler."

"And did he?"

"Did he what?"

"Ever get the bill."

"I don't know." She put on her sunglasses and lay back. "I lost touch with her. You just got me thinking, you know. About Larry. I hope he gets a grip on himself. It's amazing how many men feel no responsibility for their children once they're no longer married to their mother."

I went straight to the porch and finished the memo. Afterward I read it through silently.

And then, finally, I took off the ring.

It was Monica who introduced me to Larry. She was my best friend at Columbia, where I went into the PhD program right after college, a bird of a woman with the warmth, vitality, and lung power of a body three times her size. We both worked at the slide library in the art department, and on the days our hours coincided we always ate lunch together at the Blue Apple, a vegetarian cafe run out of a Presbyterian church on West 121st. One day Monica recognized Larry in the lunch line, and introduced us. But it was the second time we met there that we really fell into conversation, the time he ran into me eating my sandwich standing in the narthex so I could listen to the organist practice. I remember turning as he joined me in the doorway. The atmosphere was hushed, dim, washed with stained glass hues from the rose window over the street door. He smiled so sweetly, said hello so shyly. "I came in to listen to the music," he fibbed, twiddling an almost-empty styrofoam coffee cup in one shearling-lined, leather-gloved hand. That afternoon he wowed me by sitting down at the Steinway upright in his apartment and spooling out the Bach he'd just heard.

A couple weeks later, Monica said to me: "No, Kim, he's not for you." We were filing Baroque slides; she paused, Domenichino landscape in one hand, index finger of the other marking its place in the drawer, and frowned. "I don't know why. I just can't see it." She slid the image in place, and shut the drawer with a click. That was Monica: confident and frank, qualities I saw myself lacking. I knew she had five brothers, so she'd probably learned to be assertive out of self-defense. We used to go shopping together in West Village. She'd pull shapeless garments off racks, say "This would look fabulous on you," and always be right. On Friday evenings, after the library, we'd go to parties together.

Grad school parties were a little hard to get wild at. Usually it was a bunch of guys clustered around the Coldspot in the kitchen, the kind with rounded edges and a chrome paddle for a handle. The door would thunk open and shut, as the men pulled out beer after beer and discussed string theory or capital-asset pricing models while hoping some women would show up, and then ignoring them when they did. B-school parties were slightly less grim: there'd be some chips and a little dancing, and someone might ask for your phone number. As for the law school, its primary redeeming virtue was a good Friday night film series. It might be that it was only in such an atmosphere of astounding male repression that I could have picked up with Larry: he had the instinct of the chase, so the field was his.

Monica left after the Master's to go to law school. Having been through it myself now, I'm convinced she went into litigation: she had the perfect personality for it. During the following year my adviser, a tower of intellect in a dandruff-salted navy blazer, died suddenly, and the department chair decided not to replace him. Disgusted, I was in the mood to quit the program when Larry finished his last semester of law school and, in what I could not have recognized at that early date as another one of his "seesaw" maneuvers, proposed that we move together to rural Vermont.

I often wondered about Monica, where she was now, what she was doing, but especially I thought about the way she took no nonsense from anyone, the way she spoke her mind. And I wondered: if I had made a better friend of her, known her longer, seen her dice and slice more of those arrogant bastards at Friday night parties, would some of that confidence have rubbed off on me?

Come to think of it, I had no idea how Monica had made the slight but friendly acquaintance of Larry in the first place. Larry was a law school loner. How would their paths have crossed? My soul now had an irreparable hairline crack from top to bottom; I'd never be the same, and this hung on the slender thread of Monica's acquaintance with Larry—and I didn't even know what that thread was. I never would know. I imagine her sometimes, sitting on the edge of the bed in one of the rooms in her parents' motel in New Jersey. The television is mounted on the wall, the bedspread is stiff, quilted in a muted floral pattern. She's in a sharp red business suit with her laptop across her knees, skillfully drafting a Motion for Summary Judgment, completely unaware of her indirect but long-lasting effect on my life, unaware of her role as innocent catalyst in my suffering and my joy: the suffering that lingered in the form of memory lapses and a bad right ear; and the joy in the creation of a new life, my beautiful son.

〰〰
〰〰

11

Stranded in Tulsa

MORGAN AND I WERE AT the espresso stand in the student center. "When's that hearing again?" he asked. "On the motion to quash?"

"A week from tomorrow, nine a.m. Pacific Time." I scribbled on a paper napkin. "One hundred eighty-eight hours."

"So then can we go dancing?"

I gave him a look. I was trying to cultivate the Karen look. I practiced it in the mirror.

"Hey, y'all." My study partner laid two fingers on the tabletop. He glanced around and lowered his voice. "I just got a really good Commercial Law outline."

"Better than the one we got from Courtney?"

"Much better. This guy AmJur'd the class."

"That's great, Chris. Want to join us?"

"No, no, got some stuff to do. Listen, I had to promise him our IP outline, he knows we got the only two A's. Hope that's okay."

"Sure. Don't you want a cup of coffee before Snoozeson's lecture?" That was Professor Swanson.

"No, I'm good." He hoisted his backpack again. "See you in a few."

"That is a huge weight—" I turned back to Morgan, who wore a mysterious grin as he picked up muffin crumbs with a moistened finger. "What? What?" I asked.

He shook his head.

"Was that an 'I don't want to barge in' no?"

He recrossed his long legs and turned his gaze to the ceiling. "Maybe."

"We'll have to stop meeting like this. People will think we're dating."

"What's wrong with that?"

"I'm still married."

"Don't be such a stickler."

"I'm not dating. I can't," I insisted, trying to repress an answering grin.

"So what is this, then?"

"A coffee date. That's not a real date. It's during the day."

"So when can we go dancing?"

I slid out of my seat and checked my watch. "In one hundred eighty seven and a half hours."

THE THREE OF US were in a car. Larry was driving. We were going up a winding mountain road. He was going too fast for the curves but when I pointed this out he got mad and just for spite accelerated, driving the car straight off a cliff. We plunged down toward the water. I said, "At least unbuckle your seatbelt so we can get out when the car hits the water," and he snarled, "There's no way we're going to make it out of this car." He'd done it on purpose. He wanted to kill us all.

My eyes flew open.

At one a.m. in Tulsa the silence was unexpectedly deep. It was disorienting. Was I in the city or the country? Was Tulsa urban or suburban, home or alien territory? I was afraid to go back to sleep, so I sat up in the maple bed—the same one I'd slept in as a child—and pondered the disintegration of my marriage. In his crib, baby Nathan turned in languorous, pink-cheeked slumber and poked a tiny hand through the bars. In a big city, right now, there'd be sirens, airplanes, car alarms; here, nothing. In the middle of the night, in the middle of the country, I was marooned in absolute, dustless, heat-soaked silence. The bottom dropped out of the present. The past rushed up from behind and blocked my future, and I was stranded—stranded in Tulsa, the city of my discontent.

I stuck my finger through the blinds. A narrow strip of grass lay between me and the next building in Riverview Gardens. A walkway led to the parking lot, where a cottonwood drooped over the streetlight. It blocked my small portion of visible sky; to see the stars I'd have to go all the way out and stand by the dumpster. I was never good at science, but didn't homeward-bound rockets burn up when they reentered the atmosphere? Or was that meteors? I released the blind and curled up in fetal position, pulling the covers over my head. I sat up and put in earplugs, then pulled the covers back.

Larry was driving again. This time I got out of the car and put the baby in the stroller. It rolled into the street and I ran after it to save him from an oncoming car. When I turned around Larry had driven away, leaving me with nothing. No money, no way to get home.

4:34 a.m. Nathan was rustling. I crawled to the end of my bed, lifted him over the crib railing, and lay back down. He nursed greedily, his little body warm against mine. I slipped my fingers through the mini-blinds. It was grey and quiet outside, every window shuttered. I drowsed off again, Nathan tucked into me.

I could have stayed in Chicago, lived with Bobbie, finished my last three classes somewhere downtown. I even looked into it. But something told me I needed to be entirely alone for the first time in five years. I needed to go through this, to finish it out, and I had to go back where it happened.

When I first arrived I was elated. I'd actually taken a victory cruise, after recovering my car from Dana's garage, where we'd hidden it from the long arm of Larry: south on Riverside Drive, past the booth where I'd made the Phone Call, then back north to downtown, where businessmen whose dress made virtually no concession to the heat stood on the corners of empty streets, patiently waiting for the walk signal.

From there, east on 6th, crossing Centennial Park, a buffer between the high-rises and the decrepit warehouses and body shops that formed downtown's crumbling edge. This was my new route to

108

school. A straight shot past Peoria, Utica, Lewis, the railroad tracks and the Beehive Lounge, the funeral home with the broken clock, and finally to Delaware Avenue.

There the blocks were tidy and collegiate. Quasi-Gothic limestone buildings, moored on huge expanses of dormant lawn, sat dumb, thrashed by the sun. It was heat of an overwhelming yet peculiarly hushed intensity that had stunned me when I'd arrived three years earlier, but which by now I hardly noticed. I paused in the no-parking zone outside the law school. Chenille bushes nodded somnolently against the wall of the library, where first-years were going through orientation with Morgan and the library director. My old house, the house Nathan had been born in, was a few blocks away.

The silence was deafening.

It was the silence that did it, an immense, yawning vacuum that made me feel suddenly as though I'd returned to the scene of a tremendous natural disaster nobody else could see: no ripped-up con-crete, telephone poles at steep angles, twisted car wrecks, overturned gas pumps and telephone booths, boarded-up windows. The feeling of victory evaporated.

And then there were the nightmares. That was when they'd started, when I'd returned to Tulsa.

Why was I having all these nightmares?

Larry was pinning me down in bed, squeezing me around the waist. I was gasp-ing in pain, couldn't speak, and he was laughing, gloating over how he had me where I couldn't even cry for help. But I kept trying to, and finally I did cry out loud and wake myself up, and the baby too, and the baby started crying.

5:52 a.m. Diaper change. I fed Nathan a scrambled egg, then put him on the floor with some toys, which he ignored in favor of gym practice while I read Federal Courts until he pulled over the wastebas-ket sixteen minutes later. We took a bath together. I nursed him again and put him down for his nap. It was eight a.m. and I was overcome with exhaustion. I lay down on top of the bed fully clothed and fell asleep.

Half an hour later I got up and wrapped the coffee grinder in a towel to muffle the noise. While breakfast brewed, I got a piece of paper labeled SLEEP TALLY from the utensil drawer and calculated, subtracting for the twice-nightly feedings and the nightmares: Sunday, five-and-a-half; Monday, six. Tuesday, four. Wednesday, four-and-a-half. I'd started this in order to encourage myself with progress. There wasn't any, but it had become compulsive.

Outside the sliding glass doors—my only window—a scrawny, browning boxwood hedge crouched around a cement pad the size a beach towel. The management at Riverview Gardens called it a patio. On the North Shore of Chicago, expensive landscaping service bought never-ending summer, emerald green lawns from May through September. Tulsa was poorer, drier, too far south; summer here died its natural death: a prolonged strangulation.

The motion to quash had been successful. It had only taken five minutes, according to Jessica: after the first paragraph of her opening statement, the judge had interrupted her with an immediate ruling. "His lawyer didn't even get a chance to open her mouth," she reported gleefully. Victory was short-lived, however, because Larry continued to refuse Oklahoma service. Hal Duncan got irritated, which worried me. "Washington just *rejected* jurisdiction," he said peevishly. "Where does he think this case should be heard?" He and Jessica had conferred, and now I had a detective from Bellevue on my legal team.

When Nathan woke up, I took Aunt Ginny's nursery rhyme book and we sat in the rocker. This was the only time now I could read to him, when he was drowsy, the only time he'd still snuggle quietly for a few minutes before wanting to be up and off. Ginny had been right: he was an early crawler.

> Seven blackbirds in a tree
> Count them and see what they be…

I looked up and saw my babysitter approaching with her tote bag, windbreaker zipped up to her neck. I'd installed a full-length mirror at right angles to the window. It brought light into the room and also allowed me to see anyone coming up the walkway. It made me feel safe. I opened the door before her knock.

"Saw me coming!" Loretta beamed. "How's that baby today?" She scooped him up.

"Oh, Loretta, I don't know what I'd do without you—" Tears came to my eyes. It happened frequently since I'd given birth; was it hormones?

"Honey, don't even think about that." She jiggled the baby on her hip. "The Lord brought us together and here we are. Right, pumpkin?" she asked, and Nathan crowed in response.

12

Sex after Larry

I MADE THE FIRST DATE without realizing it. I was briefing Federal Courts at the Indian Territory, utilizing the multiple-highlighter technique I'd picked up from Larry, from his stint in law school: Issue (red), Rule (yellow), Analysis (blue), Conclusion (green). I stopped now and then between colors to take a bite of chocolate cake, a treat in celebration of the fact that Larry had finally been served—one hundred and forty-six days after I'd filed. The detective had called me personally that morning.

"I had to tell you this story myself. I'm a good server, you know? The best. I've tracked people into the *woods*, for Chrissake. But this guy—man, we were running on three weeks! I can't tell you how pissed I was getting. I thought, this guy is ruining my *rep.* So what I finally did was, I went to the townhouse next door, told the lady I was a friend of Larry's, and Larry wasn't home, and I wanted to wait for him out by the pool. So she lets me through. I go out to the pool, change into swim trunks, put some ketchup on my hand, and wrap my tee shirt around it. Then I went to Larry's back gate. You know they all have these fenced courtyards. I knocked and said I just cut my hand by the pool and could he get a band-aid? He opened the gate and I handed him the papers. Man, was he fuming. He was so mad. He tried to give'em back. I said, 'Do whatever the f— sorry, Ms. Baltakis—do whatever you want with'em, you been served.'"

I almost went shopping. I thought about new shoes, or a new pair of earrings. New shoes *and* a new pair of earrings. It was, after all, mid-October; I'd been waiting for this for five months. But my legal fees so far—I kept a personal running total in my head at all times—were sixty-five hundred dollars, just to get the petition on file. So I settled for a piece of chocolate cake and a double espresso.

I noticed Forrest when he walked in. Of course, I didn't know his name then, but I noticed him; I was reading, but I knew he was looking at me. I recognized the feeling—the same one I'd had when I stepped out of the stationery store over the summer and someone had whistled at me. I thought: *I'm becoming single again.*

After a while, I took the side door out. I window-shopped at the two boutiques next door, which, along with the Indian Territory, formed a valiant little upscale cluster in the sagging retail neighborhood next to Mercy. Then I went back around the corner and almost fell over him, tying his shoe. We both apologized, and before I knew it I'd agreed to meet him at the same place the next afternoon.

When I got back to Riverview Gardens, I tucked Nathan under my arm, grabbed a few teething biscuits and went one apartment over and up the stairs, where my new friend Alison lived. The day I'd moved in, alone, she'd walked past me coming home from work and reappeared five minutes later in shorts and tee shirt to help me for two hours in ninety-seven-degree heat. It was instant friendship.

She opened her door clad in a bathrobe, with a towel over her shoulders. Nathan goggled at the little tufts pulled out of the highlighting cap.

"What are you doing?" I asked.

"I'm going a little bit auburn around the front."

"That'll look nice." Alison had a head of black curls.

"Yeah, well, I'd rather put in pink and blue streaks, but in my position I have to be a little more subtle."

"What position is that?"

She gave me a look, like Karen, and burst into a staccato peal of laughter. "No one remotely near my own age would ask me for a

113

date." She went over and opened the balcony slider. "He's not going to like this smell," she said, referring to Nathan.

I sat down at her dining table. Unlike my apartment, hers was a home, courtesy of a mother who was an interior decorator: a real table and chairs, a couch, drapes, pictures on the wall. It was her mother's style, but she didn't care because it was free. Alison herself was more given to leather and vinyl (clothing), and the only thing that prevented her from having multiple ear piercings was the fact that she taught first grade in a very conservative geographical region.

I gave Nathan a biscuit and admonished him to mind his manners.

There was modeling clay on the table. "What's that?" I asked.

"It's for next week." Alison picked up a blue ball and a knife. "This is the earth." She sliced it in half, and pointed. "This is the crust, and this yellow layer is the mantle, and the red is the magma core."

"They won't eat the clay?"

"Kim, these are six-year-olds. They're well beyond the stage where they automatically insert everything into their mouths." She jumped up and caught Nathan before he planted his biscuity hands on the sofa.

"Alison, I need to check something out with you."

She spotted the damp bready stub on the floor, picked it up with two fingers and threw it away. "And we're done with this too, don't you think?" She dampened a paper towel. "What?"

"I think I just made a date."

"You *think* you just made a date." She cleaned Nathan off while I told her about meeting Forrest. "Okay." She sat back down and readjusted the bath towel. "You started talking to this guy outside that you'd seen inside—of course you realize he followed you out—"

"He did?"

"Of course he did. That thing about 'didn't I just see you at the Indian Territory?' Come on!"

"Okay, okay. He followed me out." I began to collect clay crumbs.

"You talked to him, you exchanged names, he asked for your phone number—"

"But I didn't give it to him. I'm not that dumb."

"It doesn't matter. Stop that." She snatched the containers from my hand, forcing me to look at her. "He asked to see you again, you set up a time and a place. That is a date."

"I thought so. I'm not sure I meant to do that. I don't think I meant to. I was going to work my way into this slowly."

"Nobody's ever followed me out of the Indian Territory and asked for a date," she said.

"You never go there."

The oven timer went off.

She picked up Nathan and put him in my arms. "Get out of here," she grinned, "I need to rinse my hair."

FORREST WAS THE opposite of Larry: tall and blond. He'd gotten a football scholarship to college and been stabbed while tending bar in Dallas one summer—he told me that story right away because of the visible scar under his jaw. I liked that, a football player who'd become a doctor. It was unusual, but not eccentric. I was trying to taper my attraction to eccentricity. After dinner we went to his house, a brick ranch in Florence Park. The nice landscaping weighed in his favor. He tried to kiss me in the living room, and I started to cry. I was so embarrassed I didn't say a word all the way home.

But he called back the next evening. We had a nice conversation, during the course of which he did not ask for another date. I appreciated the tact, and when he called again a few days later and did, I accepted.

I liked his living room. The hardwood was bare, the furniture modern, and he had art on his walls I was able to inspect this time around: abstract, with some good Indian watercolors mixed in. We went out on the terrace so he could smoke an after-dinner cigar. I settled on a chair. He patted the sofa cushion next to him.

"Don't be a stranger."

I moved over.

"It's not too cold for you, is it?"

I shook my head. I was, in fact, feeling, suddenly, that my short skirt and halter top exposed a great deal of flesh.

He sat contentedly, puffing on his cigar.

115

I'd been picking up on this lately, this quality that some men seemed to have, an ability to be at rest. Suddenly I realized: Larry was the exception, not the rule.

"Beautiful night," Forrest said, putting his arm around me. "And beautiful company. Did you notice at dinner that everyone in that restaurant was looking at you? You were the most beautiful girl in the room."

"There weren't many girls *in* that room, Forrest."

He set down his cigar, put his other arm around me, and kissed me. I kissed him back.

Suddenly I sat up.

"Everything okay?" he asked.

The baby was at Dana's. She took him overnight so I could have a nice evening out and not worry about the sitter; the baby was safe. "Yes." I sat back again. "He's okay. I mean I'm okay."

"I know you've had a hard time," he said, tracing circles on my shoulder. He whispered in my ear, "This outfit has been driving me crazy all night. How did you know just what I like? Thank you so much for wearing this outfit."

It's okay to be doing this because I don't really know him, it's okay because I never dated blond guys before so it doesn't count, because I never dated a football player before so it doesn't count, because...

He carried me inside. When he set me down I clenched my hands around my shoulders. I was in the bedroom of a person I'd only just recently met and I was naked except for my stockings.

"Don't do that," he said, loosening my arms. "Let me see you." He rolled down the stockings.

"Let's get under the covers," I said.

We lay quietly. Forrest crossed his arms behind his head. "Wouldn't it be nice if you could stay over," he said.

"I...I can if you want. Nathan's at his godmother's overnight."

He kissed me in reply. We started over. He pushed the blankets away. "Go ahead, talk to me," he said. "Say anything you want."

"I don't know what to say," I cried. He took a handful of hair, turned my head to the side and pressed his face against mine. I pushed against him but he was pinning me down, and then he clutched my hair tighter and with his mouth right on my ear whispered say this, say that, and I did, in a whisper, beginning to move against the weight of his body.

How had I forgotten so completely about sex? Sex for Larry had been masturbation using a woman's body. He never touched me, never told me he loved me, that I was beautiful. He never ejaculated inside of me—he said it hurt—except once, intentionally. *We can have a baby if you do all the work and we split the expenses,* he said, and then he ejaculated.

How did I ever forget I was attractive? How could I have been so prescient in leaving him—how had I known something was wrong when I'd lost awareness that anything was wrong, had completely forgotten what it was supposed to be like between a man and a woman?

That night in Forrest's bed I dreamt I was back on the third floor of the music building at New Trier High School, trying to open my locker. It was time to set up for symphony practice. Students were going past me with their cases and folders, but I hadn't been there in years and couldn't get my locker open. The bell rang. I tried again. A voice in my head shot out: *16-22-34. Wow,* I cried, *I can't believe I remember my locker combination from high school!* I grabbed my rehearsal instrument. Mr. Kamin was sitting on the podium, one heel hooked into the bottom rung of his stool, twiddling his baton and cracking jokes while the woodwinds put their instruments together. *Please let me back,* I asked him. *I'm not very good anymore but I'll sit in the back until I improve,* and he agreed. The oboe gave the strings an A, and I began to tune. I couldn't believe I was getting a second chance.

13

The Ten Commandments are Not Suggestions

"YOU'RE NOT SUPPOSED TO CONTEST a temporary custody application," I moaned to my counselor. "It's a formality while the divorce is under-way. Now we have to wait a month for a hearing on it. And we can't get in line for the final hearing date until that's over."

"Typical," said Dee. I liked Dee. She had a cherubic face and bright blue eyes, but the gravelly voice and world-weary air were pure New York. "Typical," she repeated. "And how far out are they scheduling?"

"About three months," I responded miserably.

She handed me the tissue box.

I'd lucked onto Dee, simply walking into the Brookside office of DVS one day and asking for a counselor. Dee was old enough to inspire confidence, young enough that I could see her as a peer. Now that I thought about it, she filled a gap: younger than Thea, older than Karen. My extended family, I realized, while spread over decades, had no real representative of the hippy era.

I sat back and wiped my nose. "Dee, it's supposed to be routine, you get temporary custody with nominal support until the divorce is final. But he filed this long, crazy, rambling answer, and now we have to have a whole *hearing* on it." I wiped my nose again. "Am I whining?"

"What kind of things does he say?" She leaned over and reached a pad from her desktop. "Do you mind if I take a few notes? It's getting a little hard to keep straight." She tucked her legs beneath her again and rearranged the pleats of her Navajo broomstick skirt over her lap.

I stared glumly at the poster of the *Desiderata* in rainbow-tinted flowing cursive. It belonged to the counselor she office-shared with. It didn't hang flush because of a crack in the fake wood paneling. Out the small window was a gully lined with trashy hawthorns. If it rained a lot, it became a creek, emptying into the Arkansas.

"What?" I asked.

Dee leaned forward. "Kim, where were you?"

"I don't know. I'm sorry."

Pen in hand, she pulled at her bottom lip. "We need to talk about that—but not now. What I asked you was: what makes you think he's going to cooperate now? Given his behavior in the past?"

"But he doesn't love me!" I wailed. "Why should he be doing all this stuff to delay? Why can't he remember that he doesn't love me?"

"It's not *about* love. It's about control."

I rubbed my temples. If I could just lie down on the floor and take a nap. The night I'd spent at Forrest's I'd slept ten hours straight, my first uninterrupted night in over a year.

"This is typical, Kim. The husband tries to wear down his wife. Get her to drop the proceedings. A lot of men do this, and a lot of them succeed. Some women just don't have the financial resources to fight it. Not to mention emotional. You've got someone with a couple little kids, no money, no education…they give up."

"That's not going to happen here."

She looked me straight in the eye. "Then we know what we need to do."

I picked up Nathan from the Rainbow Room down the hall. By the time I hit the parking lot, the relief was gone. What was the point? Lawyers took notes, therapists took notes, I took notes. Everyone took notes, but nothing happened, except that every day I spent more money and every night I couldn't sleep.

Next door, the Peoria Avenue Baptist Tabernacle marquee had just been changed to read THE TEN COMMANDMENTS ARE NOT SUGGESTIONS. The ladder still leaned against the pole. I tuned to Big Country 99.5, Nathan's preferred station, pulled out and headed downtown to the

119

Federal Building. Had I committed adultery with Forrest? No, I hadn't, I decided. It wasn't that I was getting a divorce, or that we'd been separated for over a year. It was that I'd never really been married in the first place. It had only taken me one date with Forrest to realize that.

In the D.A.'s office I pushed my papers through the slit in the bulletproof glass. "This is for Ms. Lockhart," I told the receptionist. "It's overdue. I'm in her pre-trial practice class."

She pulled down her reading glasses. "How old is this little darlin'?" she cooed.

"Eight months." I saw the comic-strip calendar on the counter. "Eight months today! I'll have to take his picture."

"Good for you. It goes by so fast. Y'all have a nice day!" She put her finger on the glass. I pressed Nathan's hand against the other side.

Our next stop was the photocopy center, because babies weren't allowed in the library. Nathan sat in his stroller, happily watching the pages of a subciting assignment for the junior staff at the journal shoot into the tray, oblivious to the discrimination. Then back to campus. Since it was autumn I could move faster now; I didn't have to open all the windows and blast the air conditioner before strapping him in.

I saw one of my old classmates in the lobby examining job postings. She'd graduated in May with the rest of my class. "Hi," I said.

She glanced at me. Her eyes slid over the baby, then returned to the bulletin board.

I blushed and pretended to examine the listings. "Anything interesting?"

She shrugged. Finally she said, "Heard you were still in town."

"Yes."

"Heard from Courtney lately?" she asked.

"Not since graduation. She's down in Houston now, with Corman Glazer."

"Yeah, I know."

Another silence.

"Well, I gotta go." She turned on her heel.

Back home I lay on the living room floor while Nathan napped, staring at the ceiling and feeling sorry for myself. There was a knock at the door. I pressed my eye against the peephole. "Who is it?"

"Parson's Flowers. Delivery."

"Are you sure?" I said, opening the door. "This is number 2127—"
I broke off, gaping at the size of the box.

"Looks like you have an admirer," he smiled.

The card read: *Looking forward to tonight. Forrest.*

Who cared if Courtney had dropped me, and then done a little
well-poisoning for good measure? I was going out with someone she
would have given her eyeteeth to date, Howard or no Howard.

I grabbed the phone and called Alison. "Do you have a vase?"

"He sent you flowers."

"Just get your posterior down here and bring a vase. A big one."

I lifted the roses out carefully. Something small and tissue-wrapped
lay beneath. I took it out, and unwrapped ivory satin lingerie. I shoved
it into the utensil drawer before Alison tapped on the door.

"So you're going out with Forrest," his friend Tracy said. We were in
the ladies' room at Southern Hills Country Club. "Did he tell you
we've known each other since kindergarten? We went to Holland Hall
together." She opened her handbag and took out a lipstick. The light-
ing was supposed to be flattering but it made her tan look fake. I
perched next to her on another seafoam-plaid vanity bench.

"It's only our third date," I said.

Exactly what I'd told my babysitter when she'd seen the roses and
cried *Oh, my stars! Do you think he's the one?* even before she'd taken off
her windbreaker. I wondered why everyone was in such a hurry to make
assumptions. To pair me off so quickly. That's precisely what I *wasn't*
going to do anymore: be impulsive about men. There was obviously
something about single women with infants that made people anxious.

"All right," Tracy said, "Not going out. We won't use the word.
But you've certainly made a conquest. Forrest just can't stop talking
about you at work, Chad says." She smiled at me in the mirror. "No,
don't be embarrassed. You're living up to the billing. Where do you
get your hair done?"

"Miss Jackson's."

"Good, good." She nodded. "Is your divorce final yet?"

"Almost."

"Who's your lawyer?"

"Hal Duncan."

"Good, good. That'll be okay then." She capped her lipstick and turned to face me. "I just dragged you in here because…well, you're the first girl he's gotten really enthusiastic about since his divorce."

"And that was two years ago?"

"Yes. She was a nurse. From Joplin. They met at the hospital. Barely finished high school. Completely boring. I can't think what possessed him. I knew from the beginning it wouldn't work, of course, but you can't tell Forrest anything. She didn't even play golf."

"Who left who?"

"She left him. If you can believe it. Well. We'd better go." She stood up. "Look at those ankles! You could be a hosiery model. Do you work out?"

"I swim a little, play tennis. Or used to. Lately I've been running. Not a lot."

"I knew it. It's genetics. That's what I keep telling my husband the medical doctor, but he won't believe me."

We rejoined the men in the dining room. "Is the interrogation over?" Forrest grinned at Tracy. She knuckled the back of his head. To me he said, "Do you like steak?"

"Sure."

"We'll have the Kansas City strip," he told the waiter, "rare, and the Caesar to start with."

"Chad, honey," Tracy said, "how come you never order for me?"

"Because we're an old married couple."

Forrest put his hand on my knee and slid it up until he found the lace garter. I looked out the window at the empty eighth fairway.

"Do you play?" Chad asked.

"Not very well."

"Me either," said Tracy, taking a gulp of gin-and-tonic. "Maybe in the Spring we could take some lessons together." She passed Nathan's picture to Chad. "Isn't he adorable? Where did you deliver?"

"At home."

"At home?" Chad's head snapped up. "On purpose?"

"Yes. With a lay midwife."

"My God." He looked at Forrest, then me. "You're not Seventh Day, are you?"

"No. I just wanted to have a home birth."

He gave Forrest another look, and returned to sawing his veal. "You were very lucky."

"How brave," Tracy said quickly. "All I know is, I want those drugs. Ashley was ten pounds, and that was mostly cranium. Honey," she told Chad, "I think I'm going to order a gold brick sundae for dessert."

"It's your funeral," he replied glumly.

In the parking lot Forrest took me by the waist. "I just couldn't stand it. The whole time. I knew exactly what you had on under your clothes."

He took me along a gravel path through a grove of weeping willows. They were staggeringly beautiful in the moonlight; I felt like I was on another planet. When we came to a chain-link backstop protecting a terrace, I grabbed Forrest's hands and pinned him to it, curving mine over his. Then he lifted me up and turned me around, trading places. I kicked off my shoes and wrapped my arms around his neck.

"No, hold on, I've got you," he said. I grabbed hold of the fence.

The lights of a golf cart approached: a security guard making the rounds. I let go and he pulled me under a weeping willow.

"Just in the nick of time," he panted.

Back at my apartment, after the sitter left, Forrest set me on the kitchen counter. "I didn't get to see the bra yet."

"We'll wake up the baby."

"Hmm. Slight logistical problem."

I buried my face in his neck.

"Do you want me to leave?"

In answer, I tightened my arms.

"How about we go over to my house? Pack a little bag, bring the playpen, we can set him up in his own room, all comfy-cozy."

"I never thought of that."

"Let's see." He held out both hands, palms up. "You've got a single bed, I've got a double bed, you've got a single bed..."

"Okay, okay," I laughed. "Put the baby seat in your car, and be quiet. Maybe we can do this without waking him up."

When we got to his house, he started setting up the playpen in the living room. I stopped him.

"Can we put him somewhere further away?" I moved down the hall, Nathan snuggled on my shoulder, and pushed open the last door with the toe of my shoe. "In here."

"Will you be able to hear him?"

"I could hear this child through ten-inch concrete. If you fold the blanket in quarters it makes a softer mattress. Perfect." I lowered him in, tucked another blanket around, and laid a stuffed animal on either side. Forrest put his arm around me as we watched him settle back in, and I shuddered involuntarily. *This is what normal couples do,* I thought. *They look at their baby together at night.*

I left the door ajar and we went back down the hall. "Don't think I'm weird or anything. I couldn't...I just couldn't have him so close."

"Don't worry about it. Don't think so much."

"That's hard. I've always had a problem with not thinking."

"That's what sex is for."

"Now you get to see the bra, I guess," I said, hugging my elbows.

He kissed me. "Stop thinking," he said, "and just do what I say."

~~
~~

124

14

Seven Blackbirds

"WELL?" SAID DANA. I opened the passenger door and scooted in beside her. It was seven o'clock on a Friday night, and we were going out.

"Eighty-two dollars a month," I said.

"Shit. Didn't he just buy a Lexus?"

I'd gotten something for my money from that detective service. A few extra details.

"It's the lowest possible amount of child support a non-custodial parent can pay in the state of Oklahoma," I said.

She turned north on Peoria. "Girl, why are you smiling?" she demanded, pounding a hand on her lambswool-covered steering wheel.

"Because he also has to pay fifty percent of health and childcare expenses."

"And you pay your sitter what, I forget—"

"Three hundred dollars a month."

"Which brings it up to..." Her eyes narrowed. "Two hundred thirty-two. That sounds better. And he can't get out of it?"

"Nothing he can do. It's a court order."

Dana whooped. "Just send him the bill!" she shouted out the open window.

"That's exactly what Hal said! 'Just send him the bill.'"

"Send him the bill," we sang all the way downtown, over the railroad bridge, and into the Brady District.

The Tin Horn Gallery was on one of the old brick streets, a block down from Cain's Ballroom. At the curb, two scrubby trees were strung with white lights. Smokers, clumped on the steps, used their planters as ashtrays. We picked our way inside. Large abstracts filled the walls. I snatched up a glossy information card from a pile on top of a cigar store Indian. *Max Schmidt-Ebenroth: American Visions,* it read.

"Dana!" I exclaimed. "This guy's the real thing. He's represented in galleries in New York, Paris and Vienna."

"Gareth wouldn't steer us wrong." Gareth was one of her former patients at the hospital, a retired oil company executive and an art collector. He didn't go out at night anymore; he said he liked his beauty sleep.

Someone familiar approached—the man I'd met at Riverparks. "My friend with the baby!" he said. "I recognized you even without the accessory. You're…"

"Kim," said Dana, inserting herself between us with a plate of appetizers. "And I'm Dana."

"Hi, Jake," I said.

"My feelings are hurt. You come to this opening but you didn't come to mine."

"I'm sorry. The timing was wrong."

"So, are you still married?"

"Where'd you meet this guy?" Dana asked.

"Do you two always dress alike?" Jake retorted, spearing a cube of cheese.

"It's accidental," I said. "Maybe," Dana said at the same time. "At least we made an effort."

"What? What?" He grinned, plucked at his shirt, and stuck out a foot in a sandal. "What's wrong with this? This is what I always wear."

"Maybe that's what's wrong." Dana gave a wicked smile.

"Oh, I like this one. Where'd you pick her up? At least I bathe regularly." He nodded toward the featured artist. He was rolling a cigarette in a corner. As we looked over, he paused, scooped disheveled black curls behind one ear and looked straight at me.

126

"Don't tell me he's your type," Jake said.

"I don't know what my type is. The old type isn't working for me anymore. I'm looking for a new type."

"She's in dating rehab," said Dana.

"Under your guidance?"

"You bet, baby."

"Can I sign up?"

"We're only taking men who can show a W-2."

"I figured you for a union gal. You know, there's nothing wrong with being self-employed."

"That depends. Especially for creative artists. Do you have an agent? Are you a household name? Can you support this woman in the style to which she is accustomed?"

"Oklahoma City just bought one of my pieces for the new Federal Building. Does that qualify?"

"No," she said over her shoulder, hauling me away. "Too local."

"WE'VE HAD SOME developments." Hal shut his office door and pulled out a chair. It was the first time he'd asked me to come in since our initial meeting.

"Developments," I repeated.

"Larry has challenged paternity."

"What?" I scooted to the edge of the chair.

"He's challenged paternity."

"He's challenged paternity." I said. "Is he *allowed* to do that? He knows he's the father."

"It's his right. If he wants to bring it up as an issue, it's his legal right."

I looked around the room, at the jacket on the coat tree, the butterflies on the wall. The differences between the butterflies were subtle, and I was too far away to read the captions on the prints. I looked back at Hal. "I don't get it. I thought you only challenged paternity if you didn't know whether or not you were the father."

Hal tapped his pencil on the papers in front of him.

"But Hal, he *knows* he's the father."

127

He tossed the pencil down and leaned back in his chair, clasping his hands behind his head. "I never doubted it for a minute."

"I did his shirts," I said softly.

"Frankly, nothing this guy does surprises me anymore," he went on. "What did you say?"

"I did his shirts. Myself. I did them myself." Wet the collars and cuffs, scrubbed them with Fels Naptha, washed, dried, sprinkled them with water, rolled them in drycleaner's plastic, then ironed them with spray starch. "I never even sent his shirts to the cleaners."

Until I was bedridden with morning sickness and couldn't get up.

If my father were alive none of this would have happened. But how could I think that? How could I regret my son? I couldn't. I wouldn't.

Hal shook his head. "Apparently he called his lawyer on Thursday—"

I closed my slack jaw. "That's when he got the bill! The baby-sitting bill. I mailed it on Tuesday. He probably got it on Thursday."

"Yes, he complained to Toby about that too, but there's nothing he can do about it. Toby knows that. If it's work- or school-related child-care, he's responsible for half of it. That's all there is to it. Toby tried to explain it to him. He called me on Thursday to give me a heads-up about this, but I didn't want to say anything to you until I had the motion in hand." He paused. "He also told me he was off the case."

I knew Toby. He had graduated two years ahead of me. "He fired Larry as a client?"

"Larry's been hounding him on the phone, and he can't deal with it anymore. He swore he was never going to do a divorce case again. He enclosed this strange letter from Larry." Hal slid it over the desk. "He's asking for a visit. He challenges paternity and he's asking for a visit!"

"He's coming to Tulsa?"

Hal was shaking his head, lips pursed in disgust. "He can't *see* Nathan. He's just said he's not the father! Trey MacIntyre called this morning—that's his new lawyer. I told him our position was that Mr. Baltakis had no right to see the child until paternity had been determined. Trey was in complete agreement. He didn't relish communicating that to his client, though."

"Do you know Trey?"

"Oh yes. Very good. Aggressive. He might meet his match in Larry, though."

I looked down at the letter in my hand.

> I will be coming to Tulsa to see my son after my classes end on December 9. My wife has withheld contact with my son for months. She has moved him from state to state in an effort to conceal the child from me, his father. Please inform her that this is illegal.

"Hal, he's never once asked to see the baby."

"Don't worry about the letter." He waved his hand dismissively. Nobody's taking the letter seriously. His lawyer will explain the matter to him and that'll be that."

"So he's not going to come?"

"He's not going to come."

I LAY ON MY living room floor while Nathan played, trying to think of my house. Not my childhood home, the one I'd grown up in, and not the house in Vermont, but the bungalow in Tulsa with the old sash windows, the eight-inch baseboards, the dining room arch—the house Nathan had been born in. I hadn't been able to think of it at all, until after I had known that Larry had been served; but even then, even now, I could only see the floor, the one we'd stripped and refinished when we moved in. Recollection had come first as the floor. My eyes were on the floor, the hardwood floor and the sound of the bassinet wheels rolling over it from the dining room through the little hall into the bedroom. I loved the sound of those wheels. The bassinet was white, and the eyelet skirt too, with a ruffle. Larry saw it at Sears and asked, "would you like this? I'll buy it for you," but then when the bill came in, he made me pay. These things I saw were signs of hope—the refinished floors, the white bassinet, the tiny baby in it, the sound of the wheels rolling on the floor into the bedroom so the baby could sleep behind a closed door. Everything was a promise, and it all came to nothing. I could think of that house, now, but so far only of the

129

floor—the sunlight slanting on the narrow taffy-colored oak planks and the faint squeak of the bassinet wheels, the bassinet slowly traveling from one room to the next. I couldn't get my mind any further off the ground. I could only see the floor, I couldn't bear to touch with anything the physical reality of the life that occurred above the ground, between people, at eye-level, between those four walls. The whole house was a hope. Everything was a hope, and all the hopes were foolish, all the hopes were in vain. The floor, the floor, the floor: I couldn't get my eyes up off the floor and confront the reality of my marriage.

I turned my head to the side. Nathan was emptying the wastebasket. He could do it from a standing position now, instead of having to tip it over. I turned my head back again and stared at the ceiling. I was playing Delbert McClinton on the CD player I'd picked up at the Salvation Army store, and the materials for my practice deposition were lying by my ear. Next week, I had to put on a suit and grill a local attorney playing a witness in a mock trial. I could not imagine, but by now I was well-versed in the art of not thinking ahead. This Thanksgiving was better than last, but not by as much as I'd expected. I'd expected to be divorced by now, so I could finally go back to being me. But it had been so long, I was losing my grasp on who that was. I didn't know what my outlines were, what kept me together on the inside. I squeezed my eyes shut, then opened them. The apartment was painfully white. That cheap spackling—what a joke to call it "brocade." In a room so completely white, what would keep my body from expanding until it dissolved?

I levered myself up on one elbow. Two p.m. No wonder I was hungry. I got up and looked in the fridge. There was a container of hummus, half a cucumber, and a cup of my babysitter's chuckwagon chili covered with tinfoil. Nothing appealed.

On the kitchen counter was a letter from Larry. It had come yesterday—was that Friday? But Hal had gone out of town for the holiday, so I was stuck until after the weekend, with the letter, still here, sitting on the counter.

Dear Kim, I am arriving in Tulsa on the 12th to see my son. You had better be there…

"Don't!" I raised my hand. Nathan was aiming the car keys at me. How had he gotten hold of the keys? He was smiling widely, showing two new front teeth. The keys sailed past my head and hit the door. I rolled over and fumbled for them. Despite outward appearance and the march of time, I was still living in a world where the men, and only the men, jingled the car keys.

THE NURSE CAME back into the examination room, a freckly redhead living in the wrong climate. She was holding a miniature straitjacket.

"No," I said.

"Now, honey." She smiled at me, which only added yellowing teeth to the equation. I was not in the mood to be charitable. It was the end of a busy day, including an exam, a deli sandwich from Bigelow's, a nap in the car, and a trip down to the restraining order office; while Trey had made it quite clear to his client that he couldn't see Nathan until the testing was completed, I wasn't taking any chances—Larry had been leaving flight times on my answering machine. So I joined a dozen women scattered along three tables stacked with forms and tissue boxes, and dutifully filled in the blanks. I was so drained I didn't mind that I knew the supervising attorney—Sulie, a former classmate; didn't mind being walked across the street into the courthouse; didn't mind being lined up against the wall outside the courtroom. All that mattered was that I now had in my pocket a document stamped "By order of the Court of Tulsa County, Oklahoma." The medical lab on Skelly Drive was our last jolly stop of the day.

"No," I said again, rubbing the band-aid in the crook of my elbow.

"Honey, it's the only way to take a blood sample from a baby. They're just too squirmy." She took him from me and strapped him in. She had on a WWJD wristband: *What Would Jesus Do.* "Now you hold his head this way so he can't see what I'm doing."

I crooned to Nathan, stroking his hair. "We've had shots before, sweet pumpkin baby. This'll only take a minute. Then you'll have a treat."

He started to wail.

"Can't find a vein," the nurse said. "Don't worry, we'll get it.

They're just so small." She tried again. And again. And again. Nathan's face turned purple.

The nurse gave me a quick apologetic glance, brushing back a loosened wisp from her forehead with her wrist. "Those veins are so small!"

"Just do it!" I screamed.

"Let's take a break for a minute, hon."

I bent down, stroked his cheek, kissed his damp forehead.

Behind me the nurse opened the door. "Get the mother out of here," she hissed.

"I hate you, Larry Baltakis," I screamed at her before the other one could get the door shut.

The other one sat down with me in the hall and grasped my hands in both of hers. "It'll be over in a minute," she said.

"This is not what Jesus would do," I pointed out.

"He won't remember a thing," she said. "Would you like a valium?"

"How do you know? How do you *know* he won't remember a thing? I need you to tell me! This is why I left him."

Someone stood in front of me with a cardboard tray.

"No, I can't take anything, I'm nursing."

"One little valium isn't going to hurt the baby," the nurse urged. "Just give him formula next feeding and express your milk. I can call you a cab to get home."

"No, I'm okay," I said, quieting down.

The pill and water disappeared.

"I didn't know it would be so hard to get the blood," I said. "I didn't know it would hurt him. I wouldn't have agreed. I didn't know it was going to be like this. I promised him."

An old man with a walker shuffled by. He looked at me with rheumy eyes and smiled.

"Promised him what, honey?" The nurse loosened her grip.

"I *promised*," I whispered, and sagged, hands still folded, neatly, just as I'd been taught in sixth grade social dancing class.

The nurse was still holding on, she'd never let go, but suddenly she scooted closer, bringing arms and legs together as though gathering herself for prayer. Her grip tightened, but this time she was cupping her hands over mine, warm and protective, as though shielding them from the wind. I focused on her hands, her arms, until Nathan was put back in mine.

"DO YOU WANT something to eat?" Dana called from her kitchen. "I made chili yesterday. Put some turkey in it. There's plenty."

"I'm not sure I should take solid food right now."

She stuck her head around the corner. "What's he done this time?"

"Let's see," I said, settling Nathan in the living room rocker, "What's the latest?" I cocooned him in pillows and turned on a Disney video. "I made Hal wait on anything till I was done with exams, so I got it today. Remember the money thing?"

She called, "You mean where he said he couldn't pay support 'cause he didn't have an income? Well, that didn't work."

"No, and I guess that really pissed him off. Now he's sent copies of some sort of loan documents I've never seen before, that he's borrowed four hundred thousand dollars from his mother over the last four years. He says it's a joint debt. He's trying to leverage me into dropping child support."

She came back around the corner holding a dishtowel.

"Asshole!" she breathed. She wiped her hands and steered me to the sofa. If six figure amounts were very, very large for me, they were even larger for Dana. She was silent a moment, then turned toward me, tucking a throw pillow under her arm. "Listen. He can't get out of child support. You know that. Parents have to pay child support. He just won't do it until he's forced. He won't do anything till he's forced. I mean, look at that stupid paternity challenge. This bogus loan shit—no judge is going to buy that."

"He gets away with everything."

"No, he doesn't."

"But he keeps doing these scummy things."

"He's a scummy person. Everything he does is scummy."

"But he gets away with *everything!*"

"He doesn't get away with everything. Sooner or later the court will nail him. Repeat after me: he's not getting away with anything."

Seven blackbirds in a tree, count them and see what they be...

"Girl, you've got to get a grip. You've got to put this behind you," Dana said. "Maybe you should come to my meditation class." She got up and started back to the kitchen.

One for sorrow, two for joy, three for a girl, four for a boy...

I looked at Nathan's profile, round eyes shining, chubby cheeks smooth and pink, rosebud mouth parted slightly as he stared, entranced, at a world that was for him, at this point, an entirely equal plane of reality.

Five for silver, six for gold, seven for a secret never to be told.

Aunt Ginny was right: they picked up on everything. They picked up on more than you realized.

"He made me have sex while nursing the baby!" I blurted.

Dana turned, came slowly back, hissing something I couldn't quite hear. I must have said something really bad. *Did I say something bad? She's mad at me now.*

"Bastard," she repeated. She sat down and gripped my arm. "That was abuse."

"No, no. He was my husband."

"That is sex abuse and it's wrong." Her mouth shaped the words slowly. That was such a good shade of lipstick on her. She wore it all the time, a bold red that went well with her long black hair and pale skin. It was all she needed. It made her look strong. Maybe Larry was right, Nathan didn't know what was happening. How could I know for sure?

"Girl." Dana shook my arm. "Girl, you have to tell your counselor."

"Okay."

"You have to tell your lawyer."

"Are you sure?"

"I'm sure."

I picked up the baby and sat in the rocker. I wanted to get away from her. "Okay," I said. *"Okay."* Pooh was flying up, up to the honey tree. I pressed my face into Nathan's hair. Dana leaned over the back of the rocker and put her arms around mine and the baby.

"Dana, I'll be a good mother," I whispered.

"Oh, girlfriend," she said, in a tone I'd never heard before or since from her or from anyone but somehow recognized by its resonance as the ancient voice of abiding witness. Of woman who creates, bravely, knowingly, over and over, accepting the price she has to pay, generation after generation, for remaining open to the depths of love. Staring at the television screen, I wrapped my hand over hers. We embraced each other, and within that embrace we held the child.

〰〰
〰〰

15

Burial at Sea

FOR ONCE I WASN'T HOLDING a wet diaper when Hal phoned. "I thought you might want to know the results of the blood test," he said.

It was Christmas again. I was sitting at my mother's breakfast table with Karen. I grinned at her. "I already know the results of the blood test."

He chortled. "You're right. 99.99%."

"They couldn't be any surer than that?" I rolled my eyes at my sister.

"I'll mail you a copy."

"I think I'll forward it to his mother."

Karen suppressed a laugh and snapped a thread with her teeth. She was sewing buttons on a sleeveless denim blouse. She wasn't even showing yet and her entire maternity wardrobe was almost done.

"Now we can move forward toward settlement," Hal continued. "The first step is to send out interrogatories so we can get a fix on his finances."

"The only thing I want to know is, when's the court date?"

I heard him shuffle papers. "The dockets are really full right now. Judge Byson just retired and he hasn't been replaced yet. So we don't know who our new judge is. We're probably looking at April, May."

I hung up the phone. Karen looked at me.

"April or May," I said.

"That's a whole *year* from when you filed!"

"Don't tell Mom, okay?" I could see Bobbie outside, shaking snow off the overloaded evergreens with a broom. "I'll just say he's conceded paternity and everything's chugging along."

She skewered the next button into place. "Now you know why people go out and buy guns." I turned back to her. It wasn't the Karen look this time. Her face was serious.

THE NEXT DAY, New Year's Eve, late in the day, I couldn't wait any longer. The world was not far off anymore, the way it had been for us as girls, when we searched for it along distant horizons or in the lines of our bones. The world was here, and I had to meet it. I bundled up the baby like an Eskimo, put him in the stroller, and walked to the beach.

The snow had melted, but it was bitter and overcast. Wind whipped the sullen water high. Leaving the stroller at the base of the pier I walked to the end, straight into the wind, the spray, the cruel whitecap ruffles, straight into the elements. All summer my pilgrimages to the lake had been fruitless; it hadn't given me any answers, and I figured now there must have been a reason for that. Some things you just have to work out on your own. So I wasn't asking the lake a question, this time. I was giving it an answer.

The wind was from the north, so I turned to the south, and when I threw the ring it went surprisingly far and I saw the little plunk it made in the water; it was satisfying to see the actual, tiny point of contact, proof of its destination. I turned and retraced my steps, wheeling the baby back across the boardwalk, past skeletal boat racks, up the ramp to the bluff. I felt bold but also frightened; a marriage, a ring, were sacred things. I turned one last time. Across the beach, toward the pier, toward greenish-gray waves mercilessly indifferent to my offering, I blew a last kiss.

"Thank you for the beautiful baby," I said, and then I turned and pushed the stroller up the hill and it was over. I'd shed my marriage.

16

Tips for Stress Management

TULSA WAS A RELATIVELY BALMY forty degrees, but Dana met me at the airport dressed for a polar expedition: shearling-cuffed boots, fuzzy red sweater, matching hat. "How's my godbaby?" She hefted him onto her hip. "Good Lord, girl! What've you been feeding him up there?"

I tuned the radio to Nathan's favorite station as we pulled away from the arrival curb. *"Blue skies smiling on me..."*

I rubbed my bare ring finger. Blue skies ahead. Now that Larry admitted Nathan was his, there was really nothing more to stand in the way. And the Bar exam would be behind me soon, too. "How was Christmas?" I asked.

"Good. Dave wanted to try deep-frying the turkey but I told him over my dead body. That's white-trash and I don't care if he read about it in the Wall Street Journal. My mom gave me some Fiestaware. I'm going to start a collection."

"It's about time to graduate from those Pez dispensers."

"I've been meaning to say," she grinned. "What about you?"

"Mrs. Claus gave me an injection of cash for legal bills. She said, 'This probably isn't what your father intended you to spend your inheritance on.'"

"I'll say."

"She's going to split the bills with me until I'm supporting myself. Kind of like a matching grant. Dollar for dollar. The MacLean Foundation."

"There you go." She turned the radio down on a Cherokee Nation casino ad. "So, what's your game plan?"

"Study for the Bar." I saw a billboard for the Arms Show at the Expo Center. "Maybe buy a gun."

"When's he coming to town?"

"Next weekend."

"Guess he thought the weather was good enough," she smirked, in reference to the infamous "I'm not coming to Tulsa in one hundred and four degree heat and renting a stinking motel room just to see my son" letter of last August, Hal's favorite.

Back at Riverview Gardens I dumped two weeks of mail on the kitchen table. There were five letters from Larry; I stuffed them in a desk drawer. That was number two in my file TIPS FOR STRESS MANAGEMENT. Number one was not to answer the phone. At my first counseling session, Dee had given me a brochure on post-traumatic stress disorder. I'd thrown it in the trash and turned the ringer off on the phone. It worked wonders.

Another box arrived from Parson's. I put the flowers in Alison's vase, shook the tissue paper clean, and gave it to Nathan. He had a high time ripping it up while I turned my back to unwrap the latest addition to my growing collection of lingerie.

"HE'S BEEN HERE for how long?" Bob asked. "Four days? And he's leaving tomorrow?"

"Mmh," I said. I was in the chair at Miss Jackson's, trying to keep my head still.

"And they won't let him be alone with the baby?"

"I didn't know you could do that, but my lawyer insisted."

"And he can't see you, either."

"Right."

"He must be teed off," Bob concluded, checking the length in front.

"Nine billable hours worth." Enough for a round-trip ticket to Venice.

The woman in the next chair, her foils completed, glanced at me surreptitiously as she got up. She moved to a sofa, tucked a designer purse as big as a grocery bag against her thigh, and accepted a cup of coffee from a maid. The bag was worth five billable hours, I guessed. Or seven of Larry's monthly support payments.

Hal had not only insisted on supervision, but also on monitoring by the only psychologist in town he thought worth his salt. This had so infuriated Larry we'd had to go to court when he arrived to get an order over his objection: ninety-minute, twice daily visits in Alison's apartment, while she was at work.

The first night Larry was in town, Alison came over and slept on my floor in a sleeping bag. The second night I lied and said I'd be okay; after the baby went to sleep I filched Winnie-the-Pooh from Nathan's crib and took him in with me. The third day I was bedridden with a high fever. I dreamt Larry had a whole row of prisoners and was forcing them to give him oral sex, one after another. When I woke in the morning the fever was gone. There was a notepad on the floor with big block letters scrawled across it: SEXUAL ABUSE IS A FUNDAMENTAL VIOLATION OF AN INDIVIDUAL'S HUMANITY.

I thought of what Dana said: *That is sex abuse and that is wrong.* The *Newsweek* article too: *Jekyll and Hyde.* Had Larry changed, or was he the same as he'd always been and I'd just never noticed?

I was having trouble sorting that one out.

"Well?" Bob had his hands on my shoulders.

I tore my gaze away from the handbag and considered my reflection in the mirror. "Curls."

"You got it." He unholstered a curling iron. "We're going to give you *party* hair."

At home, Alison leaned over her balcony railing and called: "Why on earth would you want to put curls in your hair?"

"Spoken like a true curly-haired person," I called back.

I changed quickly and switched purses. The restraining order was sealed in a zip-lock sandwich bag; I'd folded and unfolded it so often it was beginning to tear along the creases. I was trying to resist the urge to keep checking it.

"My stars, look at all those curls," Loretta said, when she arrived, shortly after Forrest. She put down her tote bag and beamed at us.

"Y'all have a good time tonight. And don't you worry one bit about that little baby," she added in a whisper to me as we went out the door. "He's safe with me."

"Are you hungry?" Forrest asked, driving slowly down Peoria.

"Not yet." I should have been; I'd hardly eaten all week. We idled past Carpet City and the car wash. "Maybe a little. Let's go to the Quiktrip and get a redneck mocha."

As we got out of the car a skinny cowboy leaning on one of the newspaper machines gawked at me. "Hey, friend!" I said, as we went through the door. "That's a hell of a big belt buckle you got there!

"Wow, curls really get you noticed," I said inside, spilling powdered cocoa on the counter as I poured it into the coffee. "Whoops!"

Forrest handed me some paper napkins. "It's not just the curls, honey," he drawled, smoothing down his black turtleneck.

We went to a movie, and then to the Petroleum Club, and sat at the bar. "You need to eat," said Forrest. He ordered a Caesar salad.

"That's too healthy," I told the bartender. "We'll have some buffalo wings too." I swiveled around on my stool. "Anybody here you know?"

Forrest surveyed the room. "Not at the moment."

"Oh my God, look, over there in the corner. That's Larry's lawyer."

"Which?"

"The one whose date is wearing a beehive."

"Trey MacIntyre? He's a ballbreaker."

"There's a man who needs a drink. He's had to deal with Larry for four days straight."

"This is the first time I've ever heard you say his name."

"Larry, Larry, Larry," I chanted, as the bartender put down two place settings, then poured the champagne.

"Of course that's not *really* his name," I cooed softly. "It's...asshole, asshole, asshole." The bartender suppressed a grin and refilled my empty glass. "No," I chirped. "No, actually, it's...it's...SPERM DONOR!" I slid the knife and fork out of the napkin and shook it open with a flourish.

"You got a live one there, Doctor Sayler."

"Yes, she forgot to take her meds today."

I ignored them. "Should I go over and ask him if his client is going to comply with our—oh, now let's see—one, two, three, four requests for discovery?" I held up the fingers I'd counted. "Including a motion to compel?" I wiggled them in the air.

Forrest wrapped his hand over mine and anchored it on my knee.

"I'm only kidding." I swiveled back and hooked my foot around his leg as the bartender served the salad. I leaned close. "Forrest. I'm not wearing any underwear."

His hand leapt off my knee. He palmed his head. "Nothing like a seventy-dollar bottle of champagne to bring out the inner whore in a woman."

I stroked the silk tweed of his pants leg. "Actually," I said, inching higher, "I think my inner whore has been in the process of emerging ever since I got my hair curled this afternoon."

"Kim. Trey MacIntyre is looking at you."

"Who the heck cares? I'm just acting like the slut his client has accused me of being all along." But I took my hand away. "He's just used to eating at more wholesome, family-friendly establishments," I said loudly. "Like Hooters." I popped a crouton in my mouth and gave Trey a winning smile.

"Time to go," said Forrest.

The bartender met us in the lobby with a brown paper bag, and Forrest conducted the transaction with admirable finesse in front of the elevator as I plucked at his sleeve, insisting, "That's probably where he picked her up."

The elevator arrived with a musical chime.

"I really wanted those buffalo wings," I said to the bartender, as the door closed.

We began to descend and I looked around. "Do they have closed-circuit in here?"

"This building? No."

I inched up my skirt. "Just wanted to show you I was telling the truth."

"Don't make me drop this ninety-dollar bottle."

"I thought you said seventy."

"The price increased considerably at the door."

"And then there were the glasses. Well, don't blame Oklahoma liquor laws on me." I smoothed down my skirt. "Anyway, I'm kind of telling the truth. They put a cotton gusset in nowadays, it's kind of like built-in underwear, if you're wearing a really tight skirt then you don't get a panty line."

"More information than I need right now," Forrest said, hauling me through the lobby as I waved goodbye to the nice folks in the WPA mural. "Actually, I prefer to make my own examination," he said.

Providentially his car was in the furthest, darkest corner of the parking lot. I set my glass down on the bollard. "Dare you."

He got a pants leg off in record time.

The metal was cool against my cheek. The hood ornament swam in a dim sodium-vapor haze. I closed my eyes, then opened them again. "Publicly knowable object."

"What?"

"'Beauty consists…in the active perception of harmony…in the publicly knowable features of an object.' Kant."

"I'm actively perceiving harmony in your hips right now, baby."

"Oh, wait." I pushed myself up. "We forgot."

"I thought…you kind of caught me by surprise." He zipped his pants back up.

We got in the car and took Riverside Drive south to 71st, then turned around. "I want that Tom Petty song. Where's the Tom Petty tape?" He lifted his elbow and I scrabbled in the armrest storage. "'Even the losers / They get lucky sometimes,'" I shouted along out the open window. "Park here, park here," I cried, drumming on the dashboard at 31st.

We went onto the pedestrian bridge, and leaned over the railing, looking north at the electric plant, branded in white neon PUBLIC SERVICE COMPANY OF OKLAHOMA. The bridge was empty. "Quick." I lay down. "Before anyone comes."

"Listen," he said, complying immediately. "You know I don't have anything with me."

"It's okay. I counted. It doesn't matter." I turned my head and looked through the slats at the water, glistening with reflected neon light. The single word *Electricity* in red script made a fiery glint along the surface. *Fuck you, Larry! Fuck you!* I screamed in my head.

"This stuff is getting to you, isn't it," Forrest said afterwards. "The legal stuff." I leaned against the railing, staring at the water. He stood behind me, his hands around mine.

"No. It's just...don't you want a blond bimbo?" I tried to laugh, but he turned me to face him.

"No. When did I ever say that? I tried that before. It didn't work."

"Okay. Well then. That's what the philosophy major and the law degree are for."

He wouldn't let me look away.

"Forrest," I cried, shaking loose. "I tried being a good decent wife before, and look what happened!" I appealed to him. "And now look where I am."

"Yes," he repeated slowly, "Look where you are."

ALISON STEPPED OVER the boxwood, onto my patio and through the slider. "Your blinds are open, Larry must be gone," she said.

"One if by land, two if by sea."

"Thank God, he was using up all my coffee." She looked at the jumbo index cards in my hand. "Mint green?"

"I'm color-coding. This is Con Law. Con Law is green. It's also Baroque."

"Why?"

"Structurally elegant." I turned off the harpsichord music. "You know, they didn't come this morning. He canceled out and changed his flight to leave earlier."

"Why am I not surprised?" She took another step in and looked around. "Where's Pep Boy? Just asking, 'cause I'm wearing panty hose."

"Sleeping." I paused. "Why are you not surprised?"

She held up a finger. "Let me grab a sandwich first. I know there's nothing to eat in your fridge."

She came back a few minutes later, through the door this time, a formidable book under her arm and a pint carton of half-and-half suspended between thumb and forefinger. "I had to show you this," she said. "Hazelnut-vanilla-flavored."

"Yuck."

"Yes, well, it was an educational experience for me too." She opened the plywood cabinet beneath my sink and dropped it in the trash. "Good riddance."

She sat down in the basket rocker. "You need some curtains."

"Among other things."

"My mom might be able to get you some material cheap." Nathan crawled over and pulled up on her knees. "Hey, big boy. Watch out for my Sunday clothes. I thought you said he was asleep."

"Yeah, well, he heard me say it."

She sent a terrycloth car on wheels across the floor. "I just made a date at church."

"At church?"

"Yes, at church. Don't you know that's why any single person between the ages of eighteen and twenty-eight goes to church in Tulsa? My first date in ten months. Thank God. I haven't had real sex in I don't know *how* long."

"Is he cute?" I sent Nathan's car off again.

"You're supposed to ask his name first," she drawled.

"What's his name?"

"Rob. Gordon."

"In that order?"

"Yes, smarty pants."

"Is he cute?"

"Very. And a great sense of humor."

"Well. That would be a deal-breaker for you."

"You got that right." She took the car from Nathan. "Does he ever get tired of this?"

"You started it. Here, buddy." I put the car away, and dumped the blocks out in the corner. "Okay," I said. "Tell me."

"Well, let's see." She leaned back in the rocker. "You know, it's good that I actually got to see this person in the flesh when I was there on Saturday and see him in action, because I was getting to the point where I was just not believing the things you were saying anymore. But I'm here to say that if anything, you could be accused of understatement."

"What did he do?"

"What *didn't* he do?" She ticked them off. "Didn't have any idea what to do with the baby; didn't have any interest in the baby; didn't talk about anything but you. Basically, his friend played with the baby and he pumped me for information. *Tried* to pump me," she amended.

"Who was his friend?"

"I don't know. Skinny, business clothes, updo, groovy glasses."

"Lisa. From his old office. That's funny, she didn't tell me…well, I haven't talked to her in awhile…"

"I let them take the baby out in the stroller. Hope that was okay."

"Yeah, since *she* was with him."

"That's what I figured. This guy, on his own? I wouldn't trust him not to leave him in the middle of traffic."

I winced.

"He didn't do that, did he?"

"Only in a nightmare."

She patted the book. "I brought you my brother's *DSM IV*. The Bible. I want you to read about psychopaths. I think it might help."

"What's a psychopath?"

She held out the book.

"Great. A little light reading between Bar study sessions."

She stood up and put it on my desk. "I'm not going to tell you. You have to read it." She patted the book again. "But you know what his real problem is."

"What?"

"He's gay."

"Don't be silly."

"Girl, it's as plain as the nose on your face. The minute he walked in the door."

"But Alison, he married me. He wouldn't have done that if he was gay. Why would a gay person want to marry me?"

She put her hand on the doorknob. "Kim, you're paddling down that river in Egypt. Get over it. Not only is he psycho, he's conflicted. He's lying to himself and doesn't want to admit it. That's why he's so nasty to you. Kim. Kim, look at me. Kim!"

I looked at her.

"Read the book."

"No, honestly, I don't think..." I said to her retreating figure. "He's just...a misanthrope. He hates everyone."

〰〰

17

Capital D Dating

DELBERT MCCLINTON WAS BACK at Cain's Ballroom. After the first set, Dana walked over to one of the long tables and commandeered two chairs with a simple "Hi, y'all!" She was good at that.

I tucked the disposable camera into my fanny pack. "Nathan waved bye-bye for the first time today," I said.

"Don't forget to put that in the baby book." Dana tried to flag down some service.

"We're not having much luck here," I commented.

"'Cause we're not guys," Dana said loudly, adjusting her tank strap. "She thinks we're not going to tip her. Which is stupid."

"Dana, I need to run something by you."

"Two longnecks, please," Dana smiled at the waitress, who was now standing at her shoulder. "Shoot," she said to me.

"Forrest is getting serious. What should I do?"

"Maybe stop sleeping with him?"

"What's that got to do with it?"

She rolled her eyes.

"Please, Dana."

"Okay. What's the evidence?"

"Well, he's escalated the floral arrangements…"

"Uh-huh."

"And he's starting to make references to children…"

"Uh-huh."

"I can't go steady with anyone. I haven't gotten divorced yet. I can't think that far."

"If you sleep with a guy more than twice, he's going to."

"Dee kind of said that too."

"Connect the dots, hon."

I started scraping the label off my bottle.

"Listen," said Dana, "you're thinking far enough to take off your clothes. How come you can't think any further? Forrest is a good person. He's like the perfect husband. That's what everyone at the hospital thinks. I *know* the story. And his ex was a bitch."

The man next to me pushed his chair back to fit a friend on his lap. Only at Cain's could you have a completely private conversation in public at full volume.

"What does Dee say?" Dana asked.

"She uses the big words. Like interpretations, responsibility, blah, blah, blah..."

"Sounds good to me. Especially that 'blah' part."

"Well, why can't Forrest put the same interpretation on sex that I do?"

"Because obviously it means more to him. And if it doesn't for you, then you're either a tramp or there's someone else you care about. What other *adults* are in your life? Chris? John?"

"Chris is just a friend. I haven't seen him for a couple of months actually. John either. John isn't *in* my life. He lives on the West Coast."

"You talk to him on the phone. You write him letters. You told me."

"Two letters."

"Stop shredding that label."

"I've just made a huge mess out of my life and I'm not dragging anyone else into it! I'm not thinking about John!"

"I rest my case."

"What about Morgan? Maybe I'm thinking about him. Actually, I *am* thinking about him."

"Not a good bet, hon. Don't sign on with another professional student. You're a woman with a law degree and a child to take care of! I don't care how smart and wonderful he is. He's not grown up. He doesn't own a car."

"He said he doesn't drive because he got tired of getting pulled over by the cops here late at night just because he's black."

"That's an excuse. Really it was his girlfriend's car when he moved up here, and he couldn't afford to buy another one when they broke up. That's what I got out of my conversation with him on the subject."

"Well, lots of people don't have cars," I pouted. "Look at New York City."

She swung her arm around. "Is this New York City? Do you see lots of people here in black, with small hair, and Bloomingdale's bags? Do you see all those little checkered cabs? Do you see public transportation? It's just not *normal* to live in Tulsa and not have a car," Dana concluded. "You're just afraid, is all. It's easy to think about someone on the other side of the country. It's easy to hang around campus and go dancing with Morgan."

"I don't want to be a doctor's wife."

"Then keep dancing with Peter Pan and writing letters to someone who's two thousand miles away. Do what you always did, get what you always got. Inappropriate relationships that don't work. Be scared forever and date people you couldn't possibly marry." She looked over my shoulder with an expression of horror. "Good God, girl, did you invite him?"

I turned around. Morgan was waving to us from the door.

"You didn't invite him on our date, did you?"

"No, I swear."

"But you told him where you were going tonight," she accused.

"I mentioned it. When I was in the library. He asked. I said I was going to Cain's with you. With *you!*"

She shook her head. "We need to have another rehab session. Soon. I can see I've neglected some of the finer points."

OUTSIDE QUEENIE'S, beneath a budding curbside magnolia, Nathan pulverized a saltine packet and flung it, hitting a blade of the stationary

150

ceiling fan. It ricocheted onto the specials board (chicken cashew salad and Mount Saint Helen's fudge cake) before bouncing onto the sandal of a startled passerby.

"Sorry." I retrieved it from her path. "Aren't you glad we got an outside table?" I said to Forrest.

"I don't *mean* to be moving too fast for you, Kim. I just thought…" Forrest took a bite of sandwich and chewed morosely, staring at a convertible with a license plate frame that read *"I'd rather be sailing!"*

"Can he play with your ID badge?"

He slipped it around Nathan's neck. "I mean, I'm looking for a wife. Aren't you looking for a husband? Especially under the circumstances?"

"I'm still married," I hedged.

"Are you sure you're not delaying the divorce? That it's not you?"

Nathan got the ID badge off and threw it on the ground.

"No, Forrest, it's not me." I took some of his French fries and put them in front of Nathan. "I haven't been sharing all the gory details, but rest assured. He's thrown a wrench in the works every possible step of the way."

"You could, you know. Share the details. I've been through this too."

Not this you haven't, I thought but didn't say. "In ten months we haven't done much more than serve him. And establish temporary custody. What we're trying to do right now is find out how much money he has. Hal says we can't proceed without financial disclosure."

"Maybe you should rethink that. I mean, with your lawyer," Forrest said. "Maybe you just need to run with your best guess. I…the longer this goes on, the older Nathan gets. You have to balance your priorities. A few dollars more or less in child support may not be that important in the future."

Nathan threw a fry into a Harold's bag parked under the next table. I got down and fished it out from between the tissue-wrapped clothing, apologizing to the elderly gentleman it belonged to.

"Good pitching arm," he smiled.

Forrest persisted, "The older he gets, the harder it will be for him to establish with a new dad. That's what my friends say who have steps."

"I can't think ahead, Forrest. I have to get through this process one step at a time. That's just me. I know you want children. And clearly," I joked, inserting another fry into Nathan's mouth, "there's no fertility issue here."

He almost jumped out of his chair. "Who told you that? That's not true."

"I don't—nobody said—"

"That's *not* why my marriage broke up. And that's not why I'm dating you." He slumped back down. "She didn't even want to try fertility drugs. When it didn't happen, she didn't seem to care. She just...wasn't interested. Not in children, and then, not in marriage."

Just like Frank's ex-wife, I thought. My brother-in-law. There were more of them around than I'd guessed: women who didn't want to settle down. "I don't even know if I'm going to *stay* in Tulsa," I said gently.

"Wouldn't you stay if you met the right person?"

"Forrest, right now everything in my life is temporary. Temporary custody, temporary child support, temporary everything. I don't know what the next step will be until I get there."

"You'd know if you'd met the right person."

"Don't push me!" I burst out. "Can't you see? Maybe I don't want to be a doctor's wife, and play golf at Southern Hills, and be a docent at the Philbrook! I'm not sure I want that! I don't know what I want!"

"That's just it, Kim. You only know what you don't want. That's not going to get you anywhere."

The waitress served a plate of fudge cake to the man at the next table. "Back in a minute, hon," she told him. "We just ran out of whipped cream. I'm going to whip you up some fresh."

He lifted a forkful to his mouth. He was well-dressed—khakis, crisp dress shirt, silver bola with polished tassels—but his clothes were almost a size too large: he was old enough to have shrunk, considerably. *He already knows his whole life story* I thought jealously. *Everything is behind him, everything except some fresh whipped cream.*

"Forrest," I implored, "should it surprise you, that I'm afraid to make decisions? When every one I've made so far has been wrong?"

"That's not true. What about me? I'm not a bad choice. Healthy, heterosexual, willing to take you to Cancun every winter…"

I didn't laugh.

"Don't be so serious! Listen, the Bar is really getting to you. It's too much stress. We shouldn't talk about this right now."

"Not just men, Forrest," I said glumly. "Careers. Everything. Music was the only thing I was ever good at. I dropped it. Then I got into academics. That was a mistake. Now I have an expensive legal education, but I went and had a baby, thinking, I can work and raise a baby, no problem! And that was the biggest mistake of all. I had no idea. I made a wrong choice. And who suffers for that? Nathan."

"Don't be so hard on yourself. You didn't know you'd be doing it alone. And you don't have to do it alone. It's not hard when you have a real partner. And you can work part-time if you want. Nobody's asking you to play golf, for Pete's sake."

This wasn't going the way I'd intended. It still sounded like he was working up to a proposal. I knew that kind of conversation, I reflected. I had a lot of experience with it, in my previous life. Why was it that everyone slept with me a few times and then wanted to propose? Except Larry. Had that been his appeal? That he hadn't been in a rush to get married? Larry hadn't proposed, he'd just asked me to move in with him—almost a relief, when it came down to it.

And maybe that was because…I shook my head. Maybe I'd liked the idea because it hadn't appeared to involve a decision.

Forrest misinterpreted the head shake, took my hands and smiled. "All right, you can work *full-time* and not play golf."

I was trying to break up with him and we were talking about golf. Where was Dana when I needed her? Practicing this conversation at Cain's had been easy but now the right words failed. There had to be a way to convey, without being impolite, that I did not feel as serious about him as he felt about me. In the past that had never been easy; I hated disappointing people. But somehow I'd been able to do it. Maybe it had been easier because I'd done it sooner. Which raised the question of why I had let things go so far with Forrest. Because I was afraid of hurting his feelings? Or because I really didn't, in point of fact, want to break up? Because I *did* feel serious about him? Or, at least, serious enough that I was unable, even in the face of the mildest opposition, to be direct.

Especially when he was holding my hand.

I gently extracted it and tried again.

"I—I think you're right about the Bar, Forrest. There's just a few weeks to go. I can't do anything but study from now until then. It's so hard with the baby." I wiped a spot of ketchup off his ID badge. "I mean…go out or anything." I tried to look at him. "I don't want to go out," I said, then added hastily, "I have to focus."

"Okay, okay." He wiped his mouth and nodded. "I've taken boards, I know how it is. Concentration, that's important. Don't worry about it. Don't think about anything right now. We can talk about all this later." He shook his wrist to check the time. "I have to get back." He pulled a bill out of his money clip, anchored it on the check with the salt-cellar, and got up. "You don't know what you want. But I know what I want. And it's right in front of me. And I just want you to know that." He bent down. "And think about this: you may not be the one delaying the divorce, but the fact that the delay is occurring is serving your fear." Then he whispered in my ear: "You know you can't say no to me."

I couldn't help kissing him back.

Hands in pockets, he strolled back across the street to the hospital.

I brushed Nathan off and checked around the table. No personal possessions, only food debris. When I straightened up I saw Jake the artist inside, sitting at a window table with a girl who looked like a teenager. He waved cheerily. I turned my back. A moment later he was at my elbow. "So the rumors are true," he grinned.

"Who let you in here?" I tried to stuff Nathan into the stroller. "What rumors? Cradle-robber," I added, glancing in the window. "That girl's young enough to be your daughter."

"She is my daughter."

"Oh. It's just that she's so good-looking. There's no resemblance." I gave up trying to get Nathan into the stroller and helped him wrap his hands around the handles.

"Are you dating this guy?" he asked.

"No! Just going out with him."

"What's the difference?"

"I don't know. There's a difference. We're not capital D dating."

"You are if you're having breakfast on Sunday in the same clothes you wore Saturday night."

"Jake, you're outrageous!"

"My spies are everywhere."

We pushed away from the table. "Say bye-bye, Nathan."

"Now clarify for me again: which one of those categories includes sex, dating or going out? Because I'm interested in that one."

"Jake, I'm not in the mood for this right now. Go back and have lunch with your alleged daughter."

"I'm just wondering why you won't go out with *me*."

"Because you've never asked me on a real date."

"If I do, you'll say no."

"The likelihood is increasing every minute."

"Then I'd better stop now and cut my losses."

"Good idea." The electronic carillon in the department store tower started up. I pulled Nathan off the ground, where he was busy wedging discarded French fries between the patio slates. They were an exact fit. It was enchanting, except that every third fry was going into his mouth.

Jake turned back again. "So—is this doctor *really* rich or just *kind of* rich?"

"Say bye-bye, Jake," I caroled.

"Ba," said Nathan, flapping his hand. He pushed the stroller in front of him like a drunken midget, improvising his own descant to Pachelbel's Canon, as we made our slow and unsteady progress back to the car.

I sat in the driver's seat after buckling him in and reflected again on the fact that sometimes—often—it was easier to be blunt with people who didn't matter: Jake; the belt-buckle man at the Quiktrip; the cowboy on the other phone at Riverparks, when I made the Phone Call. The people in my life who really deserved the benefit of clarity from me—Larry in the past, I supposed, and Forrest now, though they stood at opposite ends of the spectrum and I hated even to breathe their names in the same thought—those people who really deserved the benefit of clarity from me didn't get it. Was it a cruelty instead of a kindness to be elliptical with Forrest? And what might have happened on that long ago day, the first time Larry hit me, that I only remembered last summer, the time he broke my glasses—what might have happened if I'd said to him, *You can't do that. If you do that again I will leave.* Not just: what would have happened to me. But: what would have happened to him?

MORGAN KNEW everything and everyone by virtue of his position at the law library, and he had a lead for me on Bar study materials. I swallowed my embarrassment at the fact that he discussed my situation with all and sundry, because pride was a luxury and I had a Bar to pass, and drove to Sulie's home early the next morning. She was the classmate who'd run me through the protective order process. It was a decent first-out job.

I rang the bell.

"Come on in, Kim." Sulie nudged a large box with her foot so she could open the door fully. "Here it is." A little girl in denim overalls peeked out from behind her bathrobe. "Sweetie, say hello to Mrs. Baltakis."

"My mommy's a lawyer now. She doesn't need these books anymore."

Sulie smoothed the bow in her daughter's hair. It was pink, to match the flip-flops. "I'll be happy never to see them again."

"You sure you don't want anything for them?"

"No, I should pay you to take them away." She took a sip from a mug emblazoned *Girl Scouts of Magic Empire Council.* "The multi-state stuff is a couple years old, I got that from my husband, but it's not going to be much different. They reissue it every year, but there's never much change. I threw in all my outlines, too, for what they're worth."

"Securities Law! Great. I didn't take that."

"The nutshell's in there too." She followed me as I lugged the box out to my car. "You're going to do fine without the prep course. You've got the discipline. Most people don't."

"It's not that I don't want to take it. But the child care on top...that would be huge."

Sulie took her daughter's elbow between thumb and forefinger. "Don't pick those flowers, honey, Mommy just planted them." To me she said, "That jerk ex of yours ever come back to town that time?"

"No, and I think it was because I got the restraining order. He was embarrassed."

"You were really smart to get out of it right away. A lot of these women, the average is seven times. They'll go back to their husbands seven times before they'll take any steps. I'm not kidding." She picked up the little girl and closed her hand over her wrist to keep her from opening her robe. "My husband wants me to get another job. He thinks the stress is keeping me from getting pregnant again." She shook her head and sighed. "I see them at the shelter. Seven times."

I drove to Brookside, popped the trunk, and pawed through my stash, feeling like a criminal. I picked out Securities and settled down in my favorite corner at Gold Coast. If TU's law library hadn't been in a windowless basement, I might not have spent so much time studying in coffee shops. As it was, I couldn't concentrate. I kept thinking about what Sulie had said. *Seven times.*

I couldn't have done that. I couldn't have gone back to Larry, after I'd left. Not even once.

Someone spoke. "Do you remember me?"

I looked up. It was Max, the artist. I capped my pen. "Of course I do. I never got a chance to tell you how much I liked your show."

He put down his tobacco can and pulled out a chair. "I did that as a favor to my landlord. He owns the gallery. What is this book you are hiding?"

"It's on Securities Law. Someone loaned it to me. I'm not really supposed to have it." I flipped it over and back quickly to show him the cover. "Did anything sell?"

"No. I didn't expect it. Technically, I can't. I'm under contract with my dealer in New York. Do you want to go to a table outside, so I can smoke?"

We resituated, and he embarked on the process of fabricating a cigarette, which, I was realizing, took much longer than the actual smoking of it. "You know, I have not seen many girls in America reading books."

"Maybe you haven't been in the right places."

"I came to Tulsa six months ago. I was driving with my friends, since the summer, when we got in New York. I said, 'Let me off here, this is where I'm staying.' Because it was in the middle of America. The middle of nowhere. Where are you from?"

"Chicago."

"Ah, I haven't been there yet. You can take me." He took a tiny sip from his cup. "This is the only place in Tulsa that has good espresso. You know, when I saw you, I knew you were an intellectual. I knew it."

"Do I have a scarlet 'I' on my forehead?"

"I could tell."

"I tried to reform once, but it didn't work."

He raised his head and blew smoke at the row of Harleys parked across the street at the Blue Rose Bar. "The second floor of my building is empty," he remarked. "The building next door to the gallery. You should rent it. The landlord only wants two fifty."

"For the whole second floor? I'm paying three fifty for a shoebox. Are we talking running water?"

"You should come see my apartment. They are…how do you say…identical. Except that I did a mosaic tile work all over the floor."

"I don't know how long I'll be staying in Tulsa."

"Me either." He shrugged.

"I speak German," I said shyly. "I did my junior year there."

"Das ist ja fantastisch. Come to see me. I don't have a phone. Come by any time you want. Just give the bell three short rings, then I'll know it's you and come down and open the door. People are ringing my bell all the time."

"If you got a phone they wouldn't have to."

"I know. But then they would be calling me all the time."

He balanced the miniscule remainder of his cigarette on the table's edge and took my pen. "It is easiest if I call you. What is your number?"

"It…it might be hard to get hold of me right now. I'm screening all my calls."

"For what?" He tucked the number in his pocket and picked up the cigarette again.

"My ex likes to harass me on the phone. I usually let the answering machine pick up."

"Okay, so we make a system. I ring once and then hang up, then I call again. That way you know it is me." He drained his cup, and ambled away. At the corner, he turned around and gave a little wave. Then he tucked a curl behind his ear and crossed against the light.

"ADMIN, ADMIN," I muttered, opening dresser drawers. Where were the first four pages of Administrative Law? It's not like there were that many places to lose things in my apartment. The phone rang. I checked the schedule taped to the wall. February 27. Larry's deadline for the interrogatories. Yesterday.

"Well?" I asked.

"Nothing," Hal said.

"Can the judge order him now?" I pulled open a kitchen drawer.

"No, we need to file a Second Motion to Compel."

"A second one? You're kidding."

"That's the procedure. He'll get another thirty days from the time it's granted, and then, *then* if he doesn't respond, we can file for contempt."

I pulled out another drawer. "There's no way we can go ahead? Without this?"

"We can't proceed to settlement without this information, Kim. Remember, he already has all of your information."

"Yeah, because we were good and gave it to him when *he* asked." I got down on my knees to look in the bottom kitchen cabinet, where Nathan sometimes put his little rabbit, Smushy, with the pots and pans.

"Remember, the judge is going to have to impute income to both of you because neither of you is working and neither of you have W2's. It's going to be a judgment call on her part. We need to make our best guess as to what things might be so we know where to peg our settlement offer."

"Right." I stood up and opened the stove. The first four pages of Admin lay on the top rack along with an oven mitt, a gel-filled teething ring and a size four sneaker. "How did this happen?"

"Kim, you know as well as I—"

"No—I mean he isn't strong enough to open this door."

"Who?"

"Nothing, Hal. I just found my Admin outline in the stove."

"I'll let you go then. Hang in there, Kim. I want to do everything I can going into this to maximize the support. Remember, this new judge hates moms and loves dads. We have our work cut out for us."

Yes, especially when you play by the rules and you still get screwed. Aloud I said, "There's no way a judge could love this dad."

"He's definitely got too much time on his hands. He needs to take up petit-point."

I added that to MY LAWYER'S FUNNY JOKES, hung up and opened the slider to catch Alison as she went by.

"Hi, stranger," she said. "How's the studying going?"

"One week left. I did five straight hours today."

She shifted her grocery bag to the other hip and waved away a piece of cottonwood down. "Well, now that you've stopped studying in *coffee shops*, where you get picked *up* all the time..."

"You're just jealous. Speaking of which, how was that date with Mr. Rob?"

"We went to Woodward Park after dinner and he climbed up in a tree and started singing to me. He was plastered. He was singing in this awful accent, his name was Raoul, and he wasn't going to stop until I agreed to marry him. I said, 'Get down out of there before the cops come,' and he said 'Not until you say you'll elope with me.'"

"So what did you do?"

"I agreed, of course. We were starting to draw a bit of a crowd."

"He can't hold you to that, you know. It could be construed as duress. 'Threatening conduct which creates in the defendant a reason-able fear—"

She held up her hand. "Stop!"

"All right, I'm going. I have to get Nathan at the drop-off center before they give him Snackables for dinner."

When we returned, Max was on my patio, smoking and trying to catch the cotton as it floated by.

"You didn't answer your phone," he said accusatorily, as Nathan drag-ged the diaper bag to the door and smacked on it with the flat of his hand.

"I had the ringer off. I was working."

He stubbed out his cigarette. "Let's have dinner. We can go to my place. But I don't have any food."

We got back in my car and drove to Bigelow's. I pushed Nathan in the grocery cart, feeding him bites of banana, while Max picked out our meal. At the end of the bread aisle I turned and came face to face with Forrest in his scrubs, ordering a sandwich at the deli counter. He brightened. Then Max came around the corner. Max put the pack-age of spaghetti in the cart, and looked at us, from one to the other.

"How's the work going?" Forrest finally said.

"Great!" I said brightly. "Five hours straight today."

In a prolonged silence the girl behind the counter finished Forrest's sandwich, wrapped it and handed it over.

"*Ja und...*" said Max. "I would like you to know that I have not slept with this young woman."

"Thank you for the information," Forrest said icily, and headed for the cash register.

Back in the car I gave Max a look.

He shrugged. "He was worried. I could tell."

At his apartment I got to work chopping vegetables at the table that passed for a kitchen. Max had taken down all the interior walls, so the sink and stove backed up to studs. Nathan crawled around on the mosaic paths.

I finished on the onions and started on the carrots. I didn't know who I was more irritated with, Forrest or Max. Despite the apparent inability of the male sex to believe it, the fact remained that it was entirely possible for women to have satisfactory platonic relationships with men. Moreover, I was *not* the kind of girl to go sleeping with more than one man at a time. But I certainly didn't need to have that pointed out in public. I chopped myself out of my bad mood and melted some butter in a saucepan.

"When are you going to play your cello again?" Max asked at dinner.

"I don't know. It's in Chicago."

"Go get it. I'll go with you. We could get it together. I would like to see Chicago."

After dinner we played chess in front of the woodstove, with Nathan nested in quilts. Max said, "Listen. That fellow." His fingers trembled as he rolled a cigarette. "How could you go out with someone like that?"

I bridled. "What do you mean? You don't even know him."

"Er ist aber ein echter Dummkopf," he went on, vociferous, poking his dirty curls with a tobacco-stained finger. "There is nothing about him, you can see it quite clearly, you deserve someone much better."

"Achja," I teased, *"Jemandem wie du,* you mean, someone like you!"

He laughed. "Kim, you know what I thought, when I saw you again at the coffee shop," he said, becoming very quiet and serious, "reading a book, and I thought, 'If I ever marry any woman, that will be the one.'"

Chin in hand, he fell silent, studying the board.

〜〜
〜〜

18

Invisible Boundaries

REPUDIATION OF A CONTRACT requires statement of breach plus voluntary affirmative act rendering obligor unable or apparently unable to perform without breach.

A pair of loosely clasped hands appeared over the top of my library carrel. I looked up. Morgan bent down and hooked his chin over the imitation veneer. "How's it going?" he whispered.

I covered the page in front of me with my hand and shut my eyes. "'Repudiation of a contract requires statement of breach plus voluntary affirmative act rendering obligor...unable or apparently unable...to perform without breach.'" I opened my eyes. "Fine."

His lips curved up. "Want to get supper?"

"What time is it?"

"Four-thirty."

I mentally recalibrated. Sunday, four-thirty p.m. Two days before the Bar.

"You weren't here this morning," he continued.

"I was studying at the hotel. My mom and I are trading off with that room. I'm glad we got it. I retain better when I can recite. Which makes me wonder what I'm doing here."

"Did you know you're the only one studying for the Bar who's not wearing sweats?"

"Surely you jest." I tipped my chair back to peer around the carrel wall.

"No, and I've been deputized by the males on the staff to express their appreciation."

"All two of them?" I tipped my chair back down.

We met at the front desk an hour later and went to the closest Chinese restaurant, on 11th Street. "It's the strangest thing," Morgan said, divvying out packets of sauce and paper napkins. "Nobody in Atlanta ever thought I was gay, but here people ask me all the time."

"They actually ask? What do you say to them?"

"I fix them with my steely gaze, smile, and say 'Why do you ask?'" He handed me a pair of chopsticks. "Did you know that Tulsa has the third highest gay population per capita after New York and San Francisco?"

"I don't see them." I switched to a fork. Sleep deprivation had taken a major toll on my manual dexterity.

"They're all in the closet."

"But you!" I exclaimed. "You were an all-state wide receiver. You lift weights. You date girls. You...were married!"

He broke open his fortune cookie. "Lots of gay men are or were married."

"But why?" I blurted.

He shrugged.

I looked out the grimy window into the middle bay of Speedway Auto Body. I needed to know this. I didn't understand the impulse, and possibly it had screwed up my life.

I looked back at Morgan. He was grinning at his fortune. He turned it around and held it up, a tiny banner. I leaned forward to read it: *Your love life will be happy and harmonious.*

I unrolled my fortune. *"You will be very successful in business.* I'll take that as a portent."

"Then so will I mine." He tucked it into his pocket.

In the parking lot he got on his bike. "Going back to the library?"

"No. I have to go home and play with my son before he forgets who I am." I put one foot in the car, and hesitated. "Wanna come over to the hotel later and watch a movie?"

He nodded.

"Let's see…finish Contracts, go through Securities again, and then Crim Law." I looked up. "Brain rot will probably set in around ten."

He pushed off, and rode away with a backward wave along the row of red paving stones that ran down the sidewalk, marking Route 66.

Back at Riverview Gardens, Nathan was pushing his wooden lawn-mower around the carpet, wearing a dinner bib over red overalls. He looked freshly adorable because I hadn't seen him all day.

"Perfect timing." Bobbie sat down carefully in the basket rocker. "Do you know they show *The Rockford Files* here? It comes on every night."

"Welcome to the wide world of cable, Mom. You should break down and subscribe."

Nathan climbed up on my lap and pulled at my shirt.

"Maybe I will. I got him to eat some broccoli. Did you know he'll eat broccoli?"

"Not for me."

"How's it going?"

"All right. Luckily time is too short now to get hysterical." I shifted him to the other side. At twelve months he made short work of emptying a breast.

"This is just one of those moments, Kimmie, when you're going to have to put your perfectionism aside and give it your best shot."

I went into the bathroom and turned on the tub. Sometimes I wished my mother were not so wise and sensible. I bathed Nathan, put him down, and went back into the other room. Bobbie was fixing her dinner plate during a commercial: chicken, the aforementioned broccoli, homemade cole slaw.

"Don't study too late," she warned. "The main thing is to get sleep. At least you're sleeping better."

"That's true." It was only a partial lie. Separated from the baby I was sleeping for more than three hours at a time, but sometimes it took two hours of staring at the ceiling before I drifted off. I was still sleeping with Winnie-the-Pooh, but I was too embarrassed to traipse out of the house with it in front of my mother, not to mention carry it through the hotel lobby.

"How are *you* doing?" I asked.

"Oh, I'm fine. I nap when he does, that's the key. But he's missing you, I can tell."

I kissed her and left hastily.

At ten Morgan knocked on my door at the hotel. I bathed my face with cold water, took two aspirin, and piled my books in the corner. We ate ice cream from the carton, then stretched out with our chins propped in our hands watching *The Spy Who Came in From the Cold* on the television inside the armoire. At the end, after escaping over the Berlin Wall, Richard Burton climbed back to help the woman he suddenly realized he loved, knowing this meant certain death; choosing, in essence, to become human even at the cost of his own life.

I switched to MTV with the remote.

Morgan stroked my hair. "Do you want to have sex?"

I looked away, at the desk, at my piles of workbooks on the floor. I nodded.

"No. Say it." He took my chin and turned my face to his. "I want you to say it."

"Yes."

"*Say* it."

I took a deep breath. "I want...to have sex...with you."

He peeled off my shirt. "After supper I just wanted to lay you over the hood of the car and do you right there." He set me on the desk. I wrapped my arms and legs around him and crossed the invisible boundary I'd stepped back from over a year ago in the car at the Chicago airport, shocked and confused, because I was a married, pregnant woman and couldn't understand why I suddenly wanted to kiss another man.

Now I could.

I hadn't been able to allow myself a relationship with Morgan when I'd started over in Tulsa. Because I'd known him when I was married, known him when I was pregnant. Kissed him when I was pregnant. Now it was okay. I could cross that line now. I'd actually crossed it, I realized, the moment I stood on that row of red paving stones on 11th Street and invited him back to the hotel.

What a lot of time I'd wasted obeying unwritten rules which had been stacked against me from the beginning, which Larry had disobeyed with impunity! I didn't want to think about the boundaries Larry had crossed, the ones he might have crossed with young Andre who mowed our lawn. Suddenly I was full of anger at Larry for denying me a normal sex life, for the sudden easy accusations of affairs during the past few years, a time in which I had been wholly and completely and unknowingly inhabiting a loveless marriage. Making his coffee, ironing his shirts, trusting him.

Then I realized: he'd tried to break me, but it hadn't worked. I shot past my marriage and was back with Morgan, feeling him with one set of limbs and looking at him, and only him, with one set of eyes. I wiped my lips across his face, held his face with my hands and kissed him. This was sex, pure and simple. Massive. Olympian. No strings, no agenda, no past, no present, no future.

Afterward we sprawled on our backs. He turned his head to look at me, smiled, and tapped two fingers on his breastbone, acknowledging breathlessness.

I got up and opened the drapes. From this height, urban Tulsa was silent, orderly, well-lit. The downtown blocks were brightly-outlined quilt squares, huddled together against the vastness of the plain, obeying secret, invisible boundaries of their own: the river on the west, Peoria on the east, 2nd Street, 18th. Morgan got up and wrapped his arms around my waist. A police car dawdled through the intersection of 5th and Houston.

"You have the most perfect hips," he whispered in my ear.

I leaned forward, hands on the sill, forehead against the glass, and closed my eyes.

Later, when we were in bed again, Morgan suddenly and with no prelude started to make the sound of the wind, a delightful, uncannily accurate imitation of a capricious breeze whistling through the trees of

167

a miniature forest, no louder than the ocean in a shell. I lay curled against him. I was in a new place, a strange one, a place I didn't know very well yet, but Morgan was my anchor. He took his cupped hands away for a moment and whispered, "Close your eyes." I pressed more closely into his chest and listened as the sound of the night wind blowing through lonely trees enveloped me, lulling me to sleep.

19

Get Your Kicks on Route 66

I GOT BACK FROM Oklahoma City at nine p.m. after the second day of the Bar exam, raced into the bathroom and threw up.

"I guess I don't need to ask you how you feel," joked Bobbie.

I slept on and off all through the next day, rousing at four in the afternoon, when I choked down a few spoonfuls of hot cereal after nursing my greedy child.

"What are you going to do now that this is over?" asked Bobbie.

"This might not be over."

"Don't worry about it. 'Let the day's troubles be sufficient unto the day.' I've heard a lot of people walk out of the Bar exam thinking they've failed."

Who are all these people my mother is talking to, and where can I find them? I remember thinking, before falling asleep again.

The next morning she arrived from the hotel to find me upright, fresh and clean, and pouring a cup of half-caf out of my Mr. Coffee Junior. "Oh, good," she said. "I was going to change my ticket if you needed me but I'd hate to miss another Sunday. He's so short on altoes. And you washed your hair." She smoothed it with two hands. "I always feel so much better after I wash my hair."

"Mom, if you break into that tune from *South Pacific* I'm going to throw up again."

"I don't do show tunes," she sniffed.

We were on the way to the airport and almost there before she ventured to ask, "Have you given any more thought to what you're going to do?"

"Sleep some more and reacquaint myself with my child."

"I was thinking long-term."

"Mom, you know I can't go anywhere until I have a finalized decree."

She reached out and snapped off the country-western station. "Do we have to listen to this?"

I glanced at Nathan in the rearview mirror, but he didn't seem perturbed.

"Maybe you could come down again in April," I suggested, pulling up at the departure curb. "The azalea festival in Muskogee is supposed to be beautiful."

She opened the door. "You've got time, Kimmie. Get the divorce behind you. You'll get everything figured out. Just... remember that wherever you settle, that's where you're going to...meet people." She put her good foot out first, then grasped the other calf with both hands to guide it. She saw me notice and said, "It's just because this seat is so low."

She leaned on the door to pull herself to standing and looked around. "Goodness! Is the airport closed?" She waved off the sole porter as I set down her bag. "Just pull the handle out for me. That's why I bought this thing, so I could do it myself. When we took that trip to Sweden last year. I don't know how I ever did without a wheeled suitcase. You should get one." She hugged me. "Oh, I forgot to tell you, your friend called a couple times yesterday. Forrest? You were asleep. He sounds nice. What does he do?"

"Why do you ask?"

"Oh Kimmie, don't start. I'm too old for it. *You're* too old for it."

I relented. "He's a cardiologist," I said. "He's a lot older than me, Mother."

"That's not necessarily a bad thing." She leaned in to kiss Nathan, then loosened his grasp on her necklace. "He doesn't seem to have too much of an accent."

"He *is* from Oklahoma, Mom. He grew up here. Some people in Tulsa have accents and some don't."

"I've noticed that." She straightened up. "Well. Just remember what I said." She smiled and disappeared into the airport, pulling her bag behind her.

SHOULD I FEEL bad about basking in the admiring gaze of a man who had a real job and a full wallet? I tussled with the question for a moment, then shoved it into THINGS TO THINK ABOUT LATER. By the time we'd had a margarita and a bowl of chips, I'd already told Forrest I was wearing lingerie outfit number two (blue mesh lace) under my sweater and jeans.

"When I grow up I'm going to have a Mexican kitchen," I said, looking around the restaurant. "White brick, exposed beams, the works."

"You are grown up."

"I don't think you ever grow up. You just get older and have kids, who serve as a constant, humbling reminder of how immature you really are."

"Where did you learn to be so hard on yourself?"

"I'll have to research that."

We went outside for coffee so Forrest could smoke a cigar. He put his coat around my shoulders. It was late March, and still cool at night. I wasn't going to bring up Max, because there was nothing to say. I was certainly under no obligation to go around pointing out all the men in Tulsa I hadn't slept with.

A busboy came out and plugged in the white lights in the bushes.

"Now that you're finished maybe we could go down to Mexico together. You and me and Nathan. For a week?"

"Forrest, I couldn't accept a gift like that."

"You told me you wanted to take a break. Before you went on to the next step."

"But that's so extravagant. It wouldn't be right. Not until I'd been working maybe for a year. You know, really earned it." I buried my hands in the pockets of his coat. "I wouldn't feel justified."

He parked his cigar and pulled my chair closer. "Kim, you're such a Puritan. You're the most erotic Puritan I've ever met."

"Listen, it took several generations to develop this formula. Just enjoy the finished product."

"You need a vacation, I'm offering you one. Just tell me you'll consider it."

"Okay. I'll consider it."

In the car his voice was hesitant, for the first time. "Should we go get Nathan?"

"Let's stop by your house first."

The instant the door closed, he dropped his keys on the marble-topped table and backed me up against the coat closet. "This has been torture. Please don't ever take the Bar again."

"I hope not to have to. Don't even say the word." I helped him get my jeans off.

We slid to the floor.

"I think…" he said thickly, "I think—the condom broke."

I leapt off.

He heaved himself into a sitting position and leaned against the wall. Above him, a row of Hopi mudheads were framed, frozen in dance. I switched on the lamp, but it cast no more than the glow of a candle. I sat down again and tried to calculate. "It's…ah…well…it's probably okay."

"I'm sorry."

"It's okay," I repeated, pulling on my underwear backwards, taking it off, turning it around. "It's not like we haven't done that before, I mean gone without, and nothing happened. I'm not going to worry about it." I found my sweater. "But I was thinking, Forrest. Before, not because of this. I was thinking I'd like to go home and sleep in my own bed tonight."

"Still, think about the trip," he said, reaching out for my breast before it disappeared beneath the sweater.

IF THERE WAS one aspect of home ownership I missed on a routine basis, it was my own washing machine. Nathan and I were on our third trip over to the laundry room the next morning when he spotted

Alison on her balcony reading the Sunday *World*. He abandoned the jumbo detergent box he'd been pushing in the stroller and ran over to the stairs. "Heads up," I called.

She looked over the railing. "See you in ten minutes," she joked, as Nathan began his laborious hand-over-foot ascent, but she was ready at the door when he knocked.

"Mmmm. O!" he cried, when she opened it.

She handed him a piece of Zweiback. "Now let's get this straight. *She's* Mama. I'm the Other Lady."

"What do you say, Nathan? Say thank you. Thank you! You're welcome!"

"Oh God, you've started already. That talking-for-your-baby stuff."

"It's genetically programmed. Wait and see."

She returned to her balcony and started putting the paper back together. "Let's go in. I missed the sun. I only get it for twenty minutes. Want some sweet tea?"

I shook my head.

"Heard you slept sixteen hours on Thursday. And that was just during the day."

"Rumor has it. How would I know? It's all a blur."

"I love your mother. Wanna trade?"

"I don't know. Is she going to come through with those drapes?"

She cackled. "Come out with us tonight. You need to celebrate. Rob, me, Cheryl and that guy she's dating, what's his name, the pocket-protector guy. We're going to go down to Eclipse and rub shoulders with the teenyboppers."

EXCEPT FOR THE disco ball, Eclipse was very dark, and very crowded. One or the other would have been okay, but both together guaranteed that, unless you were roped together, you were going to lose your friends. Which was exactly what happened. But I was confident in my ability to manage. I had just crossed the invisible boundary! Already I was thinking *What was the big deal?* Navigating the world of social relations was not as difficult or as fraught with peril as I had imagined.

It was just a dance club, for heaven's sake. A bunch of people having fun. No one was even going to touch me. I knew the rules from dating rehab: a guy does not slow-dance with a girl the first time he asks her out on the floor.

But then one—he had three studs in one ear—wrapped his arms around me and pulled me close. "Um," I began, but he stopped me by thrusting his tongue down my throat.

"Listen, how old are you?" I said, when I managed to pull my head away.

"Nineteen," he murmured, rubbing his hands up and down my back.

"Well, I'm twenty-eight."

He cocked his head, then smiled. "Good joke." He covered my mouth with his, clutching me tighter when I tried to pull away.

"Don't you get it?" I pulled his arms off. "I don't *want* you to do that! I don't even know you." I pushed my way off the floor.

Alison was nowhere to be seen.

There was a double door in front of me. "Hand?" said a voice.

"What?"

"Hand." Someone grabbed my wrist and stamped my hand.

"I'm not *coming* back." I stumbled out and sat on the curb, rubbing the stamp. It wasn't ever going to go away. It had been almost a year. How was I going to make it go away? Maybe stuffing Larry's letters in a drawer and turning off the ringer were not enough. Maybe I'd been trying to do it on my own for too long, and I did need serious help, more than I could get from an hour a week with Dee. Maybe I needed medication, or a week in a mental institution, or a week in Mexico. Maybe I needed a new approach.

I heard a voice, a male one. "Are you okay?"

I turned.

He took a step closer, hands jammed in his front pockets. He smiled and bent his knees a little to see my face. "I saw what happened in there," he said, jerking his head towards the door. "You okay?"

"Oh, yeah. That. That kind of threw me for a loop."

"He was way out of line. That guy." He sat down on the curb and extended a pack of cigarettes.

"I've never been here before," I said, taking one.

He lit it for me. "It's a pretty young crowd. I'm twenty-four," he added.

Personally, I wasn't about to make any declarations. This fellow looked old enough, though, to keep his testosterone under control. He was good-looking too, in a kind of muscle-bound way that had never appealed to me before. Maybe this was my new approach.

"I'm in the Reserve," he went on. "Spend the weekend in Tulsa once a month. Then I like to go out. There's not a lot going on in Fayetteville." He shifted his cigarette and extended his hand. "Randall."

"Kim."

"You feel okay now, Kim?" Randall asked. "Your friends still in there?"

"It's too dark in there. I'd never find them without a GPS device. I drove my own car anyway, I didn't know how long I'd last. I'm pretty beat." I hesitated. "I just finished the Bar exam."

"No way! Congratulations!" He shook my hand again. "My sister's a lawyer."

"What about you?"

"Oh, I haven't figured that out yet. Probably I'll end up teaching. My dad's an English professor at Fayetteville. Listen." He ground out his cigarette and flipped it through the chain-link fence into the wide cement culvert that angled past the club. "Wanna go somewhere, get a drink, or a Coke, or something?"

That culvert. Wherever I was—in my apartment, in the car, at Dee's office—there was always a creek or a gully that led to the Arkansas. That was the problem with Tulsa: all roads led to the Arkansas. That was why it would always be the city of my discontent, despite the fact that my son had been born there. All roads led to the river, and there, Larry was forever standing on the bank, sneering at me: *You look woebegone.* That was the problem with the whole state. As long as I remained in Oklahoma, I could never be in that new territory. I was trapped in one place by my endless husband's endless and perverse legal machinations.

A lowrider rumbled by toward the street. The work of a moment had destroyed months of repair; I couldn't go home and be alone with Larry's arms, Larry's body. A million gauzy watts of sodium vapor hid the stars from my view, and the curb was getting chilly. I took a last drag on my cigarette, stubbed it out and pushed it through the fence. "Sure," I said to Randall. Sooner or later I was going to have to stop running every potential date past the handwriting analyst.

"Great." He stood up and held out his hand. "Let's turn this night around for you. What do you say?" He pulled me up easily as a feather. Larry would have called him "beefy," like our old next-door neighbor, the one he didn't like. Larry wouldn't have liked Randall, either. Or maybe he would have.

"One thing for sure," Randall said, "*I* won't kiss you without asking first. Promise."

I climbed carefully into his pickup in my short skirt.

He helped me in. "You know, most of the gals in there are wearing jeans. That was the first thing I noticed about you." He shut the door and walked around the truck.

"What was the second thing?" I asked, when he'd gotten in.

He removed a flask from the glove compartment, took a pull, then tucked it against his thigh. "The second thing." He put his hands on the wheel and stared out the windshield. Then he smiled. "I like the way you move," he said, nodding. "You dance like the rain."

The catch in his voice was husky and unexpected. But it wasn't like Larry all those years ago at Columbia. Larry was a musical savant who collected instruments, a stellar triathlete who collected trophies, an intellectual snob who collected degrees but then didn't use them, because that would entail working with other people. Anything you could do alone, Larry did, and did well. But when it came to relationships, Larry was a fake. Larry played pretend until he got what he wanted. He kept pretending until he was sure he could get it without expending the effort, and then he stopped.

Randall was not about manipulation, I could tell. Randall was simply, unwittingly, showing me he was human, that he needed and wanted a warm body close to his and wished it were mine.

"Ask me," I said.

"What?"

"Ask me if you can kiss me." I knelt on the seat.

"Can I kiss you?"

I began unbuttoning my shirt. "Where?"

"Sweet Jesus," he breathed. He turned off the ignition, whipped off his seat belt and wrapped his arms around me, moving from my mouth, to my neck, to my shoulders.

"You want to go somewhere?" he said finally, detaching his mouth from my breast.

"Why?" I unzipped his pants.

"Sweet Jesus," he said again. "This is my lucky night."

"It is if you've got some condoms." I liked the way he held me tight. I wanted his arms around me. I needed a warm body as much as he did, if not more, to keep the ghosts at bay.

In the QuikTrip parking lot I sat and watched him make his way through the bright fluorescent aisles like a man driven. I took a sip from the flask, then propped my chin on my hand and closed my eyes. A cool breeze fanned across my face. When I opened them a skinny cowboy in a pearl-buttoned shirt stood in front of me.

"Jesus has your answer."

His voice had such a lilt I waited, thinking it might be the first line of a song.

"Jesus has your answer," he said again.

I took my chin out of my hand and gave him my best smile. "Well, that's just dandy. Thank you so much."

He tipped his hat and walked away.

"What'd he want?" Randall asked, getting back in the car.

"Who cares?" I tucked the card he'd given me into my pocket, rolled up the window and took another drink. I wasn't generally a whiskey person, but it was part of my new approach. "Some fundie. Think I've seen him before."

"I don't know why they always hang out at convenience stores."

"Jesus has the answer."

~~~~

THE NEXT MORNING I checked the parking lot and found my car pulled in reasonably parallel to the dumpster, which meant I'd been the last one in the lot last night. Good: I'd driven myself home. Randall didn't know where I lived. Unless I'd given him my phone number. Had I given him my phone number? Then it struck me.

Oh my God. A one-night stand.

I was consumed with shame. I hadn't had sex with a virtual stranger since that road trip to Amherst freshman year, when my roommate's older brother's frat brother had persuaded me to leave the mixer and take a walk with him in the woods behind Hitchcock Field.

Forrest was always telling me, "You think too much." My problem right now seemed to be that whenever I stopped thinking, I took my clothes off. It probably should not be an either/or situation. Well, I thought, as Dee was fond of saying, "identifying a problem is halfway to solving it."

Dee—I'd have to talk to Dee about last night. I couldn't put it into THINGS TO THINK ABOUT LATER. At our session the other day I'd told her about that file, and she'd given me one of those straight-in-the-eye looks and said, "Later is now." We were working on that file.

I went to Dana's to pick up Nathan from his sleep-over. On the way home I stopped at the health food store and piled the cart with organic baby food, vegetables, whole grains and wheatgrass juice. But by the time I finished loading the car, I was starving. I pulled into a Burger Street drive-through and waited forever behind a black Cadillac. When I got to the microphone I ordered the largest hamburger on the menu.

Back home I took all my Bar prep materials, put them in a box in the back of the closet, and pulled on rubber gloves. I attacked the bathroom first, with a scrub-brush and all the noxious cleaning supplies I did not want to have out when Nathan was awake.

"Kim?"

I put my head around the corner. Alison stepped through the open slider in a skirt and twinset.

"You look very 'Miss Rumphius,'" I said.

"I haven't changed into my civilian clothes yet." She looked around. "This is the first time I've seen your patio door open."

"Just airing out the toxins."

"You mean from the Bar exam?" She stuck her head in the bathroom door. "How come you don't have a shower curtain?"

"The reason is asleep in the other room. He pulls it down."

"I hope you ran that by your *feng shui* consultant."

"I thought you were my *feng shui* consultant."

She plopped into the rocker. "Okay. So tell me."

"What?"

"What happened to you last night?"

I wasn't quite ready to come clean about a one-night stand, so I gave her a slightly edited version. Dee would be the first to get the full one.

"Good God, girl, he kissed you right on the dance floor?"

"I swear. We'd danced like two songs together."

"That's outrageous!"

"It was a bit of a setback."

"I can imagine. You okay now?"

I held up my rubber-gloved hands. "Disinfectant works wonders."

"You didn't give that other guy your phone number, did you? He sounds nice, but a gun rack in the pick-up..."

"No, I didn't. But I'll have to pencil that into my DRM." That was our abbreviation for "Dating Rehab Manual."

"Let me clarify. It's not the pick-up. Pick-ups are okay. Pick-ups with gun racks are not. Did I just wake Pep Boy?"

"It's time anyway." We went into the bedroom. Nathan was on his side curved into a half-moon, one foot wrapped in the blanket. He flexed the toes of the other and smiled serenely at us.

Alison hung over the crib railing. "This is my favorite part," she said. "When he's quiet."

I lifted him out. He made a beeline for the kitchen and started beating on a stockpot with a whisk.

"Notice how he completely ignores the hand-painted, personalized toy box I gave him for his birthday," she drawled.

"Pearls before swine. Speaking of swine, we're going to send out a settlement offer this week."

"Don't hold your breath."

"Believe me, I'm not." I pulled my rubber gloves back on. "Did you know there's a temp firm in town called 'Bar Belles?'"

"You mean like e-l-l-e-s?" She emitted the staccato peal of laughter I loved so much. "That's awful! How much do they pay?"

"Nine dollars an hour."

"That'll give you two bucks after you pay the sitter."

"That's what I told her."

"I would have just hung up on her." She stood up. "Well, gotta go hide the dildo, Mom's coming over."

Nathan looked up from the floor and beamed. "MAMA!" he cried.

"Oh my God! That's the first time!" I jumped up and scrabbled in my desk drawer. "Where's the baby book?"

"Leave out that part about the dildo," said Alison, gliding back out the door.

〰〰
〰〰

20

Haunted by the Question

MORGAN HAD ANOTHER JOB LEAD: a hotshot who'd recently made partner at Prentice Schroeder, dropped out into solo practice, and had more work than he could handle. I eagerly accepted any tips; I only had three months left of the six-month grace period on my law school loan, but the contacts he'd generated hadn't amounted to a substantial amount of work yet. I was trying to avoid taking an eighty-hour-a-week associate's job because of Nathan, but establishing myself as a solo contractor was proving to be difficult. It seemed that a large pool of potential employers was necessary in order to get regular cash flow. I was beginning to worry about achieving that in Tulsa.

The address was on a quiet stretch of Harvard south of 41st. I drove past a Silver Dollar Pawn, then a tailor shop with a cardboard sign in the window: *Pant Hems While U Wait.* My heart began to sink. What I was really looking for was a top-notch, overloaded solo practitioner who'd take me on as a silent partner, and I'd had high hopes of this lead: Prentice Schroeder was one of the best firms in town. They'd knocked on my door twice, but I'd turned them down because I was trying to forge my own personal "Mommy track." I continued down the block, and on the other side of a church driveway, I came to an ashlar professional building with a landscaped parking lot. I decided to go in.

The receptionist's desk was unmanned. The lawyer, Brian Duggan, wafted out to greet me in a fog of nicotine. He was tall, dark, and would have been handsome in his pin-striped shirt with a banker's collar except that his skin was sallow and his eyes bloodshot. *Is this what law practice does to you?* I thought as I shook his hand.

He led me to his office and cleared a chair. After the obligatory initial chat, one cigarette in duration, he swiveled around to the credenza, picked up three files, and handed them to me.

"What kind of cases are these?" I asked.

He laced his hands behind his head. "Three med mal cases, just got dropped into my lap. I don't really have the time, but I thought you might be interested. If you did some research we might be able to address them together. They are, of course, contingency," he said, as though in afterthought.

"How much would you be paying me?"

"These are contingency cases," he repeated, busying himself with his lighter. "We'd work out a split, but I wouldn't be paid for them until settlement, assuming we were successful."

"In other words, you want me to do all this work without being paid for it."

He tapped ash into one of the trays wedged around his desk. "That's what contingency means."

I looked down at the files in my lap.

It had taken me the entire morning to get ready for this appointment. To wash my hair, dress decently, apply hairspray and mascara, and suck down enough coffee to hold a pen without dropping it. In other words, to successfully assume the disguise of a normal, functioning human being. All in those spare moments between feeding, changing, playing with, feeding and changing a very active baby boy. Brian didn't have any work to contract out. He just wanted to make a buck off me at no risk to himself.

"Brian," I said carefully, "there's been a misunderstanding. I need paying work. I'm a single mother with a small child to support. I'm not in a position to front services. I'd be happy to prepare these cases for you if you could pay me an hourly."

"I'm not able to do that. I just thought you might be interested. Morgan said you really needed work."

"I do. Paying work. I can't assume all the risk of a contingency case for your benefit. You never said contingency on the phone. If you had, I wouldn't have wasted your time."

Afterwards I stopped at a Git'n'Go and bought an orange slurpee to recover. Screw Brian Duggan and his righteous indignation. This was my alternative to Bar Belles? He was never going to throw me any work anyway. Any real work.

On the radio, Stormtracker reported a funnel touching down at B10. I checked the map on the car seat. D2, nowhere near. I switched to the classical station and sucked greedily at the slurpee. At a red light, Ellie Ameling began to sing "An die Musik," a favorite Schubert aria. I closed my eyes.

> Du schöne Kunst,
> In wievielen grauen Stunden...

Gray hours. Jekyll and Hyde. The time Larry knocked my glasses off. The time he'd hit me on the head, three years later, before the baby was born—I'd liked forgetting that one. The problem with remembering your memories, was that then they wouldn't go away again. *The past is just the present of another day.* My mother's marriage, like mine, was over, but hers had been happy and successful. Her memories were all good, weren't they? What did I do with my memories when they came back? Dee and I had talked about this—but I couldn't remember just now what she'd said.

The car behind me tooted its horn. I opened my eyes. The light had changed. I was dogged by a staggering inability either to read signs or to respond to them, or maybe both. Because of this I'd failed at marriage. Now I was failing at divorce, motherhood, even lawyerhood. On impulse I switched my signal in the other direction and went north on 31st to Woodward Park.

The azaleas were blooming and it was crowded. I parked behind two buses unloading high-schoolers from Pocola and moved away from the hubbub to the rose garden, wandering along the gravel paths among scrawny bushes that had just begun to flag their colors.

183

I'd known the appointment would turn out like that. I'd known it would happen. Brian wasn't being quite straight with me on the phone, was omitting certain pertinent facts to get me down there, where, he felt, I might be desperate enough to work for free. His intonation had been false. But I'd gone anyway. It wasn't his fault. It was mine.

I sat down on a stone bench and scuffed at the gravel. In my previous life, I'd had a good ear. I never worried about being in tune. My hand knew where to go when I shifted positions on the fingerboard, leapt from the scroll to the very top. I'd relished that silent partnership with my cello, our conspiring to perfection. Why had I given it up? The question had been haunting me ever since I'd taken the road to Tahlequah. *This is the voice of your soul. Never let it go.* Well, I had, and I'd lost it. I'd lost that voice. Once upon a time, I was really, really good at something. I had that mastery once, but couldn't believe it. I denied talent, and since my whole life was woven out of music this flowed over into everything else too. It broke me as a musician, that I didn't trust my intuition, and that dammed reservoir of awareness and love and trust then washed back empty to its point of origin, and broke me as a person as well.

Why had I given it up? In order not to compete with Karen? That was foolish; Karen would certainly have welcomed a sister at Julliard. It was also a negative reason, the kind that didn't get you anywhere. I was learning that now. Because ever since then, I hadn't known what else to do. Now I realized the endeavor had been doomed from the start. I'd quit because I was afraid of being too good, and afraid I wasn't good enough. I'd gone out into the world already handicapped, carrying the weight of those fears around with me, everywhere. I'd never gotten past them. My whole life was one big contingency case that hadn't yet settled, and I was close to thirty.

I looked around. Roses out of season really had nothing to recommend them. I got up and started strolling again, thinking back to that time when I still had my cello, my sister, my home, and how blithely I'd left them behind.

The September after high school graduation, at the end of that summer together in Civic Orchestra with Karen, my parents put me on the train for Wellesley, but first, to underscore the importance of the occasion, they took me to lunch. It was Labor Day weekend; the Loop was deserted. We went to the Conrad Hilton because it was the only place we could find open, and sat in the high-ceilinged dining room among two dozen empty tables laid with starched linen, glasses and silver as though a large celebration just about to begin had been indefinitely postponed. At a signal from my father, my mother launched into a vague speech about strangers and men, on the train, and in the world at large. Embarrassed, I looked down at my plate, but mostly I was excited about college. I was about to begin my new life! I contained myself, though. There was a heaviness in the air, something stiff, perhaps regretful, that I felt but did not understand until they took me to the station. As my train lumbered out, I stuck my head out the window and waved, and at the very last moment my mother turned to my father and his arm went around her shoulder, a gesture I'd never seen before in public.

Karen had already flown back to New York, but I didn't want to take a plane the first time. I didn't want my feet to leave the ground. I wanted to personally cover all the terrain between Illinois and Massachusetts, so I'd know exactly where I was and where I'd come from. I didn't know why; I just recognized the imperative. Also, Bobbie had gone back and forth to college by train in her day; I wanted to try the same. I even used her suitcase.

In the dining car I met a sophomore from Iowa on his way to Harvard. That evening he worked his way back from coach to the Pullman cars to find me. It was true, then. In this new life I was going to meet new people, and they were actually going to be interested in talking to me.

The last time I'd been on a train I was seven, going west to the Rockies on our first family vacation. Dad spread his handkerchief on the seat for me because the upholstery was scratchy. When we got to Kansas he crouched beside us, steadying himself on the armrest. "Any minute now, you'll see jackrabbits everywhere, all over the fields," and we watched, but there weren't any. "Where are all the jackrabbits?" he kept repeating. "I can't believe there aren't any jackrabbits."

All during my childhood I asked my father incessant questions. Questions about how machines worked, why the sky was blue, what happened to shooting stars. He always knew the answers. He was an architect by profession, but he knew the answers to everything. Then I got older, and things changed. We spent time together, but didn't talk. The conversations that did occur were few but gratifying, because he spoke as one adult to another. I wondered what it was that made him reticent; but even more, what inspired the confidence. It seemed they were connected. If I knew, perhaps I could believe in it, too.

A few months before his death, he spoke the words *I love you* for the first time. Had he spoken sooner, perhaps I would have gone into young adulthood better armed. I might have made better choices. Even, maybe, made a better job of marriage.

We spent two weeks in the Rockies every summer after that first trip. We progressed from dude ranches, to rented cabins, to the wilderness. One evening on a backpacking trip during college, we sat over the campfire. He was on a downed tree, ankles crossed in front of him, holding his tin cup of coffee. We'd been silent for a while. Then he looked up. I could see the flames reflected in his eyeglasses. "You'll make it," he said. "You're a survivor."

We let the fire burn down to coals, then went to bed. The coyotes howled that night, echoing from ridge to ridge, until I couldn't tell which were the cries and which the answers, and where they were coming from, and I fell asleep. I'd been too bashful to ask what he meant.

The opportunity was gone now, but I wanted it back. I wanted *him* back. I knew he wouldn't be angry with me, for what happened. For how my marriage had turned out. He'd say: *Your mother already told me.* He'd let me scratch his back, and we'd watch an old movie together, and he'd talk to me from a man's perspective, and give me the advice and comfort only a father can. I wanted him back, so I could ask him all my questions. I would say, "Remember the jackrabbits? Why weren't there any jackrabbits? Why did you think there would be?" And it wasn't just old questions. New ones cropped up all the time.

How did I end up in an abusive marriage?

And: *How can I keep it from happening again?*

It hurt to accept the stasis of eternity. What Karen missed most was showing Dad things: her engagement ring, her dissertation, her prenatal ultrasound photos. She craved the sight of him. What I missed most was the chance to ask him questions. There was a whole universe of lost answers out there I'd never come to find. What Karen missed most were the things he'd never see; what I missed most were the things I'd never hear.

I thought of my cello again, remembered what it was like to hold the instrument in the crook of my thumb and among the infinity of scale tones on wire-wrapped catgut find just the right ones, then reach with the little finger, a gentle breath not a pressure, for the harmonic: the single delicate place on each string, where the tone was a ghostly whisper containing within it echoes of the lower octaves. Harmonics are shadows, shadows thrown back by the future or forward by the past to the place where time meets timelessness, that seamless junction, eternity. But art can be perfect; real life can't. I'd given up one and stumbled at the other. And as I moved further and further into adulthood, shifted from theory to practice, I'd accumulated moments I wouldn't want to stand in for eternity, grasped meanings I'd rather not have learned. I couldn't stand in that place, that seamless junction, like my mother could, like Karen could. I couldn't abide it. It hurt too much. I could never be whole like them.

I'd always been attuned to harmonics in real life. But what had it ever profited me? I'd been unable, unwilling, or just too plain stupid to translate understanding into action. The wages of philosophy were unemployment and solitude. I threw my empty slurpee in the trash can, and trudged back through naked bushes to my car.

〰〰

21

Strangers and Men

GARETH WAS LEADING A TOUR of his art collection. I stepped away and
drew a cup of coffee from the urn on the sideboard, then sat down and
closed my eyes. Eight weeks after the Bar and I was still exhausted.
Things hadn't been turning out quite as I'd expected when we'd had
the Bar celebration party a month ago. Then, Gareth had dusted off
his grand piano and hired a singer; I'd worn a turquoise leather
miniskirt of Alison's so short it would have made my mother gasp
(something borrowed, something blue), and my hairstylist, Bob, had
done me up in a beehive taller than Larry's lawyer's girlfriend's.
Dana and I had invited everyone we could think of. Everyone, that is,
except Forrest. I hadn't invited Forrest.

I'd called him up after the Bar to spite my mother; we went out,
and I had a good time. But then the condom broke, and ever since then
I'd been running away from him. Because I remembered what a wonderful man he was, and it would have been so easy to fall back into a
relationship, and maybe he *would* be the kind of person my mother
would like to see me with, even though he lived far from Chicago—
but he wasn't the *one*. It was my conviction. Or was I just reacting
against my mother again? Maybe, just maybe, I was staring my future
husband in the face—but was too immature or screwed-up or scared
to admit it. Maybe I was fated to perpetual adolescence.

Gareth moved the group down the hall to a charcoal drawing of

Taos Pueblo. I really wished—I wished Forrest were here. Everything seemed to be sliding downhill. And my energy had never picked up either. I took a sip of coffee. It tasted odd. I went through the swinging door into the kitchen, where the waitress was replenishing a platter of roast beef, deftly tucking slices all around the edge.

"Is this decaf?" I asked.

She looked up. "No, hon. I can make some if you want."

Dana came in. "There you are! You know those two guys from American I introduced you to? They're in the library now, arguing about which one of them you liked better."

"No way."

"Would I lie to you?"

"Well, that's very flattering, but what I need right now is paid employment." The two-carat rock I'd thrown into Lake Michigan at New Year's would have bought me quite a bit more time, but it had been more than a gesture and I was not going to allow myself to regret it.

"Job, job. I know. We're working on it," Dana said, stealing an olive on her way back out.

"A contact in the legal department would be nice," I called after her.

I stared out the wall of glass at the late-blooming rock garden nestled in the shady woods below. The waitress went out with the platter. I set down the cup and slipped out the back door. I got my datebook out of the car and scrabbled through it, looking for the tiny x. *When? When? When?* I hadn't marked it down. I flipped the pages, backward and forward. I couldn't be pregnant, I couldn't possibly. With Nathan, it had been like night and day. I'd known even before I missed my period. It was the Bar exam. The stress of the Bar had thrown my system off.

I started the engine. I had to go slowly on the winding one-lane road in case I met a car or a horseback rider. At Lewis, I peeled north as fast as I could, stopping at a grocery store far from home turf to buy a stick test. Fifteen minutes later I was back at Riverview Gardens, sitting on the edge of my bathtub, watching the double pink line grow brighter and brighter.

The broken condom. Damn him!

Then: *How can I do this to Nathan?*

Then, staring down at the plastic tube, I realized with horror that within the last month I'd also had sex with two, count'em two, other men: Morgan and Randall. However unlikely, I could not absolutely rule them out.

Three partners in one month! Single-handedly, with no help from anyone at all, I had just torpedoed my own self-image.

All my life people had told me how much I looked like my mother, how much our voices sounded alike. Significant differences were now beginning to appear. I sank down into the rocker. I could imagine the psychologist's report:

> The child's mother, already overburdened by her parenting responsibilities, has exhibited irresponsible and promiscuous behavior and is now expecting a second child out of wedlock, rendering her even more incapable of providing a stable home environment for Nathan.

I remembered a billboard picture of a pink phone with a curling cord that turned into script: "Pregnancy Hopeline." I got out the phonebook. But it turned out all they wanted to do was help me find adoptive parents. "You don't understand!" I said. "I can't *have* this baby. I already have one baby, and I can't even manage him! I'm *not married.*"

"Honey, I hear you, but we can only help you if you're fixing to have the baby. We don't do abortion referrals. Have you talked to your minister?"

I hung up. Then I had a bright idea: look under A in the Yellow Pages. There it was—there was only one. But I couldn't bring myself to make the call. I couldn't bring myself to say the words.

"DO YOU WANT to get married?" said Max.

I stared out his window at the barbed-wire fence around the Borden Milk truck lot. "What?"

"Do you want to get married? I will marry you."

The opposite corner was full of wire bales and scattered pipes, and a shed with a rusting corrugated roof. It looked like a storage lot for a construction company. Just beyond it was Cain's Ballroom, where a month ago Dana and I had been pasted against the stage, clapping our hands as Delbert McClinton sang "She's like rolling a seven / Every time I roll the dice."

I scraped loose flakes of paint from the windowsill.

"This is exactly why I can't tell Forrest," I said. "He'll propose."

"You can't marry him."

"I know."

He turned back to his canvas.

"Don't gloat," I said. I saw what I was doing to the sill and stopped. The wood was gritty. It bothered me, that someone had taken the trouble to strip and sand the window, but not clean it off before painting. "He's a great guy. It just…it wouldn't work."

"*I* can be the father."

I walked over and put my arms around him.

"Come here," I said. "I want to do something for you." I led him to the doorless bathroom, ran water in the tub, and folded a towel for him to kneel on. Then I began to wash the matted hair that hung to his chin.

"When I was little," I said, "my mother washed my hair in the kitchen sink every Saturday night. I lay on my back on top of the counter. She stopped when I was twelve." I poured water over his head and his hair flowed down, clean, black, arrow-straight. "I guess I got too long for the counter." I blotted his hair with a towel. "I miss her hands. She had gentle hands."

"So do you."

I moved him to a chair in the middle of the room. He sat with his legs crossed, a towel around his neck, and rolled a cigarette, holding it aside while I warmed his cheeks with a washcloth. I applied the razor slowly and carefully, stopping every now and then to let him take a puff. We were surrounded by his paintings. The canvases were large, stacked around the room, like a museum that had run out of space.

"You know the Galerie in Munich, at Lenbach Haus?"

He nodded, eyes closed.

191

"The room on the second floor, with Kandinisky improvisations all the way around? I went there all the time junior year, just to be in that room. The first time I saw it, I started to cry. I walked in and sat down and just started to cry."

"'Art is the axe for the frozen sea within.'" He felt his chin, looked up at me and smiled. "Kafka."

"Max, I just can't see a wife and small children fitting into your lifestyle."

"Maybe. Maybe you're just a coward." He lit the cigarette he'd rolled, shook out the match and flipped it into the sink.

I smoothed his hair with one hand while combing it with the other. "I remember one time my friend wanted to come with me to the gallery, and I practically threw a fit because I wanted to go alone, I can't even remember why now, it was so long ago. The math professor, I told you about him, from Athens. He didn't want me to go anywhere alone. He said I was too independent." I ran my thumb over the comb. "Maybe I'm just a loner. I certainly married one."

He propped his elbow on his knee, thumb on mouth, cigarette wedged between two middle fingers, studying me the way he did his canvases. Then he tapped me on the chest. "You're not a loner. You're a coward," he said. "Afraid of a real relationship. That's what you'd have with me."

I looked down at the folded towel on my lap.

"If I...would you go with me?" I said quietly. "Would you go with me when I go to the clinic? I need somebody to drive me home afterward."

He combed two hands through clean hair, tucking it behind his ears. "Yes, of course. Of course I will," he said, then turned away and picked up his brush.

〰〰
〰〰

22

Ironing Handkerchiefs

I LEAFED THROUGH THE MAIL: a dry cleaning coupon, a legal bill, and envelopes from the IRS and the title company; Hal had told me to request those last after reviewing Larry's financial information. I slit them open. There they were: tax refunds, real estate proceeds checks, front and back copies, with my name in his handwriting. Forgery. Not recent, either, not just from the sale of the Tulsa house, but from the two little houses we owned in Vermont, and the rental property we'd owned our first couple years in Tulsa. For that one, I'd put up the down payment from my own savings, and in the end he'd claimed we'd lost the equity.

He'd done this before.

Then it dawned on me: Larry had done something wrong I could actually prove.

I had no marks on my body, and the other scars were invisible, the pictures I had to live with in my head forever of what he did while I nursed the baby because unless we had sex every day he'd kick me out of the house and he only wanted sex when the baby was crying. He refused to wait, and I was afraid, so I took the baby out of the bassinet, took him out and held him and cut myself off at the waist: I watched the baby, and pretended I was just lying on the bed, nursing. Pretended, pretended, pretended.

We never had bought a crib.

I held the papers in my hand. I could prove this. This was a fact. I'd asked a routine question, and the universe had dropped a lost answer in my lap, one I hadn't even known to ask for: I'd never seen the checks in the first place. And it was one kind of paper Larry couldn't rip up. It wasn't in my dresser drawer, where I kept the diary, the blood test results, the x-ray in its tiny envelope. It was in the bank. The legal system up to now had clearly been unable to call Larry to account for anything, much less to afford redress. But this wasn't divorce court. It wasn't he-said-she-said. It was an indisputable fact—after all, I knew my own handwriting—and not only that, it was a crime. I called the police department.

The issuing bank for the Tulsa proceeds was nearby on Peoria. While Nathan chewed a biscuit in the stroller a woman wearing a nice enough suit but a little too much jewelry scrutinized my driver's license, filled in the blanks on two florid Affidavits of Forgery, and notarized my signature. I wheeled Nathan back out, unbuckled him, strapped him into the car seat, went down to the police station at 71st and Riverside and reversed the process, staving him off with another biscuit.

I laid the folder down and opened it up for the officer at the counter. Behind wire-rimmed glasses she had a brook-no-fools gaze of the less intelligent variety, and her blond hair was as short as it could possibly be and still take the curling iron. She looked over the affidavits carefully. "Ma'am?" she said.

"Yes?" I answered brightly.

"Is this man your husband?"

"No. I mean yes. He was. That is, he is. We're in the process of getting a divorce."

"At this time," she said, picking up the checks between thumb and forefinger, as though they were wet, "you were legally married at this time?"

"Yes." My smile faded.

"If you were husband and wife, at the time, it's not theft. In Oklahoma, assets of married couples are jointly held, whether it's a joint account or not. Legally, he didn't take anything from you."

Dana's mouth, shaping the words: "That is sex abuse and that is wrong."
The note on the floor: SEXUAL ABUSE IS A FUNDAMENTAL VIOLATION
OF A PERSON'S HUMANITY.

"But it was my money, and he forged my signature. I never even saw this check!"

"That's the way it is in this state. A married couple is a legal unity and the state is not going to interfere in how they divvy up assets."

Nathan dropped his biscuit on the linoleum. I snatched it up, blew on it, brushed it off, and handed it back. "The officer on the phone—"

"He obviously did not understand the situation," she said officiously, pushing the folder back. "I'm sorry, but that is the state of the law on this matter. It's not an actionable offense."

In the parking lot I sat sideways in the driver's seat, one foot out the open door, staring across Riverside Drive at the cottonwoods on the edge of the Arkansas. They were completely leafed out now; summer was almost full-blown. It was mid-May, a year since I'd filed, and more than a year since the Easter afternoon he'd hit me, then later stood on the riverbank—this same riverbank, a few miles up—and laughed at me. I looked at the affidavit on the passenger seat. *Not an actionable offense.* I knew it wouldn't work, I thought. I knew he'd get away with it.

All roads lead to the Arkansas.

IT WAS AN EASTER afternoon, as well, that I'd last seen my father. Three years ago, but it seemed like a lifetime. I was visiting alone, as usual. On Saturday morning I borrowed my mother's car and drove downstate to attend the wedding of a friend from Mount Holyoke finishing a doctorate in microbiology at Saint Louis. This was the cover for my trip home; the real reason, unvoiced even by my mother when she'd called me to come, was that my father was failing. The wedding was held at a state park on the bluffs of the Mississippi, in a nineteen-thirties lodge built by the CCC with huge timbers and a massive fireplace of river rock. The day after the wedding, I awoke at dawn, got in my car and sped north on back roads laid like soft ribbons through faint green fields, pulling up at stop signs, making ninety-degree turns right, then left, then right again as I cut through the fertile heart of Illinois toward Chicago and the lakeshore.

Four hours later back on the Dan Ryan I felt a little foolish for that urgency downstate, in that different world I woke up in, of rolling Thomas Hart Benton landscapes, buckled asphalt, shoulders that crumbled off into the grass, fences notched with DeKalb corn signs. So I got off the highway and stopped at a shoe store to prove to myself that I wasn't in any hurry.

When I got home, I watched an old movie with Dad and gave him a backscratch. It was the last time I ever touched him. A few hours later I got on a plane to go back where I lived with Larry—I never thought of it as home—already mourning, knowing after laying hands on him that I'd seen him for the last time, that death was approaching like a slow, relentless tide—an intuition so clear and overwhelming it never occurred to me to deny its truth.

I loved those shoes. I still had them: low-heeled black suede pumps, with a crossover vamp and contrast stitching. I could wear them with anything, and did, all the time. They were my favorite shoes. They reminded me of my father, even though they were the result of a stalling tactic; of my father, the backrub, our last, silent hour together. Reminded me that I was human, that when faced with immense and desolating abstractions, we all of us energetically champion the quotidian in ways sometimes amusing, sometimes touching and profound, like the way my mother had painstakingly ironed three handkerchiefs for my father's overnight bag for the hospital after Christmas, for the lung surgery he had just warned us he might not survive, and barely did.

But aren't we allowed our coping mechanisms? Allowed to assuage our grief, to insulate ourselves, even if only momentarily, from things too painful to bear? Was ironing handkerchiefs an inherited tendency I needed to root out? Maybe; maybe not. If denial was an anesthetic, then perhaps the key to it, as with other potentially dangerous substances, was in amount and duration. When your marriage fails, you can persuade yourself that you're just going through a phase. Death, on the other hand, does have finality going for it. So perhaps the shoes were okay; they gave me a moment of relief from pain I never denied and from a truth I was able, with time, to accept: I knew the cancer wasn't my fault.

But after that Easter Sunday with Larry, I'd ironed handkerchiefs for far too long, committing significant errors and omissions: lying to Dana about why I needed a dentist, hanging up on the Phone Call, walking into the law school with a smile on my face, telling my nursery school teacher I was moving to Seattle. And I'd done it because I couldn't admit it was me. I thought it must have been me. I thought the abuse—that is, the parts I'd allowed myself to recall at the time— I thought the abuse was my fault. It was unbelievable to me now: that I hadn't been able to recognize the malice in Larry's hands. That I was convinced *I* must have done something wrong.

I WAS ON THE floor again. I jacked myself up on my elbow. Weather-tracker was on with the sound off; Nathan sat watching the garish patterns swirl over and over across the aerial map. Dee had wanted me to write down every time this happened, and what triggered it, but the problem was I could never remember.

I thought about emptying the dishwasher, then lay back again and crossed my ankles. I got different results with the ceiling at different times of day depending on the angle of the light. This time I saw something that looked like the giant Praying Hands statue on the Oral Roberts campus, in the corner over the television.

Larry's hands, moving fast. Larry's hands, on my head, forcing me down. Larry's hands, thrusting the real estate papers at me.

I sat up. "Dee, I got it!" I exclaimed. "The forged checks. I remembered!"

There was a piece of paper on the floor. It read:

1. Took out the garbage.
2. Made rice
3. Went to counseling.

I put a period after the word "rice." Then I crumpled it into a ball. I missed the wastebasket, but it didn't matter. Nathan was going to tip it over at some point anyway. I opened the refrigerator and shoved a few broccoli stalks in my mouth, then picked a recording at random: Cecilia Bartoli, singing from Berlioz's *La Mort d'Ophelie.* It was the CD of opera arias the handwriting analyst had given me—right before he asked me for a date.

I sat down in the rocker and listened as Nathan ran a terrycloth car over and over into the sliding door. School was over. The Bar was over. Now I had to confront my mistakes in marriage.

The biggest mistake I made was marrying someone who didn't cherish me. The second mistake was believing his lies because I was pregnant and wanted to believe they were true. I got another piece of paper and started a new file. I was putting them on paper lately, instead of in my head. Dee said this was an improvement.

> LIES MY HUSBAND TOLD ME
> I've changed my mind—I do want children.
> We can have a baby if you do all the work and we split the
>   expenses.
> Your problems are intrapsychic, not interpersonal.
> You're mentally ill.
> There was no tax refund.
> We lost money when we sold the house. (Repeat three times.)
> We lost our equity on the rental house.
> I'm your best friend.

THE BLEEDING STARTED at ten o'clock, just after I'd gone to bed. My first reaction was gratitude. I fervently promised the Lord never to have casual sex again, took two ibuprofen and got back under the covers with Winnie-the-Pooh, waiting for the painkillers to kick in.

After awhile I peeked through the mini-blinds. Every window was dark. The cottonwood rustled gently over the dumpster. There were few stars in my wedge of visible sky. I decided to call the hospital.

"I was just wondering if I should come in and get looked at. I'm having an early miscarriage, and the cramps are getting really bad."

"Who's your doctor?"

"I, uh, I don't have one...I wasn't planning...I hadn't been yet..."
I'd been ironing handkerchiefs, like my mother before the lung surgery.

"Well." She was silent for a beat. "I guess the Lord works in mysterious ways, hon. How far along are you?"

The abortion had been rescheduled four times. First, I'd canceled it, then there was a bomb threat at the clinic, then I canceled it again, then the doctor was out sick.

"About eleven weeks—"

"Eleven weeks!" she squeaked. "I thought you said early. You need to come in to the emergency room, hon. Is there someone can drive you?"

"Yes," I lied.

Max was the only one who knew I was pregnant; he didn't have a phone. I banged my head softly on the table. *Stupid, stupid, stupid.* I'd thought I was going to put this whole thing behind me with nobody the wiser, not even Dee.

When I could stand up I put on an old pair of sweats and moved Nathan out to the car. The streetlight shone straight in his window, so I shielded his eyes with a receiving blanket and waited to make sure he settled back. Then I locked him in and went back for the diaper bag.

As I put a folded towel down on the driver's seat, I realized I'd forgotten to lock the apartment the second time. I felt around on the floor for my keys. Another contraction hit; I shifted my weight to my arms and counted slowly to twenty, as I'd done in the early stages of labor with Nathan. Then I opened my eyes, found the keys, and went back to lock the door.

At the emergency room I rolled down the window and put my head on my arm. I closed my eyes through another contraction.

"Tell me what's wrong, honey," said a nurse.

"Miscarriage, I'm okay, the cramps just got really bad."

She lifted my elbow, opened the door, helped me into a wheelchair. "When did the bleeding start?"

"Ten o'clock. Why does it hurt so much?"

She turned her wrist and checked her watch. "You'll be okay, dear. We'll get you inside, get you cleaned up. Don't worry."

"There's a baby in here," said the other nurse.

"What's his name?"

"His diaper bag's there," I croaked. "Nathan. It was late...I didn't want to call anyone."

In the cubicle, one took my blood pressure and pulse while the other rattled off questions: age, marital status, date of last period, time of onset of bleeding, any drugs or alcohol in the last twenty-four hours, had I introduced anything into my vagina prior to the onset of bleeding.

I looked up at her incredulously.

She put a calming hand on my arm. "It happens."

The doctor was waiting in another room, gloved and masked. "Okay sweetheart," he said, "you know what a D&C is? Okay. We've got some anesthesia here, she's going to sit right next to you with this mask, when it starts to hurt, tap her hand, and you can take a few whiffs."

There was a surge of nausea. Then it was over, and I knew what a D&C was.

The doctor stripped off his gloves. "Next time, sweetheart, do us a favor, shave your legs before you come in."

The nurse's eyes widened over her mask. "Let's get you some ginger ale," she said.

"Your little boy is just fine," the other nurse reported, drawing the curtains around me again in yet another cubicle. "He's made quite a few friends out there."

"That's a blessing," I said, then started to cry. "Call Doctor Sayler!"

Fifteen minutes later Forrest was there in his Sooners sweatshirt and jeans, hair uncombed, feet shoved sockless into loafers. He grabbed a stool and wheeled it under him as he took my hands. He closed his eyes for a moment and I realized he was trying not to cry.

"I'm so sorry," I said.

"You weren't going to tell me."

"Forrest, it was an accident."

He nodded bleakly.

"I didn't want to hurt you."

"That was a foregone conclusion, either way."

"I hadn't made a decision yet." Because I didn't know what I wanted. Only what I didn't want: to be the single mother of *two* children. But I couldn't get around that. So I hadn't thought about it.

I kissed his palm and folded my hand over it. "Forrest? I love you, but I don't want to marry you."

"Well, I guess it's good we're clear on that."

"I don't know why. That's just the way it is. I don't *know* why," I wept. "It just happens that way. I didn't want to hurt you."

"It's okay, Kim." He took his hand back. "It's just…a lot of loss for one night." He sat up suddenly. "Where's Nathan?"

"I brought him with me. I didn't know what else to do." I pulled the acrylic blanket up to my neck. "Forrest, that doctor, you know what he said to me? He told me to shave my legs before I came in next time."

He shoved aside the curtain. I could see the two nurses gaping after him.

"Someone's about to get his butt kicked," one said, bringing me more ginger ale.

Driving me home Forrest said: "You should have called me. We could have done all this…privately."

"Forrest, I wasn't thinking. I wasn't thinking about what your friends at the hospital would say."

He shook his head, past Carpet City, past the car wash.

"Mercy is the closest hospital," I said stiffly.

He stared out the windshield.

We hit the stoplight at 41st. I looked over at the Quiktrip. The belt-buckle cowboy was nowhere to be seen. *Jesus certainly had the answer this time.*

"I'm just…why didn't you tell me?" he cried. "Maybe I could have done something. Maybe this wouldn't have happened. Do you know how long I've wanted? Even if you didn't *want* to get married. We could have talked about it. It might have made a difference. You didn't give me the chance. They were still my children."

"What do you mean?"

He blew out a breath through his lips like a beached fish.

"Don't tell me," I cried. I put my hands up to my ears. "How could they know?"

After a few blocks he said, "They have to analyze it. To make sure they got everything."

I put my hands to my ears again.

Finally I said, "They must have been sick, Forrest. There must have been something wrong. Otherwise...why..."

He just looked at me.

My grandmother had had twins, and one of them had died at eight months. The stronger one was Bobbie.

When we parked the car I took Nathan out and clutched him to me. Here was a healthy baby, at least, even if he didn't have a real father.

Forrest took him away. "You shouldn't pick him up for awhile. Until the bleeding stops."

I threw the bloody towel in the dumpster and followed him in. I never wanted to see it again. What he had said was true: maybe this wouldn't have happened. If I'd told him early on. He was a doctor, after all. Weren't there things they could do nowadays? It wasn't just the luck of the draw to make it past the twelfth week anymore, was it? Maybe if I'd started taking pre-natal vitamins the minute I missed my period, this wouldn't have happened—maybe something as simple as that.

Forrest carried Nathan inside, laid him in the crib, stood there cradling the little head in his hand, his beautiful, strong, long-fingered hand. I remembered: I loved Forrest's hands. He could have been a cello player, I'd told him, or a pianist. But his hands were skilled in another way, he inhabited another whole amazing universe of knowledge. He knew what was going on inside people, he fixed them, he made them whole. And he, of all the men of my acquaintance, was the one who desperately wanted to be a father. Even if there had been something wrong with the baby—with *a* baby—it wouldn't have made a difference to him.

I thought of Larry, standing at the kitchen table with the blood test results: *I called the midwife and asked her for an abortion.*

Forrest slid his hand gently out from beneath and smoothed Nathan's hair. I remembered how we'd stood together once before, watching Nathan sleep, and he'd put his arm around me. I couldn't stand it. I went into the other room.

"I'm sorry," I said, when he came out.

"You should have your feet up."

"I'm *sorry.*"

I was disappointing someone, hurting someone, on a magnitude I had previously considered unimaginable. All the other times—my cello teacher when I gave it up, my college advisor when I got mono senior year and dropped an honors thesis, my parents when I missed a *summa* by one one-hundredth of a point—all the other times evaporated into utter meaninglessness.

He stood there, bleak and deflated, looking around my cheap, bare apartment. "It's not your fault," he said. "It's nobody's fault."

"I don't always deal with things gracefully. I muck things up."

"No, graceful is *everything* you are." He took my hand and looked right at me. "Twins," he said, and uttered a short laugh. "Well," he said, "guess we know I'm not shooting blanks."

"Forrest, stop."

He wilted onto my shoulders.

"I was afraid to tell you because I knew you'd pressure me to marry you and I might not have been able to withstand it."

"Would that really have been a fate worse than death?"

"That's not what I mean."

"I know," he said miserably, faced buried in my neck.

"Forrest, I was going to tell you but I was scared to, I didn't believe it, and I hadn't decided what to do yet—not about the baby, about *you*—and I didn't believe it, and the appointment kept getting put off. Please don't be mad at me." My voice was ragged. I realized: it was the truth. I always told the truth to other people. The only one I really lied to was myself. To others I told the truth, when it came down to it, though it might—in the hands of someone like Larry, for example—

redound to my harm. Pressing my face against his shoulder, I hugged him harder than I'd ever hugged anyone before in my life, grabbing handfuls of his sweatshirt as though it were a life preserver, imploring over and over, "Please don't be mad at me."

He released himself from the embrace slowly, in stages, moving his hands from my waist to my shoulders, then cupping my head, lacing his fingers in my hair, before letting go. "Oh, I probably will be," he said, hand on the door. "Tomorrow."

23

Square One

NATHAN DANCED INTO THE KITCHEN. "Oh my gosh, do you need a dia-per change," I exclaimed. "Right now." I abandoned the dishes in the sink and scooped him up, holding him well away as I moved into the bedroom. I unrolled a beach towel with one hand and flopped him down; the changing table had long since been dismantled. "What has your mother been feeding you? You've leaked straight through." I ruffled his hair and set him upright again.

Back in the other room I hit the replay button on Burl Ives' *Little White Duck.* Larry had, of course, absconded with *Baby Brain,* so I'd reverted to the tried-and-true. It didn't matter so much what the music was, I thought, as long as he had the opportunity to sing and dance. As he began to jump around again, I returned to the dishes, and a mem-ory floated to the surface. I was very little and I was dancing in the living room of my parents' first small house, the one with the fold-down table in the kitchen and the sandbox under the maple tree. I was whirling around to a scratchy folk music record after dinner, dancing with imaginary friends, while my parents sat in the dining room, through the arched doorway. In this memory Karen and Baby Douglas were absent; I was alone and dancing, with my parents nearby.

I lifted my hands out of the soapy water and rested my forearms on the sink. A comfortable feeling stole over me that I hadn't felt in decades. I could hear their voices, one low, one higher and more musical, the fairy-bell sound of spoon in cup, the chink of cup on saucer. The tiny scratch as my father lit a cigarette, the squeak of their chairs as they settled more comfortably. I was held securely within the web of their lives. They were on the other side of the arch. They were near. I was safe. I could dance.

Nathan chortled. I stuck my head around the kitchen wall. Hands planted on the mirror, he was crowing at himself with unadulterated self-admiration, knees flexing excitedly. His little thighs were creased with baby fat below the elastic of his romper. I walked over to him and saw myself, a grown woman picking up a tiny boy. I put him down for his nap, closed the door, and something hit me square between the eyes: *I just want to be* myself *every minute of the day no matter what I am doing or who I am with.*

I went back to the mirror, stood in front of it to see that grown woman again. Suddenly I was a child, with my parents, my age now, standing on either side of me, saying, "All we want is for you to be who you really are."

It had been flowing into me, lately, at odd moments, how intensely unhappy I'd been in my marriage without realizing it. At the moment Larry and I weighed the move to Tulsa, before his sister's Boston wedding, I'd heard a voice in a dream saying *No lies, no lies, no lies.* Now I understood that dream: it meant no lying to myself. The problem with my marriage, the mistake I'd made, was that I'd betrayed myself. I'd violated my own integrity. That had to happen first, before anyone as strong and smart as I could let anyone else do the same. I crouched on the carpet before the mirror, arms wrapped around my knees, bowed over by the arduous weight of the truth, a slow river of grief flowing through my body, finding its way out.

I had to go back to absolute square one. Not just back to living on my own, not just back to being single, but back to the absolute beginning, the fundamental core of who I was, and then I had to move outward from that core, never doing anything incompatible with it. I'd always known, deep down, that I was valuable; I just had to hear it echoed back from someone else. I needed to hear my music antiphonally, sung back to me, faintly, from the other side of the room or of the world or from heaven to earth or generation to generation. I was always good at tracing, in my face, the lineaments of my family, but when I tried to see myself, I drew a blank. Hearing the antiphon was like seeing my reflection. My father and my mother, on either side of me, again; this time, my father had taken the lead, because he'd seen these things were difficult for Bobbie, and he answered my question, the question of how I could keep this from happening again.

All we want is for you to be who you really are.

Messages from the universe of lost answers did, in fact, arrive. They came unexpectedly, often freighted with remorse or regret, but they were the truth and they came when you needed them. The blessing was that they came at all.

From now on, I had to listen to what trusted others said about me and believe in it. I had to listen to the voice inside myself that was saying the same thing, and believe in it too. I wasn't Bobbie, and I wasn't Karen. I was Kim. Crouched on the floor, before the mirror, I grew to fill my outlines. My voice reappeared and filled my throat.

〰〰

24

Word Count

THINGS TO DO BEFORE DR. DELANEY'S HOME VISIT
Clean apartment.
Change crib bedding—cover stain with stuffed animal.
Stock refrigerator.
Scrape crud off high chair.

I tipped back in my chair while the list printed and examined the ceiling. This morning, it looked like the vanilla glaze on doughnuts that had been left out overnight: dry, but not quite stale.

John called from Oregon.

"I'm going out to stock the fridge," I told him, removing the television remote from Nathan's mouth. "The psychologist is coming tomorrow."

"How is that connected with the fridge?"

"Alison told me. She said he would look inside. She knows. Her brother is a social worker. I don't know if I can compete with Larry's refrigerator, though. It's probably full of lobster."

"I don't trust psychologists. I never met one that wasn't whacked."

"He's getting a nice vacation out of this case. He just came back from four days in Seattle."

"You didn't have to pay for that, did you?"

"No. But everything else is fifty-fifty. He wouldn't even start the official study until he'd gotten a four thousand dollar retainer."

"Maybe I'm in the wrong profession."

"No. Remember: you are not whacked." I picked up a pencil and added chocolate chips to my grocery list. "I also have to bake cookies before he comes, so the house smells nice."

"Listen, uh, I just got assigned to a due diligence team working on an acquisition in New York and, I was wondering…I could book my flight through Dallas and take a side trip to Tulsa for a day if that's okay."

Ten days from now. I put the pencil down, laid both hands flat on the counter. I remembered when he'd left Tulsa after graduation last year. He'd bought a new car, and drove by the house to show me. The upholstery was tan, buttery soft, new-smelling. I was jealous. I thought: *his life is just beginning.* I wished I could just climb in and go with him.

Just before he drove away, he leaned out the window and kissed me. I'd never said a word about filing for divorce, but it must have been obvious that my marriage was falling apart. Since then, since that kiss, for over a year, he'd lived in my mind, in the last little remaining corner of the world of the hypothetical. I didn't really know him all that well, when it came down to it.

"Yes." I said. "Thank you for being so patient with me."

"What choice do I have? I'm two thousand miles away."

"I had a lot of stuff to get done. Counseling, and stuff. I didn't want to mess it up with you."

"Don't worry, Kim," he laughed. "Nobody would ever call you too impulsive."

Luckily, he couldn't see me blush.

DOCTOR DELANEY was a big man. He filled the doorway, making my bedroom look even smaller than it was.

"I didn't realize Nathan didn't have his own room," he said, making a note on his clipboard.

"I signed a lease on a one-bedroom apartment," I replied. "That was what seemed right at the time." I fussed with the crib bedding.

"And he's still in a crib?" He made another note.

209

I took my hands away and stuck them in my pockets. "Well, yes. He's only seventeen months old."

"But he can walk."

"Yes."

"Shouldn't he be in a toddler bed then?"

"My mother told me to leave him in the crib until he's able to climb out of it."

"When he is, *then* would you put him in a toddler bed?"

"Well, my m-mom said to just move the adjustable side down. Then he can get in and out on his own."

He nodded. Another note.

"My mom said they're a waste of money," I blurted. "They can go straight to a twin bed with a safety gate when they grow out of the crib."

I needed to sit down. I was sounding defensive, and talking too much about my mother. I leaned against the dresser. Thank heaven Alison had done a walk-through this morning. She'd plucked the affirmation cards out of the mirror frame (*I am calm, I am serene. I love and approve of myself*) and tucked them in a drawer.

"You should see the room Larry has for him in Seattle," said Dr. Delaney.

"Custody hasn't been placed in issue, has it? Has something happened?"

He looked at me, kindly, and I realized I'd put my hand to my throat. I busied myself refolding the baby quilt. It was identical to the one Aunt Thea had made for me when I was born, the one I'd dragged everywhere until kindergarten. When I'd unwrapped it the Christmas before Nathan arrived, Bobbie had grasped my wrist and chided, *This one we're going to save.* I smoothed it over the crib railing. Aunt Thea had made it for Nathan by hand. Shouldn't that count for something?

"I'll take you up on that coffee," Dr. Delaney said.

I put Nathan in the highchair and gave him half a cookie, then poured the coffee, taking care to pick matching mugs.

Dr. Delaney folded himself into the single chair at the table. "Larry has a very nice space for Nathan in Seattle," he remarked. "Of course, he has a three-bedroom townhouse."

"Do you know how much temporary support he pays?"

He shook his head and reached for the sugar bowl.

"Eighty-two dollars a month. If we had been divorced a year ago, and he were paying adequate support, I'd probably be in a two-bedroom apartment by now. Especially with the thousands I'd have saved in legal fees."

"I know Larry's been doing inappropriate things to delay the divorce. He can't separate his anger toward you from his relationship to Nathan." He lifted a bushy eyebrow. "Yet." He finished stirring and took a sip. "I just wish—you need to see the room he has for him in Seattle."

I brought over the desk chair, sat down, and folded my hands on the table. "No. I do *not* need to see the room he has for him in Seattle."

"Kim. You need to be able to visualize him as a parent. Your concerns about his parenting abilities…there are a lot of them, and they're valid, but we're working on that. You need to see that things are changing. It's important for this mix to increase your comfort level with Larry spending time with Nathan."

"What would that achieve?"

"Obviously, it will be better for him in the long run if his parents get along."

"Dr. Delaney." There wasn't a desk between us now, as there had been at our meetings in his office; we were in my home, at my table. My grandmother's table, hand-joined a century ago by a German immigrant in whose painstaking work, in whose delicately carved ornamental corner fillets and perfectly-turned legs, one could, perhaps, see a deeper understanding of what was important and sacred in life than that evinced by the lettered doctor with his Lucite clipboard. "I'm not sure I'll ever be able to get along with someone who abused me, Dr. Delaney. And I think, I hope it's obvious to you by now, that I would never stand in the way of a reasonable visitation schedule. Whether or not he can spend big bucks to outfit a lavish nursery will not affect my compliance one way or another. I just don't want anything to do with him, myself. We're divorced. Almost."

"The fact remains that you do have a child together."

211

"We are not raising this child together! Co-parenting is a concept designed to alleviate guilt on the part of divorcing couples who want to pretend their selfish desire to split up will have absolutely no effect on their children. What's so funny?" I said thinly, as he stroked his mustache.

"I was just remembering the first time we met at my office, how hard it was for you even to speak."

"Yes. Well. Much has happened."

He leaned forward. "I really think I can reassure you that Larry has no desire to take Nathan away. As for visitation, I've been working on trying to get him to understand what's appropriate given Nathan's age and developmental level and the distance between the parents."

"Guess you've got your work cut out for you." I let Nathan down from the high chair and he climbed up on the doctor's knee.

"Larry...doesn't really know what he wants. He's very confused at this point, and like I said, he's got some boundary problems. But he does seem to show signs of genuine interest in Nathan. If he can work through some of his issues, I think this could very well possibly be the first *real* relationship he will have had in his life."

So what? I thought, as the doctor spooned sugar into his second cup. What exactly was I paying for here? "What's the focus of your study?" I asked. "Rehabilitating Larry? I thought the purpose was to figure out a visitation plan in Nathan's best interests."

"Of course, of course. But all of these elements are related, Kim. There's a dynamic. I need to look at both parents. It's a complicated situation, and the ultimate goal is to give Nathan an optimal relationship with both of you. Obviously it's the father here who's the one having adjustment difficulties. So there's more to be addressed there, with Larry, than there is with you. You seem to be doing a wonderful job." He let Nathan down and ruffled his hair. "He's very well adjusted, gregarious, cheerful...I'm just trying to clarify some things, eliminate any concerns that your experience with Larry is going to negatively impact your attitude toward your son, or to visitation over the long run."

"Dr. Delaney, the proposals we've made to Larry...those are what Hal felt were ballpark. I've really let myself be guided by Hal on this stuff. I'm not on a vendetta. Everything we've offered has been reasonable."

He left. I plugged Nathan into a Disney sing-along video, sat back down, and put three cookies into my mouth, one after the other, whole.

Alison tapped on the slider. I motioned her in. "Take these away from me," I said, pushing the plate across the table.

"That bad?"

"Oh, I guess not. I probably got a few points off for not having the Periodic Table of the Elements tacked over the crib."

Nathan climbed up in my lap and tugged at my blouse.

"Thank you for not doing this while the doctor was here," I said, unbuttoning my bottom shirt buttons and hiking up my bra. The nursing bras had long since been disposed of. "That would have been one for the clipboard."

"You really don't like him, do you?"

"I must admit, I'm a little sour to be paying a PhD three thousand dollars to diagnose my ex-husband as stubborn."

"He's supposed to be the best in town."

"And I'm overprotective and have an anxiety disorder."

"Of course you're going to come out of this feeling judged, Kim. It's unavoidable. Don't let it get to you. Did he look in the fridge?"

"Yes."

"Told you." She nibbled at a cookie. "Listen, first of all, he's there to make a third party recommendation to the judge about the schedule, because Larry is being such a jerk, right?"

"Right."

"And we know that no matter what he says, Larry isn't going to like it, because it's coming from somebody else. It's not his own say-so."

I nodded again.

"So part of the doctor's job is documenting that you keep him clean and fed and dressed and don't lock him in the closet" —she held up her hand— "because, *just* because, if he *doesn't* do that, then the other side will attack his methods, thereby discrediting his opinion.

213

He has to cover all the bases. You should know this. It's just like the law. So don't worry about it. It's just word count."

IT WAS HALF past eight in the morning, early enough to open the slider to the outside air. I lay on the living room floor, feet crossed, listening to the birds. In an hour, I'd have to seal myself in and turn on the air-conditioning, but now, I could breathe. I'd never really gotten used to the timing of the seasons in Tulsa; each year, daffodils in February, high summer in May, came as a surprise. I stretched and opened my eyes. Sunlight spanked off the building opposite. Its paint was starting to peel. Riverview Gardens had been built five years ago; things weathered fast in Oklahoma.

The phone rang. I flinched. I knew who it would be: Lisa, Larry's former colleague.

"I understand now what you mean about Larry," she said, in the husky voice which was so unexpected paired with her baby-doll face. "He is the most incompetent person I've ever seen around a baby. I'm doing everything. It's almost like I can't leave the room. Nathan went out the back door and Larry didn't even know. He was like, 'I was reading.' I mean, I guess I just didn't notice it in January, when we had those visits in little chunks at your friend's apartment," she went on. "The only time he pays attention is when the doctor comes over to check."

I rolled onto my stomach, pulled over a copy of *Urban Tulsa,* and opened it at random: "Everything You Ever Wanted to Know about Azaleas, but were Afraid to Ask." I didn't want to hear what Lisa had to say, because I couldn't do anything about it. The court was in charge of my baby, and the court had given him to Larry for the weekend.

When I'd dropped Nathan off at Lisa's house in south Tulsa the previous morning, I saw Larry for the first time in a year. He looked handsome and perfect—more perfect than ever. Even his hair looked thicker and fuller. And it was clear that his training schedule hadn't suffered. He made a show of playing with Nathan on the lawn, rolling a ball back and forth to him and looking over at me as if waiting for the Good Housekeeping Seal of Approval. Nathan, of course, had no idea who he was. It had been four months since his first visit: light-years in baby time. Four months was how long it had taken Larry's new lawyer, Rhonda Shanks, to arm-wrestle him into agreement with supervision after he'd left in an insulted huff the last time. Actually, she'd never quite succeeded. She and Hal had agreed between them-selves, and when Larry's plane landed in Tulsa, they'd hauled him into court on an emergency basis to have the terms dictated over his objection: visits at Lisa's house, under Lisa's supervision, with daily checks by Dr. Delaney. Larry renamed this concept "facilitation" and found it palatable.

"...and he's rearranged all the furniture in my daughter's room and set it up like a study for himself and he's making long-distance calls on my phone all the time and I bought all these groceries and he hasn't made any contribution at all even though I told him money was tight this month."

I felt sorry for Lisa. She'd gotten a huge house and custody of the three kids in her own divorce, but she worked on commission, so cash flow was often problematic. "Lisa." I closed the magazine. "You'll have to be a little more direct than that."

Even then, it might not work. Didn't she know that already? I'd heard her complaints many times, even before he'd left. How he never reached for the check when they went out to lunch, how he changed the financial restructuring on a couple of her deals that really didn't need it, so he would look better. But I had to let her vent. I owed it to her. She was the one taking care of my son, she was the one keep-ing him safe. And I knew I could count on her. She was doing a beau-tiful job raising her children single-handedly, while working fulltime. Why she put up with Larry was more than I could guess. Larry was always using motherly, capable women. Suddenly I wondered: was that what I was?

"Where is he now?" I asked.

"He took him around the block in the stroller. I thought that was okay. That's okay, isn't it?"

"Just make sure you're around when he gets bored."

She laughed. I didn't. So she agreed with me! She understood.

215

That was nice, but so what? Every time someone confirmed reality, reality got more real. Reality kept laying me flat. By now I needed something more than sympathy, more than empathy; something different, something else. Resolution—that's what I needed. Legal resolution. Throwing my ring into Lake Michigan hadn't been enough. I needed a legal divorce as well. The institution of the law needed to stop standing upon the rights of abusers and pay some attention to— I'd never considered myself a victim. I refused to do that. I was in a bad situation, and I got out of it, that was all. But there were other women who were real victims, who couldn't afford the good lawyers. Dee knew them. Sulie knew them. What about them? What protection was there for us in a system that insisted on settlement, above all, and sometimes even required mediation? That did nothing but give an opportunity to manipulate the legal system for further abuse. Justice couldn't see the forest for the trees. If anyone was going to make Larry let go of his ring, it was going to have to be me, personally.

"You know, Kim," Lisa went on, "I really think you could influence him about things, getting through the divorce and everything, getting him to pay child support. He hangs on your every word."

"I don't believe it."

"No, really. He talks about you all the time. I think you really have some leverage here."

"Lisa! How can I work with someone who wants me to FedEx a baby across the country twice a month?"

She was on friendly terms with her ex-husband. Her road back to singledom had been quite different; she'd traveled through a different checkpoint to arrive at a place which was as good as another country to me, a place where people who were splitting up were reasonable, sensible, and civil. I wasn't sure if Lisa had a true grasp on the difficulties of my situation. On the other hand, she did know Larry pretty well. Maybe she was right. I decided to take her up on it. What did I have to lose? I'd have to do it tomorrow—Larry's last day.

~~~~

WHEN I SAW the rental car through the window the next morning, I was out the door with Nathan, locking it behind me. I'd done this each day; Larry's feet would not poison my walkway, nor his knuckles sully my door. I set Nathan down and stepped back.

"Hi, sport!" Larry said, with forced cheer.

Nathan gave him a blank stare.

Larry picked him up and glared at me. Then, just as suddenly, he smiled. "I brought the highchair I bought for Lisa's house," he said. "I thought it would make more sense for you to have it."

Well hell, yes. Why buy baby furniture and then leave it at someone else's house, especially someone whose own children are teenagers? You made me spend sixty-five hundred dollars just to get you served; if you think I'm going to say thank you for a highchair you've got another think coming. As Doug would say: "Fuck. In. A."

My silence disconcerted him, and he fumbled with the latch on the car seat. He seemed peeved that Nathan wasn't googooing all over him; of course, to state the obvious fact that Baby had no idea who Bio-dad was would insult an ego as mammoth as it was fragile.

I took a breath, licked my lips. Could I do this? Why not. He was an asshole. *Asshole,* I repeated silently, relishing the word. "I'm not coming to pick him up this afternoon before you leave," I began. "Lisa's going to run him home for me."

He palmed his head. "So I won't see you then."

"I'll say goodbye to him now," I said crisply.

He moved back two inches.

I didn't budge.

He heaved an ostentatious sigh and took a large step away.

I kissed Nathan goodbye and shut the door.

Larry took the highchair out of the trunk. "The tray snaps in under here," he said, demonstrating eagerly. "And this is how you take it apart again."

He tried to hand the pieces to me, and I flinched.

His upper lip curled. "When are you going to get over *that?*"

I pointed at the two-foot strip of grass between curb and buildings. "Put them over there."

He did as I asked and came back, shaking the car key in a loose-cupped palm. "Well?" he said.

I was sweating. *You can't touch me anymore.* I realized it was true. He hadn't. If Dr. Delaney was concerned about word count, so was I. I was going to give Larry some *real* word count.

"Thank you for the things," I heard myself say, "but I also want to share my feelings of resentment at having to thank you because I have spent thousands of dollars in support of this child since last May and I'm supposed to thank you for this piece of baby equipment which is really just a drop in the bucket?"

My voice was going up the scale. I paused to get it under control, and saw that he was taking it.

"So while I want to thank you for these things nicely, I can't help feeling resentful too." I was on the downslope now. "You are the closest thing to a deadbeat dad there is without actually *being* a deadbeat dad."

He recoiled. "I don't want to be a deadbeat dad." He turned and put a foot in the car, then swiveled back around and growled, "You shouldn't try to interfere in my relationship with my child either."

The meanie face looked so put on. I didn't know what it was, exactly. But I felt big. I was bigger than he was. I realized: for me it was all about Nathan, but for him it was all about competition.

"I don't want to hinder your relationship with Nathan, and you know it. I'm talking about your financial responsibility for him and your reprehensible behavior since the divorce began." The words tumbled out smoothly, without the stutter. I was tall, expanding beyond my normal outlines; I felt like the fifty-foot woman in the sci-fi movie Alison and I rented last week, the one who stalked down a California valley, ripping telephone poles out of her way, her measured, purposeful strides shaking the mountains. Except that in the movie, they had to make her dumb when she turned big, as though a woman who was both large and smart was too powerful and they had to handicap her somehow. But that was a movie. That was then. This was now. I was large and smart together. I didn't sound like me; I sounded assertive. I sounded like a lawyer.

218

"Child support is not dependent on whether I am nice to you or how much visitation you have. It's your duty regardless of anything else. So get your shit together and do the right thing."

His jaw dropped.

"And oh, yes. I am *not* moving to Seattle. So stop sending me those promotional materials," I said, and turned on my heel.

〜〜〜
〜〜〜

25

The Same River Twice

MORGAN AND I STOOD ON the 31st Street pedestrian bridge after an evening dancing at Club One. There was nothing I liked better than dancing with Morgan. In college I'd dreamed of a hieroglyph of numerals or musical notes that was moving, alive; I bolted upright and fumbled for a pen, and in the morning I found a scrap of paper on the floor: *those perfect and living figures.* At the time, I hadn't understood; the bridge was out, the signals jammed, the distance between head and heart to great to brook. I'd carried that slip of paper around in my wallet for years, aware of its importance, waiting for the moment of translation. Since I'd started dancing with Morgan, after the Bar exam, every Saturday night, it had become clear: the only perfection nature wants is balance, and only in that harmony are you fully alive. The dream had been a message I couldn't understand all those years ago, a warning I couldn't heed. If I had, then—how might things have been different?

Tonight, the air was humid, and the neon reflection of the electric company sign looked oily on the water. I don't know why he brought it up. Why did he have to bring it up? I suppose because he got a promotion.

"I got a promotion. I want to move into a bigger apartment." He was leaning over the railing, hands clasped, not looking at me. "I want us to move in together."

"I'm not going to stay in Tulsa," I blurted. "I'm moving to Oregon." It just came out.

He closed his eyes and smiled.

The handwriting analyst told me Morgan was my ideal mate. He'd been mildly enthusiastic about Forrest, and John, but when it came to Morgan he'd waxed rhapsodic. If there were no more to life than dancing, I might have danced away with Morgan forever. But I had a child now, and my world was forever altered. I had to make the decision on my own. I was the one who had to live with it.

There was another dream that had stayed with me for years. It was at the Lincoln Inn, near Springfield, Illinois, the town a former American poet laureate, Vachel Lindsay, dubbed the "city of his discontent," a phrase that had stuck with me.

The Lincoln Inn was a dark, old-fashioned, timbery building, like Elmwood, or the Cottonwood County Museum in Minnesota, or the lodge on the Mississippi where my friend had gotten married. I'd eaten there with my parents a couple times, on the way to Colorado on summer vacations in later years, when I was in college, and we'd begun charting our route along back roads, for a change of scenery.

In the dream I was having dinner with a group. The man I'd come with was tall and handsome, and artistic, but childish. At the end of the meal he jumped up and left the table without paying; I emptied my pockets dutifully and followed him out.

There was another man there, intelligent, earnest, who had been watching me intently. He came after me, and in the vestibule he looked at me and I understood the question. "I came with him, so I have to leave with him," I said, almost in apology. Silently, he took my hand and lifted it to his lips.

But now, in real life, I changed the ending. I'd learned that it was okay to admit a mistake, okay to change my mind. Courtney's checklist for the ideal husband had been short: rich, good-looking, and good in bed. Mine, I hoped, was a bit less shallow. Vachel Lindsay drank an entire bottle of Lysol in his kitchen one day in final despair over his inability to provide for his small family. I'd never come even remotely near such drastic measures. But neither was I about to suborn my own needs to my child's, however compelling that might be; that was the brand of thinking I'd been in the process of discarding ever since I'd been smacked in the head. I was making a choice for my *own* reasons.

You can have a relationship with a blithe spirit, but you can't build a life with one—Morgan was not interested in fatherhood. He enjoyed Nathan, but his attitude was more that of a fun uncle. John wanted to be a father to Nathan—he'd made that clear in a letter—but for that matter so did Forrest. I'd turned away from Forrest, though, and was reaching toward John, on the basis of a constellation of reasons entirely my own, underpinned by instinct, the instinct that we were simply right for each other. I was beginning to trust myself again since I'd gone back to Square One.

Standing with Morgan on the bridge, I realized I'd made a decision. It bore all the earmarks of my usual process: a combination of doubt and impulsivity; and an apparent abruptness; but for the very first time in my history I made a conscious, positive choice about what I did want, instead of simply rejecting what I didn't, as I had so many times before. Just as important, I placed my own needs first. And that is what freed me from the poison of time.

Without knowing it, Morgan and I had danced our last dance. I could see he realized it too. He put his arms around me for a long time. Then we walked off the bridge, and I never set foot on it again.

26

The Road to Tahlequah

PASSENGERS SPILLED OUT OF the baggage claim at the airport: men in cowboy hats with briefcases, older women in flowered dresses, younger ones in jeans and high heels, with lots of gold jewelry. Then John came through the door. He wore weatherbeaten hiking boots and an aluminum-frame backpack, and carried a suit bag in one hand. Even from a distance, I could see the visible reaction to the heat, the intake of breath and widened eyes. Then he turned his head and saw me. He looked different from memory: shorter, thinner, more muscular. Fourteen months was a long time. I went around the back and opened the trunk.

"Hi."

"Hi."

We stood there.

"Hold this a minute?" He handed me the suit bag. He slipped his arms out of the backpack, put it in the trunk, and then spread the suit carefully over it.

"Sure you don't want to hang that?" I asked, but he turned, slowly and deliberately, wrapped one arm around my waist, the other around my shoulders, and kissed me for the second time ever.

He opened his eyes. and took a deep breath. "Fourteen months," he said. "That's a long time."

"I was just thinking that. When I saw you."

We got in the car. Nathan greeted him with a burst of unintelligible enthusiasm.

"Wow," he said. "Fourteen months *is* a long time."

"Walkin' and talkin'." I pulled away from the curb.

He buckled his seat belt and rubbed his knees. "So. How are things?"

"We're waiting for Dr. Delaney to finish his evaluation. Then we use that as a basis to negotiate the visitation." I flipped the rear-view mirror down. Nathan was dithering happily with his play tray, turning knobs and honking the horn to "Brown-Eyed Handsome Man." "That's the only sticking point—visitation. There's nothing else, I mean, no joint property, no alimony, no custody issue. Once we negotiate that, then we set a court date. The docket's pretty backed up."

"Dockets are always backed up. Why are we listening to country music?"

"Nathan likes it."

"Geographical hazard, I guess."

THE NEXT DAY we took the road to Tahlequah, just the two of us. I'd driven across Taylor Reservoir so many times without stopping, and John wanted to go out into the country, so we bought picnic materials at Bigelow's and got on the Broken Arrow.

At the deserted reservoir we spread a blanket beneath a scrub oak. "I'd forgotten this about Tulsa," John said, using his pocket knife to spread chicken salad on a piece of Kaiser roll.

"What?"

"How they put olives in everything." He aimed the knife at the thick rime of mud at the shoreline. "Look how low the water level is right now."

"I was just thinking about all the times I drove this road going for acupuncture when I was pregnant. I was so depressed and never even realized it. Sometimes I got this urge to drive the car off the road. I thought it was just hormones."

"Probably was."

"I feel different now." I turned to him. "Do I seem different?"

"No." He forked potato salad into his mouth. "There's this lake in central Oregon. Waldo Lake. It's the third purest lake in the world. When you come out we can go there. It can't be much longer now. A couple months?"

I looked out at the reservoir. It really wasn't a very attractive recreational destination. A few sailboats were valiantly making a go of it.

"The last opera this year was Bernstein's *Candide*," I said. "At the end, they sing this final chorus, it's so beautiful. And I thought of you. 'We'll build our house, and make our garden grow.' I thought of you, because you talked about wanting a big garden. I wished you were there."

"And now I am," said John. "I always used to wonder what it would be like to do this with you, or that with you, like normal people, on a date. And now we're doing it."

"I hope I'm living up to your expectations."

"You bet, baby," he joked.

He had a cleft in his chin—I remembered that. And his eyes lit up when he smiled. I'd noticed that at our first editorial board meeting. He came in late, and there were no chairs left, so he sat down on top of a desk in the corner, looked at me with those bright eyes, and smiled. At the time, all my energy was still focused on staying upright and not throwing up, but I remembered thinking, *Who is that? How come I don't know him?*

"*Candide* is actually from the book by Voltaire," I said. The characters go through these ridiculous travails, and there's one, Doctor Pangloss, he's always running around saying 'We live in the best of all possible worlds,' as all these horrible things keep happening. It's a satire on Leibniz."

He brushed crumbs off his pants. "I never took philosophy."

"Well, I never took econ."

"We're even then."

He nodded. We lay on our backs, looking up at the scrub oak. Sawgrass poked through the blanket. The air was thick and dusty.

"So anyways, one of Leibniz's fundamental principles was the Principle of the Best. God created the world, and since God is of necessity perfectly wise, powerful, and good, he had to have chosen the best of all possible worlds to create. So—we live in the best of all possible worlds."

He crossed his ankles and put his arm around my shoulders. "I find that a little hard to believe."

"But I have to believe that. Because of Nathan. Everything that happened to me, I can't regret, because good things came out of it too. I've been married before. I can't wish it away, because then Nathan wouldn't be here. I can take care of myself, but Nathan can't. I'm the only one he can rely on."

"I told you before, in the letter I wrote, remember? This is a package deal." He frowned impatiently. "Look at me."

I brought my eyes to his.

"This is a package deal and I know it. The past is the past. The future is ours. I want to be Nathan's father."

I touched his hand on my shoulder, and remembered what Karen had said the night before her wedding: *With him, I feel at home.* In a way, I didn't know him as well as I knew Forrest; in another way, I knew him better.

We packed up the picnic remains and put them in the trunk, next to his luggage. We were going straight to the airport. On the way back, we passed the Indian Lodge Motel again. John pulled over. We turned around and looked at the totem pole.

"'Refrigerated Air,'" he said. "Not to knock your living room floor, but it would be nice to be on a real bed, for once."

We turned the car around.

When he came back from the motel office he stuck his head in the window and grinned. "There's a sign in there that says, 'No Game in Room.'"

"My God. People would *do* that?"

"Apparently."

"Welcome to Oklahoma."

The room was stiflingly hot, tinged with sickly air freshener and cigarette smoke. "Let's get some refrigerated air going," said John, flipping on the unit below the window and closing the curtains.

"Sounds like six cylinders without a muffler," I remarked.

He tucked my hair back and kissed my neck. "Guess we don't have to worry about making too much noise."

"No game in room," I reminded him. In answer, he walked me backwards toward the bed, laying me down and unbuttoning any and all buttons within reach, all without removing his mouth from mine.

"Let's get rid of this," he said finally, pulling the bedspread out from beneath us.

"I was just thinking the same thing. It's kind of slippery."

He pulled the rest of the bedding off. "I want to see every beautiful inch of you."

Afterward, the room seemed damp and chilly. I turned the air conditioner down and pulled the blanket off the floor. We sat up against the knotty pine headboard. I took hold of his wrist and put his palm to my cheek, then turned it over. The back of his hand still smelled faintly of juniper. He'd brought along juniper berries from the slopes of Mt. Hood for me in the pocket of his jacket the day before.

"It *is* strange," he said, "coming back. It all seems so different, but it's only been a year."

"Different how?"

"I don't know. Really hot. Dry. Quiet. I mean, deadsville. Kind of hick. Nothing going on. I didn't feel that way at all while I lived here."

"Oh. Different that way."

"Portland's really great," he said enthusiastically. "There's so much going on there. You're going to love it."

I got up, went into the bathroom, closed the door, and drank a glass of water, slowly. Then I went back and sat on the edge of the bed.

"You okay?" he asked.

I toyed with the pull-chain on the bedside lamp. The shade looked like fringed burlap, but it couldn't have been. Too flammable. "A while ago," I said, "I told myself…I wasn't going to sleep with anyone again unless I was going to marry him."

"Don't tell me I haven't made my intentions clear," he laughed.

"No, it's not that."

227

He threw the blanket back and swung his feet to the floor. "Kim, we don't have to have this conversation. I've never wavered in my feelings toward you and nothing you could say would change them one iota—"

"No, you have to let me talk. Because that's you. And I couldn't marry you without telling you."

"What?" His voice was dull. "Tell me what? You don't need... listen, I've dated too, I've told you, I've dated other women since I moved to Oregon—"

"I had a miscarriage. It was a big mistake," I rushed on, "he was a nice guy, I mean, it wasn't just somebody I picked up or anything, we were dating some, but we had an accident, and it was the right time. The wrong time. It was a big mistake."

He was silent for a moment. "I'm so sorry you had to go through that."

Side by side we contemplated the fuzzy plaid window curtain. It didn't close all the way. Sunlight needled through the gap, thick with dust motes.

"Did you, were you going to marry this guy?"

"No." Out there, on the other side of the curtain, the world was hot as a frying pan. I shivered and pulled the blanket around my shoulders. "Actually, I had sex with a couple other guys, too," I said miserably.

He wouldn't meet my eye. "So, you weren't going to marry him? Then—you were going to have the baby?"

"No. Ah, well, I don't know."

"You were going to have an abortion."

How well did I know this man, really? I knew he never missed weekly Mass all through law school, even during finals. Courtney had told me.

"I think it failed because the hormone level was so low, I wasn't even sick. But," I gripped my knees, "I might have gone through with it. I would have. Yes."

He palmed his head. "Okay." He looked around the room. "I told you I didn't want to hear about it. I don't want to hear about it. I don't need to know."

228

"I couldn't...I wasn't serious about this person. We were going out, but, I mean, I didn't want to marry him. I mean, the condom broke. It was a big mistake."

He wouldn't meet my eye.

"I didn't want to marry him!" I wailed.

He got up and reached for his pants. "This is hard, okay? I never— I just have to process this."

"I feel just as guilty about the miscarriage. That maybe that little kernel of a person knew I didn't want it and died. I don't know which I feel worse about."

He looked around for his shirt. "It's not that. I mean, I'm sorry about that. But I said I'd been *dating*. Not sleeping around. I mean," he cried, "I've been waiting to see you for a *year!*" He started buttoning. "All of a sudden," he said, quietly. "I guess, you know, I thought you were Miss Perfect."

I pulled on my underwear, keeping myself from bursting into tears only through immense effort of will. Fourteen months ago, he'd left Tulsa, and he'd kissed me then, and for the first time ever I'd been possessed by the fierce desire to belong to one particular man and spend the rest of my life with him. I'd pushed it aside, in shock, then disbelief, then, for a long time, distrust, and finally, bitterness: it was too late; I'd already ruined my life and the life of the child I'd just brought into the world; I was trapped in failure while he was bounding off to success.

And all the time, he'd thought I was Miss Perfect! It hadn't been too late then, but it was now. I'd had to tell the truth, and in that moment—only that moment—I'd gone all the way back to Square One. I really was starting over now, without anything, even hope. The road to Tahlequah had finally done me in. We left the key in the room, and drove back to the airport in silence.

≈
≈

229

27

The Best of All Possible Worlds

I AWOKE WITH THE TASTE OF failure in my mouth. I'd been dreaming of a bridge of sound, had been trying, unsuccessfully, to build it. I pulled the curtain aside. Elmwood's dock lay on the bluff like the discarded toy of a giant. The sun broke through the clouds and the last patches on the big oak flared red and orange. The canoes padlocked to its trunk were gone, moved to the barn. We were at Elmwood out of season, in early November, having one last weekend, by special dispensation, because our parents—Barbara and Will and Thea and Carl, who lived in California—had sold Elmwood. "We" was Karen and Doug and I, and our cousins Jim and Chas. Uncle Carl's kids were on both coasts, and couldn't make it; Thea's children were only in high school, so they weren't invited.

I checked on the boys. They were sleeping deeply in the crib, stuffed animals strategically positioned between them. Nathan was drooling on the sheet; he was teething again. Karen's baby, Sam, also known as The Spud, was hunkered in a corner. I hung over the railing and watched him: diapered bottom in the air, tiny fists tucked in, cheek smushed against the mattress, rosebud lips sucking intermittently as he dreamed. He was five months old, the same age as Nathan when I tucked him in the sling for my walks to Lake Michigan that first summer, his first summer. Now Nathan wore real pajamas and slept like a child: flat, arms and legs splayed out. It was early

November; he was going on two.

Dr. Delaney's completed study had been a total failure as a vehicle of leverage for settlement. This had only made all the more transparent Larry's dedication to delay for delay's sake, but that did nothing to alleviate my despair. The past wasn't the problem now. It was the future: I couldn't get there. I was working at Prentice Schroeder—I'd caved, giving up on the solo route, and signed on as an associate there. I was taking mother and tot swim lessons with Nathan, and playing chess with Max, but I was still trapped in the place where all roads led to the Arkansas. The abuse continued, I had not escaped, the promised lifeboats were not coming. Almost two years had gone by, and I was still stranded in Tulsa.

In the kitchen, Karen and Cassie were unpacking far more shopping bags than I could have imagined possible in the time they'd been gone, especially in rural Wisconsin. Motherhood had done nothing to dull Karen's enthusiasm for shopping; if anything, it had enhanced it.

"Baby still sleeping?" she asked.

"Yes. I just checked on them, he's fine." I poked around. "What'd you get?"

"We stopped at the mall," Karen said. "It was close to the grocery store, I wasn't sure I'd brought up enough receiving blankets...are you sure I shouldn't go check on him?"

"He's fine," I assured her. "Let sleeping babies lie."

"So I got another package, you know they usually come in packages of four, I know he's getting a little big for receiving blankets but they're very useful, and they also had some cute onesies with short arms and long legs, those ones are hard to find."

Jim came in and opened the beer refrigerator. "What's a onesie?"

"You'll find out one of these days," I said darkly.

"What do you mean?" He turned around in alarm.

"Kim. They've only been dating since August," said Cassie.

"I know. I was speaking in general terms. By the way, what's her name again?"

Jim popped a can. "Be nice to her. I like her."

"So do we, Jim. What's her name?"

"Hilary," said Karen.

"Oh yes, Hilary. Where is she anyway?"

"She went on a walk," said Jim. "She's a little ticked because the canoes are put away. I told her we could go canoeing. I forgot."

"You know Uncle Will," Karen said, as Jim pawed through the grocery bags. "October first, hell or high water."

Jim pulled out a bag of chips. "Ohmigod. Soy and flax seed? Doug's going to freak. I'm not taking these in there."

I watched Karen rip plastic off the baby clothes and stow them in the vinyl diaper bag from the hospital, the ones distributed by formula makers with one-pound cans of product inside.

"They ought to give those bags away with coffee samples instead," I commented. "That would be something useful for new mothers."

Doug barreled in. "What's this about the chipsters? What the hey?"

Cassie smiled and continued folding grocery bags.

"Where are my fluorescent tortilla chips? You know I can't eat healthy food! My system wouldn't be able take it! What are flax seeds anyway? Are they even edible?"

"They're good for you," said Karen. She took the bag from him, opened it, and held a chip in front of his mouth.

"I like them," Frank called from the dining room.

Doug swallowed the chip.

"That's my boy," said Karen.

"Which one?" I asked, setting down my mug.

"Don't put that on my laptop," Doug said. He tucked his computer under his arm, swiped the bag from Karen, and left.

"Score," said Cassie.

"If you're going to eat junk food," said Karen, "you may as well eat healthy junk food."

Frank called again. "Kids are up!"

We fetched them down. Karen sat at the foot of the table and nursed baby Sam under a blanket. I put Nathan in the playpen and joined the game. "What are we playing?"

"Five-card stud," said Frank, shuffling.

"Where'd you find that eyeshade?"

"In the barn. We went to look at the canoes." He shot a glance at Jim, and started dealing. "Too much trouble."

"She might be worth it."

"What's her name again?"

"Hilary," said Jim. "Her name is Hilary."

"Remember the time we found that waffle iron in the barn?" Doug asked, sorting his hand.

"And it still had one of Grandma's waffles in it," said Chas.

"And we played waffle frisbee," said Jim, throwing in some chips.

"Until it landed in the lake," Doug finished.

"What does Hilary do?" Frank asked.

"She's a stockbroker—whoops!" Chas put two fingers to his mouth. "That was the last one."

Jim gave a sigh of long-suffering patience. "She's an accountant at KPMG."

"That would be good," said Frank. "This could become a very useful family to marry into. A pediatrician, a lawyer, an architect, an accountant..."

"All we need now is a midwife and a mortician," I said.

We all looked at Chas.

"Neither of those appeals, I'm afraid. I'll see you and raise you one. Can we change the subject? Like, when's your court date?"

"Don't have one yet." I tapped my hand together and spread it out again.

"How can you *not* have a court date yet?"

"We're waiting."

"Waiting for what?"

"Just waiting."

"That's what lawyers get paid for," Doug said.

A sock monkey hit him on the elbow. He tossed it back into the playpen. "Reload!" he called. To me he said, "Good thing you've only got soft toys in there."

"Hey! I'm a trained professional."

"So how come you're not raking it in then?" Jim asked.

"Can you burp him please?" Karen handed Sam the Spud to Frank.

I looked up. "Oh. I thought you meant Jim."

"Jim never needs any help with that," his brother said.

Frank laid Sam over his shoulder like a beanbag and continued playing.

"Is Max coming up?" Cassie asked.

"Maybe. He's a seat-of-the-pants kind of guy. If his car is working, he'll come."

"He really moving to Chicago?" Jim asked.

"So he says."

"Can you waive in to Illinois?"

"Not for five years. I'd have to retake the Illinois Bar."

"Too bad if he doesn't make it," said Cassie. "It's the last chance."

I looked through the dining room's glassed-in double doors. Hilary was out there, strolling along the row of cedars on the driveway, talking on her cell phone.

Frank said, "You'll have to take him on the bus tour downtown. The Al Capone tourist bus tour. It's a must-do for Germans, I discovered last year when we hosted that brass quintet from Cologne."

"You know, I don't think a flaky artist is on the preferred occupation list, sis," said Doug. He put down his hand and started rolling up his sleeves.

"And what are you then?" I picked up the sock monkey again.

"An architect."

"Every architect is a flaky artist in disguise."

He ignored me.

The cedars had been planted years ago for the five children of the farm implements magnate who had built this summer home on lake-dotted farmland that, almost a century later, was practically suburban Milwaukee. What were their names? One of them had come out for a last visit, during that first, legendary Summer of Cleaning—the house had been closed up for years. To me at age ten he'd seemed ancient of days—bent over, walking slowly with a cane. He had a nurse with him. What had happened that they'd all sold the place? Had everyone moved away? Had their own offspring lost interest?

Hilary had moved past the cedars and was disappearing behind the oaks that framed the tennis court. It looked like a long phone call; she was going all the way around the drive.

"She has a cell phone," I said.

"Who's that important?" said Doug, picking up his hand again. "I mean, who wants to be available all the time?"

"Don't look at me," I said. "I even turn the ringer off on my regular phone."

"If this Hilary chick is an accountant," Doug said to Jim, "I wish she'd been around when we were trying to brainstorm creative financing to take this place over ourselves."

Karen took the baby off Frank's shoulder, where he had been peacefully observing the back of Frank's chair. "You know we can't do it, Doug. We've been over it a million times. There's way too much lakefront. The taxes are too high."

"I guess it's just the year for selling houses," Chas said. "I'll see you and raise you one."

After we'd downsized my mother into the condo, right before the house in Hubbard Woods had closed, I'd taken Nathan for a walk around the block one last time, ending in front of the oak tree Dad planted on the parkway years ago, after Dutch Elm disease had denuded the neighborhood. I had a photograph of him: slender, in khakis and fedora, cigarette dangling from his lip, he shoveled dirt around a sapling that came up to his waist. With Nathan's hand in one of my own and his little plastic wheelbarrow in the other, I stood that day under the arching branches of that tree, one more wearying reminder that now I was an adult.

Doug took a card. "I still think we should have become a nonprofit. Filed as a 501(c)(3) corporation."

"I don't think offering one-week vacations to unemployed musicians would have flown with the IRS, Doug," Chas said.

"It only has to be for a couple weeks in the year, doesn't it?"

"Like about twelve," I said. I took a handful of peanuts. "The whole summer."

"Well," he replied, "the advantage to the unemployed musician thing was that it would be all Karen's and Frank's friends."

He looked up.

"Okay, whatever. Just don't blame me. I was the man with the plan, you didn't listen, and now there're going to be a lot of fat paper-mill executives from Minnesota running around here in their bathing trunks."

"We won't see it," said Jim. "We won't be around. I'm out."

Chas raked in the chips.

Last night in my dreams my grandmother had been walking me from the house to the edge of the yard with her arm around my waist, telling me about everything that mattered. Her hands were raw, her knuckles swollen, but her hair was still like cornsilk, in a braid around her head. Bobbie had worn her hair like that sometimes, when I was very young; she'd cut it short after Doug was born.

The yard was full of fallen leaves that we scuffled underfoot as we walked toward the gate. They had profound meaning for my grandmother, something about the changing of the seasons, which she communicated to me almost without words. She gave me a photo album of my own family. I paged through it with immense satisfaction. There were so many pictures! She let me take out the ones I really wanted to keep.

It was unusual for her to be up north this late in the Fall. She was a snowbird, and usually, by this time, she'd already left for her winter home in Florida. But an unusual cold snap down there had delayed her departure. In the dream we were together again, two women walking with their arms around each other's waists. She guided me across the yard, through the autumn leaves, to the edge of the property, to the gate and its bordering shrubbery. She was going to show me something of importance hidden in them, something that would enable me to go beyond the evergreens, but before she did that, I woke up.

Frank dealt out another hand.

"Remember the tree Dad planted?" I said.

Karen and Doug nodded. "The one by the driveway."

"That's the picture I get in my head now, every time I think of

Dad. Because right before he died, I mean *right* before he died, I dreamt there was a big wind in the night and a tree came down in the back yard, and I went out and saw it and I heard him say, 'Only the limbs that are already weak come down in a storm.'"

It was silent around the table. Karen put her nose in Sam's hair and rocked him back and forth.

"501(c)(3)," muttered Doug, shaking his head.

"Oh Doug," I burst out, "You just have to—you have to keep the things that matter and let go of the things that don't!"

"It matters," he said vehemently. "It *matters.*"

The game was finished. We sat holding the cards, carrying the heavy weight of taciturn ancestors on our shoulders. From them we'd learned to freight inanimate objects with unspeakable emotion. Perhaps they distrusted words, since they seemed to communicate the most, and most confidently, without them: my father, planting a tree, building a campfire; my mother, washing my hair, pulling weeds; my grandmother, putting her arm around my waist as she walked me to the gate. But every so often, this silent music of the hands was punctuated by actual utterances so eloquent, so profound and poetic, they made you gasp, if you were quick enough to hear, old enough to listen, wise enough to store. The older generation had sold the house, but now we were taking their place, and it all depended on us.

Outside the window, Hilary reappeared from behind the screen of shrubs and oaks, circling briskly toward the house, arms swinging. Her call was done. Nathan threw the sock monkey at the Tiffany lamp.

Jim steadied it with an index finger. "Careful, bud," he said. "That's a fixture. Goes with the house."

～～
～～

28

Six Hundred Forty Two Days

"COME WITH ME."

Hal led me into a tiny, airless conference room on the third floor of the Tulsa County Courthouse. I sat down obediently.

"Apparently he filed this yesterday afternoon."

I looked down at the papers in my hand. *Motion for Joint Custody*. It was the first of March. Six hundred forty two days after I'd filed for divorce. "Physical custody, he means?"

Hal nodded.

"But we live fifteen hundred miles apart!"

"Don't worry about it. The judge isn't even going to address it." He pulled out a chair and sat down. "I'm going to have a talk with Rhonda now and see if we can work anything out."

"You mean try to settle? After two years?" Wasn't it obvious by now to all concerned that the word "settlement" was not in Larry's vocabulary?

"This is the process. This is the way it's done. The judge asks everyone to do this."

He disappeared.

I sat on the edge of my seat in the empty room, elbows on the table, hands clasped; tense, anxious, powerless. I'd thought we were going to sit in the courtroom, the judge would look over the papers, and then lay it out. Custody. Child support. Visitation. End of story.

Now there'd be another postponement. We'd have to be reset on the docket! It would take months to get the two-day slot required!

I sat. And waited. I wished there were a window in the room. Hal had closed the door behind him, so I didn't feel I could open it. I made a mental grocery list, which didn't take very long. I inventoried Nathan's toys. What was he doing right now? Would he be playing with the terrycloth cars? Or would they be taking a walk? Loretta had brought him an old toddler trike, and he loved to wheel it around the paths of Riverview Gardens.

I wondered what the weather was like outside. It was early March, but still cold. It had been the harshest winter in Tulsa in years. And the longest. Not a single crocus had bloomed yet. When I took Nathan out, we wore hats and mittens against the brisk wind that raked through Riverparks, rattling the cottonwoods on the bank. Pushing the baby jogger against the wind was a challenge, now that Nathan weighed almost thirty pounds. He brandished toys and crackers cheerily at all we passed. Everyone smiled at him. He got a lot of attention; he always had. When he was tiny, the smiles of passersby had reminded me that the birth of a child was a happy occasion. I'd needed that reminder. That was one reason I'd persisted in my walks, despite the opposition Larry had put up to my going out alone.

The day before Easter he was insistent. He was going with me. *All right, all right!* I said. *If it's that important.* But once there, he sat on a bench and read a book while I took my hike with the baby. I thought that was silly. Not to mention insulting. So the next day, I turned him down. I reminded him of the Bargain: I got to take a walk alone every day.

I'm leaving after I nurse the baby, I said, and took Nathan into the bedroom.

I told you, I'm coming with you.

No, I said firmly, closing the door. I settled the baby on my breast.

There was a moment of quiet. Then my head snapped up. I felt the force of his rage like a tidal surge a moment before he bowled through the door. I had no time to cover—my arms were open, my face uplifted—and I couldn't cover myself mentally, either, because it happened so fast: I couldn't cut myself in two, as I did with the sex abuse. That's why it was worse. I had no time to cut myself in two, so I felt my arms cradling a tiny soft baby, and the force of his blow to my face, at the same time. Luckily the blow fell on me, or it really might have been true that he'd ruined my life. But the blow fell on me. Nevertheless, I was afraid I'd scarred my son, because I'd stayed, and, by staying, allowed him to be marred—invisibly damaged in ways that might not heal, that may yet rive his future. We might both, perhaps, have been poisoned by time.

Dana edged into the room wearing a vintage mink jacket set, a hand-me-down from Gareth's wife. It hardly ever got cold enough in Tulsa for fur and Dana was taking advantage of it. "What's going on?" she asked, adjusting the hat with a manicured-for-the-occasion hand.

"I don't know. I guess we're making one last good-faith effort to settle. He told me to stay here."

She smoothed my brow with her fingers. "Remember, the champagne's on ice."

"How's Mom?"

"Hanging in there. We're keeping her amused." "We" included her sister Trish, who had scheduled a visit around my court date. I was grateful for that because Karen was pregnant again and couldn't travel.

Hal returned.

"Well, I guess I'll go back and keep praying," Dana said, and skedaddled.

Hal ferried back and forth, hammering out the details, assessing for me what the judge would do, laying out the alternatives, what our best shot was.

"Fine, Hal. Whatever you think," I said earnestly each time, as two years of finely-crafted legal work was sledgehammered beyond recognition. What if we couldn't settle? *I want to be divorced,* I thought. *Today.* Imprisoned in that tiny, airless room by a man who was still—unbelievably! to this very day—my legal husband, I thought, for the first time: if only I could trade my horrible experience for another that might be more understandable. I couldn't go backwards, I could only go forwards, but if only the awful thing in my past could have been something different, say, getting beaten up and raped by a total stranger. Then I could explain it: I was simply in the wrong place at the wrong time. But this! How could evil be so familiar, how could I have looked straight at that face for years, and missed a side? How could I ever have felt I had anything in common with this person who had gone bad like a piece of rotten fruit, and kept getting worse and worse?

And: how could anyone possibly *ever* persuade him to come to reasonable agreement?

Kant believed that all people are fundamentally alike. Thus, all other things being equal, we can come to universal agreement. He called this the Categorical Imperative. In college, I was delighted to discover the Categorical Imperative, an appealing blend of the optimistic and the pragmatic. I especially liked the way it made goodness a given. But that was before life kicked in. All other things never *are* equal! The universe of human relations is mired with complexities both internal and external that take forever to sort out, that hamper not just our progress with others but our ability to see ourselves. "All other things being equal." I kept getting hung up on that phrase. All other things never had been equal between Larry and me. We'd never gotten to that point, that common ground. The whole time I'd thought we were approaching it—that magic moment when we would take the "under construction" sign off our marriage—Larry had been consciously and purposely skirting it.

Suddenly I realized: "All other things being equal" was a hypothetical phrase.

I imagined myself back in eighteenth-century Königsberg, and found Kant sitting in the corner of a tavern. I slid in across from him. *Immanuel! Get your head out of your ass.*

He looked up from his lonely bachelor's dinner and frowned. *There's no need for language like that.*

But you're living in the world of the hypothetical!

He sighed, and pushed his spectacles up on his nose. *Kim, we need the hypothetical. We need to be able to envision a set of circumstances other than the one we're in at any given moment.*

241

I was pretty good at doing that, and that's what trapped me.

No, Kim, think about it. Without *the hypothetical we'd be trapped. It's the only way we have to generate action out of theory. It's a kick-starter. I'm talking about aspirations.*

Sounds like you're an idealist.

I'm not talking about the best of all possible worlds. You have to work with the real, but envision the ideal. Without philosophy, we have no hope. And without hope, we're not human. Philosophy isn't life, Kim, it's a guide for life. You're supposed to have a foot in both worlds.

I know, I know, I had both feet in the life of the mind, and then I jumped headfirst into the life of the body, and boy was that a mistake.

He smiled down at the bit of roasted potato on his fork.

I said, *Now you're going to talk about the balance thing.*

Yes, the balance thing. Don't worry, I won't start talking like Dee.

Good, because I'm getting a little tired of this message. I get it everywhere.

I have a feeling life is going to keep hitting you over the head with it until you start paying attention.

Ouch!

Sorry. He took a sip of beer and wiped his mustache.

That's okay. But I am paying attention. I really am! But now I'm in the middle of this, and I don't know what to do. And I can be aspirational all over the place, but I can't accomplish anything on my own. I leaned forward to make my point. *You have to understand about Larry: other people have no meaning for him. Dialogue is nothing for him but a means to an end: material gratification. He doesn't want to interact, deal with issues and come to agreement. He just wants things: cars, degrees, electronic toys..."*

He raised an eyebrow.

All I'm saying is: he has not the remotest interest in relationships. Academics is just a cover for him. If he reads books he doesn't have to talk to people. How can I reach agreement about how to raise our child for the next sixteen years with someone who is socially and morally autistic?

He pushed his plate aside and leaned forward. *I know it's difficult,* he said, *but you have to try.*

I wiped away a tear.

Kim, he said gently. *Kim. You're doing well. You're doing a good job.*

Thank you, I whispered.

Keep going. Don't forget—collective bedrock exists. It has to! he exclaimed, suddenly fervent. *It's out there. I know. You have to believe that. It's like the road to Tahlequah—you can take it in any direction. Take it in mine. You already are.* He took my hand. *You already are. Because you recognized the necessity. The spiritual imperative.*

I stood up and started walking back and forth. If collective bedrock exists, and we're all fundamentally alike, and fundamentally good, then bad people are not bad at all, just weak. Potential fatherhood, and fatherhood itself, were adversity for Larry. If he'd addressed the problems that made normal daily life difficult for him, he could have tapped into that fundamental goodness. He had that chance with me. But it required conscious effort. It required a willingness to abandon the hypothetical—the world of the perfectly sharpened pencil, the perfectly new car, the perfectly toned body—and deal with the actual, with reality.

Larry had trouble making decisions. That was something we had in common, but not the best kind of commonality on which to found a marriage. He waffled back and forth between business and school; he'd had live-in relationships with two other women before me, and despite his initial enthusiasm as a newlywed, I realized when I looked back on it that he'd had trouble arriving at the decision to move from cohabitation to marriage. And then there was the pregnancy.

We can have a baby if you do all the work and we split the expense.

And later: *You told me it wouldn't change anything!*

It was a kind of fear, an immaturity, that stemmed from different causes but which we shared. But Larry—he hadn't climbed over the wall, he hadn't come in from the cold. He hadn't even tried. Adversity tested Larry, and he flunked. I was sorry he was weak, but it wasn't my problem. His soul was no longer my concern. What was my concern was that he never, ever touch me again, and that whatever kind of relationship he developed with Nathan remained decent and healthy.

I grasped the back of the chair with two hands. Kant was right. *Envision the ideal, work with the real.* The difficulty I faced was not admitting that Larry was evil; I could do that now. The difficulty was steeling myself to interact with him on the basis of the evil, because it was that aspect of him that had had practical effects for me and my child in the real world over the last two years and would for the next sixteen. It was that aspect I had to deal with. And I would. I understood now what Kant had meant when he'd said I was already on the road, and I was taking it in the right direction. The main difference between Larry and me was that I was strong and brave, and he was not.

Hal came back in. "What are you doing?"

"Nothing."I sat down. "Struggling with the Categorical Imperative."

"Listen, I know this is stressful, but just hang on. Once we walk into the courtroom it's easy." He perched on the table. "This is what we've come down to. Sole custody, two hundred a month, half of all medical, Dad pays his own travel expenses. We can't get him to agree on visitation so we'll continue it as it is—four nights a month in Tulsa, with reevaluation by the psychologist in September."

"September! You mean I have to come *back* here in six months and do this again? There's not going to be any difference in six months."

"I know. But we can't budge him."

"Why can't we go to court on just that issue alone, and have the doctor give his recommendations? We spent all that time and money on the evaluation."

"But it didn't lead to a settlement. That's usually what happens. Kim, you just want to avoid putting anything before the judge if you can. She's an unknown quantity—although we know she favors fathers—and this is an unusual situation, a two year old with parents on different sides of the country. We could put Dr. Delaney on the stand, but the decision would be Judge Dodd's alone, and we'd be stuck with it forever. I can't let you do that."

"Couldn't we appeal it if it was a bad visitation plan?"

He shook his head. "You know that. The only basis for an appeal is abuse of discretion. We just can't risk it. The judge doesn't have much of a track record yet. We don't know how she feels about psychologists in general, we don't know how she feels about Dr. Delaney. If the living situation were more standard..."

I looked down to control my tears. This was the deal I'd waited two years for?

"I'm a little uneasy with the psychologist's report this time," Hal said reluctantly. "It's pretty general. There doesn't seem to be anything to hang your hat on. For either side, actually. At this point I can't...no. I won't let you risk it."

"Okay," I whispered.

"So, four nights a month with reevaluation by Delaney in September. It's the only way we can get him to sign. When we finalize the decree we'll word it 'through the end of the year.' Rhonda agrees to that. We just can't think of any other way."

If he and Rhonda couldn't persuade Larry, nobody could. December. Better than September. "Okay, let's do it." I was the Good Client. I was realistic. I was a good girl. And I had not a single mote of energy left for one more month, one more week, one more hour.

We moved into the courtroom. Larry was unloading not one but two briefcases onto the counsel table. He'd gone for the friendly, harmless, college-educated but nevertheless genuinely financially impoverished look: blue shirt, sweater vest, old tie. Rhonda (lawyer number three) had probably chosen his clothes. She sat next to him, looking hot and bothered. Over on our side, Hal tilted back in his chair, legs crossed, elegant in his custom-tailored suit, twirling his pencil around on a tabletop entirely clear but for a yellow legal pad.

Larry crowned his stack with a videotape and sat down. Seeing that Hal and Rhonda had pads and pens in front of them, he got one out too, and squared it up. He tried to greet Bobbie in the front row of the gallery, but she wouldn't look at him. Dana and Trish, on either side, both gave him the evil eye. In the second row sat Dr. Delaney, smiling encouragement at me at two hundred dollars an hour (courtroom rate).

A tiny brunette in a voluminous robe entered the room. This was Judge Dodd. We stood, then sat, were in turn sworn in without having to leave our seats, and stated our names, affirmed the recital of the agreement. Yes, we were married on such and such at such and such, yes, there was one child of the marriage, yes, this was our agreement, yes, we were aware that we could have a full trial on the merits of the case but chose to make this agreement. Yes, yes, yes. The judge looked up at us periodically over the rims of her reading glasses, like a teacher keeping a sharp eye on the class while grading papers.

Hal called Dr. Delaney to the witness stand. For him, the judge removed her glasses and folded her hands attentively. Yes, he had been involved in this case, the mother had always been highly cooperative, the father seemed interested in the child and had come a long way in his parenting skills, and yes, he was willing to continue to monitor the visitation and make further recommendations to this court. He returned to his seat.

Done! I looked over at my mother, who smiled back.

Rhonda stood up and shot her cuffs. "Your honor, my client would like to make a statement to the court."

The judge looked over at us.

Hal waited two beats, then rose halfway and drawled, "Your honor, for the benefit of the record, although the plaintiff finds this request somewhat unusual, she has no objection at this time."

Larry stood up. "Thank you, Your Honor. First of all I want to thank you for allowing me to address the court, because I'm a lawyer myself and I know judges are busy and dockets are full. But a divorce is a major event in the life of the parties involved, it's a big decision, it creates a lot of changes in the lives of the parents, especially of the parent who is going to become the visiting parent, so, uh, anyway, I appreciate the opportunity to make a statement to the court."

The judge smiled at him. "You're very welcome, Mr. Baltakis."

"First of all, this is a unique case, an important case, there are some aspects regarding the tender age of the child and the fact that the parents live a great distance apart, among other things"—here he shot me a glance—"so there are some factors that may bear mentioning because they may assist the court in making decisions in future cases that may be similar. And…there are just some things that really should not go unsaid about this difficult and complex situation."

Someone opened the courtroom door, peeked in, and shut it again. A light flickered on the ceiling. I wished there were windows in the room. Were there windows anywhere in this building? I stared at the tabletop and focused on breathing evenly.

Larry tapped his sheaf of papers together, then said forcefully: "I want to make it clear that I am not willingly giving up my child—I mean," he went on quickly, seeing the perplexed look on the judge's face, "I mean, in the sense that no parent would willingly give up custody of a child in a divorce. Nathan is my first-born and only son, but he is just a little guy, and I've gone through a process, I've really been able to put my own feelings aside. I know the Tender Years concept isn't really court doctrine anymore, however I have, as I said, I have been able to put my own interests aside and decide that it would be in his best interests for him to live with his mom, maybe not indefinitely, maybe only temporarily, but I've decided that would be the best thing for him right now."

"Mr. Baltakis," the judge interjected, "You do realize that you have affirmed recital of the agreement, and that the agreement awards sole custody to the mother, and those arrangements last until the child's majority unless changed by further order of the court?"

"Of course, Your Honor, of course. I'm just saying…circumstances can change."

"Just as long as you understand that," she said.

Hal was jotting on his legal pad. Without moving my head I could read:

> not willingly
> temporarily
> change of circumstances

"Kim's a great mom," he gave me a syrupy smile, "and Tulsa is a great place to bring up a child." He turned back to the bench again. "But so is Seattle! I've brought along some magazines, and a videotape of Washington State and the Puget Sound area, where I live, for you to

247

view at your leisure, showing all the wonderful things you can do there with children. It's just a fantastic place for families. Seattle is growing, many important businesses are located there and many are relocating there, it's really a destination city, and with its proximity to both the mountains and the ocean there are lots of recreational opportunities. It would be the best place for me to give him the athletic opportunities and training he'd need if he should decide to follow in my footsteps—you probably aren't aware, your Honor, but I'm a very successful triathlete with quite a few trophies to show for it. I'd hate for Nathan to be deprived of this opportunity if he shows the talent and interest." He waggled the videotape in the air, made a gesture of offer, then, seeming to doubt the propriety of approaching the bench, took the magazines, fanned them out on the edge of the table, and ceremoniously placed the videotape on top of them, jutting out over the edge.

"Also on that tape is a virtual tour of my home," Larry went on. "I have a three-bedroom condominium with a view of Elliot Bay, access to a swimming pool, and only two blocks from the park. My mother, who is an award-winning realtor in the Wellesley, Massachusetts area, helped me pick it out specifically with a child in mind."

The judge's eyes were beginning to glaze over.

I picked up Hal's pencil and jotted on his pad, *Guess he did tell his parents about the baby.* He picked up the pencil and drew a smile under it, then added *Better keep your hands in your lap.*

"In my home Nathan has a twenty-by-twenty foot bedroom, his own bathroom with a jetted tub and a walk-in closet, and my fiancée, who is currently obtaining her doctorate in child psychology at the University of Washington, has helped me to decorate it and equip it with the top of the line in regard to age-appropriate educational and developmental toys and activities.

"And oh, I forgot, I have spent over a thousand dollars on a professional child safety consultant and have worked closely with her on childproofing my home for Nathan's benefit, removing any potential hazards and making sure he would be in a safe environment."

He paused here, as though for applause. I forced myself to look at him and smile. Because this was a settlement, Judge Dodd knew no history, although the old protective order signed by a different judge was buried somewhere in the file.

"Well. Be that as it may," he continued, "I want to say how important it is that a child bond with his parents, with both of them, but especially, in the case of a boy, with his father, and that this can be problematic in the home where one parent is the visiting parent or there are problems between the divorced parents." He shot me another look.

I clenched my hands in my lap. Below the table, Hal reached over and gently gripped my arm; a comfort, a reminder, a warning.

"I'm sure the court is aware that boys who successfully bond with their fathers and maintain a close—" this time, he physically turned and looked at me, " —a *close* and loving relationship with their fathers, are less likely to find themselves involved in the juvenile justice system when they're older. As it happens, this has been a focus of my studies in the LLM program at the University of Washington, and I've brought along a compendium of the most recent published statistics in this area, to refresh your recollection if you would like." He lifted a book and added it to his exhibit pile. There were five more left in the stack.

Trish coughed. Judge Dodd examined us sternly, one by one, as though trying to determine whether this was a massive practical joke. Having apparently satisfied herself that no conspiracy existed, she continued to keep an eagle eye on all listeners to make sure we maintained decorum. Her gaze lingered longest on me, as though to catch me out.

"With regard to difficulties in the home, I did say, at the forefront, that there were other factors beside tender age and distance that make my case unique and important, and that would be the unusual difficulties we've had resolving the legal and procedural issues in this case, and that, unfortunately, I'm forced to say, can be laid at the doorstep of the mother."

Hal pursed his lips and added another note to his pad. I risked a glance at the gallery. My mother's face was white. Dana looked as though she'd been hit by a stun gun.

"Judge, because I've been directly involved in a divorce situation here where there are difficulties in the household, especially with the mother, I've made a kind of study of this over the last year or so, with the assistance of my fiancée, who is currently working toward her doctorate in psychology at the University of Washington, with a specialty in child psychology. So I've done a lot of research in the area of child psychology, post-partum depression, and female midlife crisis."

Hal threw down his pencil here. He sat back and crossed his legs. Rhonda touched Larry's sleeve and whispered something to him. He peeled off a wad of papers and put them at the back of his pile.

"I don't blame my wife in any way, I think she's a great mom, and in my opinion, and in my fiancée's clinical opinion, Nathan is a very well-adjusted and secure child. However, she will have primary care of my son here while we continue to work through this legal situation" —here the judge furrowed her brow again— "and I wouldn't be doing my duty if I didn't speak out and encourage her, suggest to her that she obtain some psychological counseling to work through her issues for the benefit of our child, even to ask the judge to order this."

The judge cocked her head and shot Hal a questioning glance. He shook his own and opened his hands in a go-on gesture. I didn't dare make eye contact with my mother. Dana had recovered from the stun gun but now her mouth was hanging open; without moving my head further I could see Dr. Delaney leaning down into his crossed legs, hand shielding his eyes, shaking his head almost imperceptibly.

Rhonda whispered to Larry. He shook her off, put down his papers, and started to approach the bench. The bailiff took a step forward. Larry wheeled around and shouted at me, "You're not *winning* this child! I'm *giving* him to you!"

There were exclamations, Rhonda stood up, and as the judge sat forward, about to speak, the ballast of one of the fluorescent light panels overhead gave way, flickered, and died. Everyone looked up for a moment.

"Mr. Baltakis!" Judge Dodd actually had her gavel in hand.

"I'm sorry, your Honor—"

"Mr. Baltakis, I shouldn't need to remind a lawyer about courtroom decorum."

"No, I'm sorry, your Honor." He palmed his head. "It won't happen again."

"That's good, because if it does I'll have to remove you from the courtroom. Could we wrap this up now?"

"I'll be brief." He smoothed down his tie. "I just want you to know that it has been very difficult for me to bond and establish a close and loving relationship with my child. My wife has even gone so far as to conceal him from me, traipsing around the country to prevent me from seeing him. Despite the fact that she has *temporary* custody I feel that this violates the spirit if not the letter of the law and I almost consider it kidnapping. I know she's a great mom and I wouldn't want to take him away from her, but on many occasions she has neglected and even possibly abused him, I may have seen evidence of abuse—"

Hal was out of his chair. "Judge, I hate to interrupt, but at this time I would point out to the Court that we have reached an agreement, that Mr. Baltakis has had a half an hour to make a statement, and I certainly don't want to hear any fictions about how things have gone or if there have been problems." His voice dripped with disdain. "We have reached an agreement from this day on as to how things are going to work out, and I think we've heard enough."

Rhonda jumped up and wrestled down her client. "Judge, we would have nothing further at this time."

Hal moved his chair a little closer to mine as he sat down. "If he wants a trial we'll give him a trial," he said under his breath. "No way am I going to let him put stuff like that on the record."

Judge Dodd gave us a prim little homily about how she was going to allow us to break the promise we'd made before the law but that we couldn't forget Nathan's interests were more important than our own childish, petty squabbles. Then with all due solemnity she pronounced the words that lifted the eight-hundred-pound gorilla from my shoulders. I checked my watch.

We stood up as the judge left the room. It was over.

"You bastard!" Dana hissed, as Larry filed past with his lawyer. She gripped the railing. "How *dare* you speak like that."

251

Rhonda grabbed Larry's arm and piloted him toward the door.

Dana leaned closer. "If you *ever* lay a hand on my friend again or do anything to that baby I'll RIP YOUR EYES OUT."

Rhonda reversed her engines and pulled Larry back in while Hal ushered our side out to the hall. He barely had a moment to put his briefcase down on one of the wooden benches before Rhonda opened the door a crack and motioned to him.

"I'll be right back," he said.

"I think I need to—" said Bobbie, then collapsed onto the bench.

Dana and I moved in on either side while Trish went to get a cup of water.

"I'm all right." Bobbie pushed her thick waves back in place. "I just got a little light-headed. We didn't eat—" She threw her arms around me. "Oh, Kim," she whispered, "I'm so glad Dana said that. I'm *so glad* she said that." Her voice was ragged. "I couldn't have done it."

On the other bench, the next pair up stared at us. Both of their lawyers wore cowboy boots. Dana turned. "Entertainment, no extra charge," she beamed at them, adjusting her mink hat.

Hal came back, smiling. "Larry wants Dana cited for contempt."

"What?"

"No way. Judge wasn't in the room."

"I *had* to do that," Dana protested. "I couldn't let him get away with that! Everyone was just sitting there. Nobody said anything."

Bobbie nodded, her eyes shining with admiration.

"Nevertheless," said Hal, unable to stop smiling.

"What's the joke?" I asked him.

"That bailiff," he said, shaking his head. He picked up his brief-case and moved us further down the hall. "The bailiff asked me if Larry was gay. He said, 'What's wrong with that guy, is he a nutcase or what? The judge thinks he's crazy and I think so too.'"

"Possibly," I said, "but that is a separate issue."

Trish elbowed me. "Stop talkin' like a lawyer. You're the client today."

"The winning client," Dana added.

"It's no-fault divorce," I protested.

"Kim," Hal said, "you earned this divorce. I would agree. You won."

He held open the courthouse door. Outside, the grass was dusted with snow. In five years here, I'd never seen snow cover. It looked magical. Just when I thought I was getting used to the seasons in Tulsa, they changed on me, for the better.

BACK AT RIVERVIEW Gardens there was a "Just Divorced" banner over my door, courtesy of Alison, who'd gotten a substitute for lunch and recess duty. When we walked in she and Sulie and Nathan threw confetti at us, while Loretta protected Nathan's bowl of macaroni and cheese with her crossword puzzle book.

Dana pulled me around the corner into the kitchen and opened the refrigerator. "Don't say anything to your mother." She took out a bottle of champagne, handed it to me, and took out another. "When Larry started making his speech," she said, "I took your mother's hand. After awhile, she started gripping it. Harder and harder. She squeezed it so hard I thought my knuckles were going to break. It's still hurtin'. I never would have believed she had so much strength in her hands. Don't say anything to her. She didn't even know she was doing it! That's why I did what I did. Everyone was just sittin' there. And nobody was going to tell that bastard off. *Goddamn him to hell.*" She threw the second cork in the sink. "Other than that," she said cheerfully, "she was fine. She was okay the whole time. Except at the end."

I took the phone into my bedroom and called Karen. "It's over."

"My God, that took a long time! I've been sitting here all morning. How's mother?"

"Oh, I'm fine," I said cheerfully. "Made it through."

"No, no, I meant *Mom.*"

I looked through the door. Bobbie was slumped at the table, head down, arms stretched out, getting one of Trish's special Swedish/Creole/acupressure chair massages. "She'll recover."

We turned off Delbert McClinton and went outside for the final toast, Dana, Trish, Bobbie, Alison, Sulie and I. Loretta stayed in; she was Pentecostal and didn't drink. We stepped carefully on the snow-covered walk out to the parking lot. In the swirling flakes, under the white-frosted cottonwood, we emptied our glasses and hurled them into the empty dumpster.

Alison popped a breath freshener in her mouth and went back to school. Deb and Trish left too. My mother and I went to Utica Square to have lunch. We'd skipped breakfast, in retrospect an act of wisdom, despite Bobbie's near-faint.

The snow came down harder while we ate, real snow, big puffy flakes. We took our time. We weren't thinking about the past or talking about the future, just enjoying the hard-won present. We were on the tail-end of the lunch rush; the last few patrons were departing. I looked around. It reminded me of my college send-off lunch in Chicago, in the empty Hilton dining room—except that my father wasn't there, and my mother was talkative. The food seemed to have revived her even more. I realized: it was the first time I'd seen her light-hearted since Dad died.

The department store carillon started up. There was something different about its sound today, and I suddenly realized I was hearing it for the first time muffled by a layer of snow. It had turned into a real flurry. The busboys had stopped work to watch it.

Bobbie looked around to signal for more coffee. The waitress had joined the group at the window. We looked out again and saw that it wasn't just the restaurant that had emptied, but the whole shopping center: cars were pulling out, one after another.

"I think—I think they're all leaving because of the snow!" said Bobbie. We looked at each other and started laughing.

"What's so funny, y'all?" the waitress asked, coming over with the coffee pot.

"We're from Chicago," I said, gesturing toward the window.

"Well, then, I guess this is nothing to you." She cleared our plates with her free hand, balancing them expertly as she turned to look out. "We get this once every ten years or so. I'm fixing to leave my car here, have my husband pick me up."

We had our last cup, and drove home light-hearted on pristine, empty streets.

In the evening I did the laundry, crunching back and forth to the laundry room through a thick white blanket of snow, just as I'd walked to Lake Michigan with Karen the Christmas before Nathan was born, rubbing my hands over the red wool coat, baby snug beneath my heart. *He hasn't told his parents yet, he hasn't told his parents yet.* There was a lot Larry hadn't told his parents, but it wasn't my place to tell them, nor my concern. Tonight, for me, the snow was benison. It was silent music, a message from my ancestors that although things may happen out of season, eventually they come around right, that a new life was meant to be born from that different rhythm, and that the beauty of the unforeseen lay before me. Everything was soft and quiet, and Tulsa was the city of my content. *Sole custody,* I thought, and was filled with gratitude. I knew I hadn't achieved this alone. Behind us in the courtroom, behind me and Hal, Bobbie and Dana and Trish, and even Dr. Delaney, were all my ancestors, all my grandmothers and grandfathers, a shining army of the good arrayed for battle and marching into the courtroom to get this finished. And just as I hadn't been alone in the courtroom, I wouldn't be alone in the future, even if I stayed single. I wouldn't be alone, as I walked through the wilderness of this world.

I loaded the diapers into the dryer. I remembered how grateful I'd been in the past, when watching the cylinder tumble had provided a few minutes of fascination for the baby, giving me the freedom to brief a case or write a grocery list.

Two years ago, I'd walked into Dee's office at DVS and said: *I need to understand how this happened, so I can keep it from happening again.* One of my college professors once said about my writing that it displayed a remarkable combination of dignity and innocence, and I suddenly realized that over the course of years, people had been continuously remarking on this, at different times, in different ways. Dignity, and innocence. I'd always thought the dignity had served me well, but now I understood that dignity was not just being gracious and quiet. It was knowing who you were, so you knew what behavior to accept from others. And that had been my lesson: to remember who I was, to go back to Square One and become reacquainted with myself.

But I would not allow the events that had bestowed awareness of this gift on me to deprive me of my innocence. I was determined to persist in innocence, because it was a fine way to be. I was not going to relinquish my faith in the Categorical Imperative. In a truly gray hour Kant had encouraged that when he'd insisted that philosophy wasn't just theory but practice, that it was aspirational, and that without hope, we wouldn't be human. I was determined to persist in innocence. That was the road I chose to take. But now I could also see evil clearly and I knew how to deal with it. I could maintain that perfect pitch between dignity and innocence that would allow me to go beyond the evergreens and navigate the wider world in grace.

When I got into bed I stuck my fingers in the slats of the blind. The cottonwood's unaccustomed frosting sparkled under the light. There was a warmth indoors I remembered from winters further north. It made me think of dancing again by myself when I was little, in the evening after supper, while my parents sat in the dining room, on the other side of the arch. The sense of union with that child was so immediate and profound I began to cry, for the first time since eleven forty-six a.m. on that morning when Judge Dodd pronounced *I grant you each a divorce from the other.* I cried in happiness and in relief, in regret that it had taken so long and wasted so much time, and in compassion for the agony and strain it had cost. And then, and mostly, I cried at having been lost from that earlier time of dancing and then restored after so many years, and I cried the pain and regret that I'd been without myself for so long and I cried fiercely that I would never let myself go again.

At that moment I discovered that there is something more beautiful than music, and that is finding lost music, your own composition misplaced then somehow found again, so it's both old and new. The interval between repetition had been no more than a breath, a single beat, but one so long the rush of air back into the lungs was profoundly satisfying. I'd been suffocating and couldn't speak, but now I had my life and my breath and my voice back. There was something more beautiful than music. There was something more wonderful than singing, and that was singing in a lost voice.

I DREAMT I got my cello and my talent back. I was playing Saint-Saens' Concerto No. 1 outdoors in downtown Tulsa, by the bronze statue of the Indian ballerina next to the Performing Arts Center. Everyone stopped to listen approvingly, even the partners at Prentice Schroeder, who seemed to take such pleasure in drowning my every memo, my every brief, in a sea of red ink. My instrument had beautiful tone, and I dug in. It was incredibly satisfying to be playing again. Karen was there, and she said: *That was really good. You can get your talent back, if you keep practicing.*